# Art of Taming Horses

*John Solomon Rarey*

# Contents

# ART OF TAMING HORSES

BY

John Solomon Rarey

# CHAPTER I.

Mr. Rarey's pamphlet first published in Ohio.—Experience of old system. — Compiled and invented new. —Tying up the fore-leg known many years ago, see Stamford Almanack.—Forgotten and not valued.—Reference to Captain Nolan's and Colonel Greenwood's works on horsemanship.—Dick Christian missed the discovery.— Baucher's plan of laying down a horse explained.—Mademoiselle Isabel's whip-and-spur plan.—Account of the Irish whisperer Dan Sullivan.—Usual modes of taming vicious horses.—Starving.— Physic.—Sleepless nights.—Bleeding.—Biting the ear.—Story of Kentish coachman.—The Ellis system.—Value of the Rarey system as compared with that of ordinary horse-tamers.—Systems of Australia and Arabia compared.—The South American plan explained.—A French plan.—Grisone the Neapolitan's advice.—The discovery of Mr. Rarey by Mr. Goodenough.—Visit to Canada.— To England.—Lord Alfred Paget.—Sir Richard Airey.—System made known to them.—To Mr. Jos. Anderson.—Messrs. Tattersall.— Sir Matthew Ridley's black horse tamed.—Subscription list of 500 opened.—Stafford tamed.—Description of.—Teaching commenced with Lords Palmerston, Granville, &c.—Cruiser tamed.—History of.—Enthusiastic crowd at Cruiser exhibition.—System approved by the Earl of Jersey and Sir Tatton Sykes.—Close of first subscription list.—Anecdote of Mr, Gurney's colt.—Personal sketch of Mr. Rarey.

MR. RAREY is a farmer from Ohio, in the United States. Five years ago he wrote the little book which forms the text of the following complete account of his system, with pictorial illustrations, which are essential for explaining the means he now employs for subduing the most refractory animals. Without these explanations, it would be extremely difficult for any one who had not enjoyed the advantage of hearing Mr. Rarey's explanations, to practise his system successfully, or even safely. The original work contains a mere outline of the art, since perfected .. by five years' further study and practice. The author did not revise his first sketch, for very obvious reasons.

He was living in obscurity, teaching his system for a few dollars in Ohio and Texas. He never taught in the great cities or seabord states of the United States. "When he had imparted his art to a pupil, he bound him to secrecy, and presented him with a copy of his pamphlet. He did not dream, then, of becoming the great Lion of the London Season, and realising from English subscribers nearly 20,000l. It will be observed, that in the original American edition, the operation of tying up the foot is described in one chapter, and, at an interval of some pages, that of laying a horse down, in another; and that neither the difficulties nor the necessary precautions, nor the extraordinary results, are described with the clearness their importance requires.

Mr. Rarey has now very properly released his subscribers from the contract which bound them to secrecy; and it is now in every point of view important that this valuable system of rendering horses docile and affectionate, fit for hacks or chargers, ladies' pads or harness, or the safe conveyance of the aged, crippled, and sick, should be placed within the reach of the thousands whose business it is to deal with horses, as well as of that large class of gentlemen who are obliged to observe economy while keeping up their equestrian tastes. After all, it is to the horse-breeding farmers and grooms to whom Mr. Rarey's art will be of the most practical use.

As it is, enough of the system has oozed out to suggest to the ignorant new means of cruelty. A horse's leg is strapped up, and then the unlearned proceed to bully the crippled animal, instead of—to borrow an expressive Americanism—" to gentle him."

Before entering into the details for practising the Rarey system, it may be interesting to give a sketch of the " facts " that have placed Mr. Rarey in his present well-deserved position, as an invincible Horse-Tamer, as well as a Reformer of the whole modern system of training horses—a position unanimously assigned to him by all the first horsemen of the day.

Mr. Rarey has been a horse-breaker in the United States from his earliest youth, and had frequently to break in horses five or six years old, that had run wild until that mature undocile age.

At first he employed the old English rough-rider method, and in the course of his adventures broke almost every bone in his body, for his pluck was greater than his science. But he was not satisfied with following old routine; he inquired from the wandering horsemen and circus trainers into their methods (it may be that he was at one time attached to a circus himself), and read every book he could lay his hands on. By inquiry and by study—as he says in one of his ad-vertisements—" he thought out" the plan and the principles of his present system.

The methods he uses for placing a colt or horse completely in his power are not absolutely new, although it is possible that he has re-invented and has certainly much improved them. The Russian (i.e. Courland) Circus Eiders have long known how, single-handed, to make a horse lie down by fastening up one fore-leg, and then with a rope suddenly pulling the other leg from under him. The trick was practised in England more than forty years ago, and forgotten. That no importance was attached to this method of throwing a horse is proved by the fact, that in the works on horsemanship, published during the last twenty years, no reference is made to it. When Mr. Starkey, of Wiltshire, a breeder and runner of race-horses[1], saw Mr. Rarey operate for the first time, he said, " Why I knew how to throw a horse in that way years ago, but I did not know the use of it, and was always in too great a hurry! " Lord Berners made nearly the same remark to me. Nimrod, Cecil, Harry Hieover, Scrutator—do not appear to have ever heard of it. The best modern authority on such subjects (British Rural Sports), describes a number of difficulties in breaking colts which altogether disappear under the Rarey system — especially the difficulty of shoeing.

---

1   Owner of Fisherman.

Captain Nolan, who was killed at Balaklava, served in an Hungarian regiment, in the Austrian service, afterwards in our own service in India, and visited Russia, France, Denmark, and South Germany, to collect materials for his work on the " History of Cavalry and on the Training of Horses," although he set out with the golden rule laid down by the great Greek horseman, Xenophon, more than a thousand years ago—" HORSES

ARE TAUGHT, NOT BY HARSHNESS, BUT BY GENTLENESS,"

only refers incidentally to a plan for throwing a horse down, in an extract from Baucher's great work, which will presently be quoted, but attaches no importance to it, and was evidently totally ignorant of the foundation of the Rarey system.

The accomplished Colonel Greenwood, who was equally learned in the manege of the *Haute Ecole*, and skilled in the style of the English hunting-fields, gives no hint of a method which reduces the time for taming colts from months to hours, and makes the docility of five horses out of six merely a matter of a few weeks' patience.

The sporting newspapers of England and America were so completely off the true scent when guessing at the Rarey method, that they put faith in recipes of oils and scents for taming horses.

Dick Christian — a genius in his way—when on horseback unmatched for patience and pluck, but with no taste for reading and no talent for generalizing, used to conquer savages for temporary use by tying up one fore-foot, and made good water-jumpers of horses afraid of water by making them smell it and wade through it; so that he came very near the Rarey methods, but missed the chain of reasoning that would have led him to go further with these expedients[2].

Mons. Baucher, of Paris (misprinted Faucher in the American edition), the great modern authority in horse-training and elaborate school equitation, under

2   See "The Post and the Paddock," by "The Druid."

whom our principal English cavalry generals have studied—amongst others, two enthusiastic disciples of Mr. Rarey, Lord Vivian and General Laurenson, command-ing the cavalry at Aldershott—admitted Mr. Rarey's system was not only " most valuable," but " quite new to him."

After Mr. Rarey had taught five or six hundred subscribers, some of whom of course had wives, Mr. Cooke, of Astley's, began to exhibit a way of making a horse lie down, which bore as much resemblance to Mr. Rarey's system, as Buckstone's or Keeley's travestie of Othello would to a serious performance by a first rate tra-gedian. Mr. Cooke pulling at a strap over the horse's back, was, until he grew, by practice, skilful, more than once thrown down by the extension of the off fore-leg.

Indeed, the proof that the circus people knew neither the Rarey plan, nor the results to be obtained from it, is to be found in the fact, that they continually failed in subduing unruly horses sent to them for that purpose.

A friend of mine, an eminent engineer, sent to Astley's, about two years ago, a horse which had cost him two hundred pounds, and was useless from a habit of standing still and rearing at the corner of streets; he was returned worse rather than better, and sold for forty pounds. Six lessons from Mr. Rarey would have produced, at least, temporary docility.

Monsieur Baucher, in his Méthode d'Equitation, says, speaking of the surprise created by the feats he performed with trained horses,—" According to some, I was a new Carter,'[3] taming my horses by depriving them of rest and nourishment: others would have it, that I tied ropes to their legs, and suspended them in the air; some again supposed that I fascinated them by the power of the eye; and part of the audience, seeing my horses (Partisan, Capitaine, Neptune, and Baridan) work in time to my friend Monsieur Paul Cuzent's charming Music, seriously argued that the horses had a capital ear for music, and that they stopped when the clarionets and trombones ceased to play, and that the music had more power over the horse than I had. That the beast obeyed an 'ut ' or a 'sol' or 'staccato,' but my hands and legs went for nothing.

3   Carter, one of the Van Amburgh showmen,

" Could any one imagine that such nonsense could emanate from people who passed for horsemen ?

" Now from this, although in some respects the same class of nonsense that was talked about Mr. Rarey, it does not seem that any Parisian veterinary surgeon staked his reputation on the efficacy of oils and scents."

M. Baucher then proceeds to give what he calls sixteen " Airs de Manege" which reflect the highest credit on his skill as a rational horseman, using his hands and legs. But he proceeds to say—" It is with regret I publish the means of making a horse kneel, limp, lie down, and sit on his haunches in the position called the '*Cheval Gastronomie,*' or 'The Horse at Dinner. This work is degrading to the poor horse, and painful to the trainer, who no longer sees in the poor trembling beast the proud courser, full of spirit and energy, he took such pleasure in training.

" To make a horse kneel, tie his pastern-joint to his elbow, make fast a longer line to the other pastern-joint, have this held tight, and strike the leg with the whip; the instant he raises it from the ground, pull at the longeing line to bend the leg. He cannot help it—he must fall on his knees. Make much of the horse in this position, and let him get up free of all hindrance.

" As soon as he does this without difficulty, leave off the use of the longeing line, and next leave both legs at liberty : by striking him on the shins with the whip, he will understand that he is to kneel down.

" When on his knees, send his head well to the offside, and, supporting him with the left rein, pull the right rein down against his neck till he falls to the near s de ; when down at full length, you cannot make too much of him; *have his head held that he may not get up too suddenly,* c1 before you wish him. You can do this by placing your right foot on the right reins; this keeps the horse's nose raised from the ground, and thus deprives him of the power of struggling successfully against you. Profit by his present position to make him sit up on his haunches, and in the position of the " Cheval Gastronomie.' "

The difference between this and Rarey's plan of laying down a horse is as great as between Franklin's kite and Wheatstone's electrical telegraph; and foremost to acknowledge the American's merits was M. Baucher.

So little idea had cavalry authorities that a horse could be trained without severity, that, during the Crimean war, a Mademoiselle Isabel came over to this country with strong recommendations from the French war minister, and was employed at considerable cost at Maidstone for some months in spoiling a number of horses by *her system*, the principal features of which consisted in a new dumb jockey, and a severe spur attached to a whip!

It is true that Mademoiselle Isabel's experiment was made contrary to the wishes and plans of the head of the Cavalry Training Department, the late General Griffiths ; but it is not less true that within the last two years influential cavalry officers were looking for an improvement in training horses from an adroit use of the whip and spur.

From the time of Alexander the Great down to the Northumberland Horse-Breaker, there have been instances of courageous men who have been able to do extraordinary things with horses. But they may be divided into two classes, neither of which have been able to originate or impart a system for the use of ordinary horsemen.

The one class relied and relies on personal influence over lower animals. They terrify, subdue, or conciliate by eye, voice, and touch, just as some wicked women, not endowed with any extraordinary external charms, bewitch and betray the wisest men.

The other class rely on the infliction of acute pain, or, stupefaction by drugs, or other similar expedients for acquiring a temporary ascendancy.

In a work printed in 1664, quoted by Nolan, we have a melancholy account of the fate of an ingenious horse-tamer. " A Neapolitan, called Pietro, had a little horse, named Mauroço, doubtless a Barb or Arab, which he had taught to perform many tricks. He would, at a sign from his master, he down, kneel, and make as many courvettes (springs on his hind-legs forward, like rearing), as his master told him. He jumped over a stick, and through hoops, carried a glove to the person Pietro pointed out, and performed a thousand pretty antics. He travelled through the greater part of the Continent, but unfortunately passing through Aries, the people in that ' age of faith,' took him for a sorcerer, and burned him and poor Mauroço in the market-place." It was probably from this incident that Victor Hugo took the catastrophe of La Esmeralda and her goat.

Dan Sullivan, who flourished about fifty years ago, was the greatest horse-tamer of whom there is any record in modern times. His triumph commenced by his purchasing for an old song a dragoon's horse at Mallow, who was so savage " that he was obliged to be fed through a hole in the wall." After one of Sullivan's lessons the trooper drew a car quietly through Mallow, and remained a very proverb of gentleness for years after. In fact, with mule or horse, one half-hour's lesson from Sullivan was enough; but they relapsed in other hands. Sullivan's own account of the secret was, that he originally acquired it from a wearied soldier who had not money to pay for a pint of porter he had drunk. The landlord was retaining part of his kit as a pledge, when Sullivan, who sat in the bar, vowed he would never see a hungry man want, and gave the soldier so good a luncheon, that, in his gratitude, he drew him aside at parting, and revealed what he believed to be an Indian charm.

Sullivan never took any pupils, and, as far as I can learn, never attempted to train* colts by his method, although that is a more profitable and useful branch of business than training vicious horses. It is stated in an article in " Household Words " on Horse-Tamers, that he was so jealous of his gift that even the priest of Ballyclough could not wring it from him at the confessional. His son used to boast how his reverence met his sire as they both rode towards Mallow, and charged him with being a confederate of the wicked one, and how the " whisperer " laid the priest's horse under a spell, and forthwith led him a weary chase among the cross roads, till he promised in despair to let Sullivan alone for ever. Sullivan left three sons: one only practised his art, with imperfect success till his death; neither of the others pretended to any knowledge of it. One of them is to this day a horse-breaker at Mallow.

The reputation of Mr. Rarey brought to light a num-, ber of provincial horse-tamers, and, amongst others, a grandson of Sullivan has opened a list under the auspicies of the Marquis of Waterford, for teaching his grandfather's art of horse-taming. It is impossible not to ask, why, if the art is of any value, it has not been taught long ago ?

In Ireland as in England, the accepted modes of taming a determined colt, or vicious horse, are either by a resolute rider with whip and spur, and violent loungings, or by starving, physic, and sleepless nights. It was by these means combined that the well-known horseman, Bartley the bootmaker, twenty years ago, tamed a splendid thorough-bred horse, that had defied all the efforts of all the rough-riders of the Household Cavalry regiments.

Bleeding a vici6us horse has been recommended in German books on equitation. In the family Robinson Crusoe, paterfamilias-conquers the quagga by biting its ear, and every farrier knows how to apply a twitch to a horse's ear or nose to secure his quietness under an operation. A Mr: King, some years since, exhibited a learned horse, which he said he subdued by pinching a nerve of its mouth, called " *the nerve of susceptibility.*"

The writer in the " Household Words " article, to which I have already referred, tells how " a coachman in Kent, who had been quite mastered by horses, called in the assistance of a professed whisperer. After his ghostly course the horses had the worst of it for two months, when their ill-humour returned, and the coachman himself immediately darkened his stable, and held what he termed a little conversation with them, which kept them placid till two more months had passed. He did not seem altogether to approve of the system, and plainly confessed that it was cruel." Putting shot in the ear is an old stupid and fatal trick of ignorant carters to cure a gibbing horse—it cures and kills him too.

The latest instantaneous system which acquired a certain degree of temporary popularity was that introduced from the western prairies, by Mr. Ellis, of Trinity College, Cambridge, which consisted in breath ing into the nostrils of a colt, or buf-falo colt, while its eyes were covered. But although on some animals this seemed to produce a soothing effect, on others it totally failed.

There can be very little doubt that most of the mysterious " horse-whisperers" relied for their power of subduing a vicious horse partly on the special personal in-fluence already referred to, and partly on some one of those cruel modes of intimi-dating the animal. It has been observed that idiots can sometimes manage the most savage horses and bulls, and conciliate the most savage dogs at first sight.

The value of Mr. Rarey's system consists in the fact that it may be taught to, and successfully practised by, a ploughboy of thirteen or fourteen for use on all ex-cept extremely vicious and powerful horses.

It requires patience—it requires the habit of dealing with horses as well as coolness; but the real work is rather a matter of skill than strength. Not only have boys of five or six stone become successful horse-tamers, but ladies of high rank have in the course of ten minutes perfectly subdued and reduced to deathlike calm-ness fiery blood-horses.

Therefore, in dealing with Mr. Rarey's plan we' are not wasting our time about a trick for conquering these rare exceptions—incurably-savage horses—but con-sidering the principles of a universally applicable system for taming and training horses for man's use, with a perfection of docility rarely found except in aged pet horses, and with a rapidity heretofore quite unknown.

The system of Arabia and Australia are the two extremes. In Australia, where the people are always in a hurry, the usual mode of breaking in the bush horses is to *ride them quiet*; that is, to let the man fight it out with the horse until the latter gives in; for the time, at any rate. The result is, that nine-tenths of the Australian horses are vicious, and especially given to the trick of " buck-jumping." This vile vice consists in a succession of leaps from all-fours, the beast descending with the back arched, the limbs rigid, and the head as low down between the legs as possible. Not one horseman in a hundred can sit three jumps of a confirmed buck-jumper. Charles Barter, who was one of the hardest riders in the Heythrope Hunt, in his " Six Months in Natal," says, " when my horse began buck-jumping I dismounted, and I recommend every one under the same circumstances to do the same."

The Guachos on the South American Pampas lasso a wild horse, throw him down, cover his head with one of their ponchos, or cloaks, and, having girthed on him one of their heavy demi-piqued saddles, from which it is almost impossible to be dislodged, thrust a curb-bit, capable of breaking the jaw with one tug, into the poor wretch's mouth, mount him with a pair of spurs with rowels six inches long, and ride him over the treeless plains until he sinks exhausted in a fainting state. But horses thus broken are almost invariably either vicious or stupid; in fact, idiotic. There is another milder method sometimes adopted by these Pampas horsemen, on which, no doubt, Mr. Rarey partly founded his system. After lassoing a horse, they blind his eyes with a poncho, tie him fast to a post, and girth a heavy saddle on him. The animal sometimes dies at once of fright and anger: if not, he trembles, sweats, and would, after a time, fall down from terror and weakness. The Guacho then goes up to him, caresses him, removes the poncho from his eyes, continues to caress him; so that, according to the notion of the country, the horse becomes grateful and attached to the man for delivering him from something frightful; and from that mcment the process of training becomes easy, and, with the help of the long spurs, is completed in a few days. This plan must spoil as many horses as it makes quiet, and fail utterly with the more nervous and high-spirited; for the very quali-ties that render a horse most useful and beautiful, when properly trained, lead him, when unbroken, to resist more obstinately rough violent usage.

In a French newspaper article on Mr. Rarey's system, it is related that a French horse-breaker, in 1846, made a good speculation by purchasing vicious horses, which are more common in France than in England, and selling them, after a few days' discipline, perfectly quiet. His remedy lay in a loaded whip, freely applied between the ears when any symptom of vice was displayed. This expedient was only a revival of the method of Grisone, the Neapolitan, called, in the fifteenth century, the regenerator of horsemanship, predecessor of the French school, who says—" In breaking young horses, put them into a circular pit; be very severe with those that are sensitive, and of high courage; beat them between the ears with a stick." His followers tied their horses to the pillars in riding-schools, and beat them to make them raise their fore-legs. We do not approve of Grisone's maxims at the present day in print, but we leave our horses too much to ignorant colt-breakers, who practise them.

The Arabs alone, who have no need to hurry the education of their horses, and who live with them as we do with our pet dogs, train their colts by degrees, with patient gentleness, and only resort to severe measures to teach them to gallop and stop short For this reason Arabs are most docile until they fell into the hands of cruel grooms.

It was from considering the docility of the high-bred Arab horse and intractableness of the quibly, roughly broken prairie or Pampas horse, that Mr. Rarey was led to think over and perfect the system which he has repeatedly explained and illustrated by living examples in his lectures, and very imperfectly explained in his valuable, original, but crude little book.

It is very fortunate that this book did not find its way to England before Mr. Rarey himself came and conquered Cruiser, and in face-to-face interviews gained the confidence and co-operation of all our horse-loving aristocracy. For had the book appeared unsupported by lectures (or such explanations written and pictorial as this edition will supply), there would have been so many accidents and so many failures, that Mr. Rarey would have had great difficulty in obtaining a hearing, and for many years our splendid colts would have been left to the empirical treatment of ignorant rough-riders.

An accident withdrew the great reformer of horse-training from obscurity.

In the course of his travels as a teacher of horse-taming he met with Mr. Good-enough, a sharp, hard-fisted New Englander, of the true " Yankee " breed, so well-described by Sam Slick, settled in the city of Toronto, Canada, as a general dealer. In fact, a " sort of Barnum." Mr. Goodenough saw that there was money to be made out of the Rarey system—formed a partnership with the Ohio farmer—conducted him to Canada-—obtained an opportunity of exhibiting his talents before Major Robertson, Aide-de-camp to General Sir William Eyre, K.C.B., Commander of the forces, and, through the Major, before Sir William himself, who is (as I can say from having seen him with hounds) an accomplished horseman and enthusiastic fox-hunter. From these high authorities the partners obtained letters of introduction to the Horse Guards in England, and to several gentlemen attached to the Court; in one of the letters of introduction, General Eyre said, "that the system was new to him, and valuable for military purposes." On arriving in England, Mr. Rarey made known his system, and was fortunate enough to convert and obtain the active assistance of Sir Richard Airey, Quarter-Master General, Lord Alfred Paget[4], and Colonel Hood, the two first being noted for their skill as horse- . men, and the two latter being attached to the Court. From these gentlemen of high degree, Mr. Rarey proceeded, under good advice, to make known his art to Mr. Joseph Anderson of Piccadilly, and his prime minister, the well-known George Rice—tamed for them a black horse that had been returned by Sir Matthew White Ridley, as unridable from vice and nervousness. The next step was an introduction to Messrs. Tatter-sall of Hyde Park, whose reputation for honour and integrity in most difficult transactions is world-wide and nearly a century old. Introduced at Hyde Park Corner with the strongest recommendations and certificates from such authorities as Lord Alfred Paget, Sir Richard Airey, Colonel Hood, &c, &c, Messrs. Tattersall investigated Mr. Rarey's system, and became convinced that its general adoption would confer an in-valuable benefit on what may be called " the great horse interest," and do away with a great deal of cruelty and unnecessary severity now practised on the best-bred and most high-spirited animals through ignorance of colt-breakers and grooms. They, therefore, decided, with that libera-lity which has always distinguished the firm, to lend Mr. Rarey all the assistance in their power, without taking any commission, or

4   Son of the late Marquis of Anglesea, one of the finest horsemen of his day, even with one leg, after he left the other at Waterloo.

remuneration of any kind.

As the methods used by Mr. Rarey are so exceedingly simple, the question next arose of how Mr. Rarey was to be remunerated when teaching in a city where hundreds live by collecting and retailing news. His previous lessons had been given to the thinly-populated districts of Ohio and Texas, where each pupil was a dealer in horses, and kept his secret for his own sake. Had he been the inventor of an improved corkscrew or stirrup-iron, a patent would have secured him that limited monopoly which very imperfectly rewards many invaluable mechanical inventions. Had his countrymen chosen to agree to a reciprocity treaty for copyright of books, he might have secured some certain remuneration by a printed publication of his Lectures. But they prefer the liberty of borrowing our copyrights without consulting the author, and we occasionally return the compliment. In this instance the author cannot say that the British nation has not paid him handsomely..

After a consultation with Mr. Rarey's noble patrons, it was decided that a list should be opened at Hyde Park Corner for subscribers at £10 10s. each, paid in advance, the teaching to commence as soon as five hundred subscriptions had been paid, each subscriber signing an en-gagement, under a penalty of £500, not to teach or divulge Mr. Rarey's method, and Messrs. Tattersall undertaking to hold the subscriptions in trust until Mr. Rarey had performed his part of the agreement[5]. To this fund, at the request of my friends Messrs. Tattersall, I agreed to act as Secretary. My duties ceased when the list was filled, and the management of the business passed from those gentlemen to Mr. Rarey s partner, Mr. Goodenough, on the 3rd of May, 1858.

This list was opened the first day at Mr. Jos. Anderson's, after Mr. Rarey had exhibited, not his method, but the results of his method on the celebrated black, or rather iron-gray, horse already mentioned.

---

5    The list itself is one of the most extraordinary documents ever printed, in regard to the rank and equestrian accomplishments of the subscribers.

Leaving the list to fill, Mr. Rarey went to Paris, and there tamed the vicious and probably half-mad coaching stallion, Stafford[6]. It is not generally known that " Mr. Rarey concluded his first exhibition by beating a drum on Staf-ford's back, and passing his hand over his head and mouth. Stafford was afterwards ridden by a groom, and showed the same docility in his hands as in those of Mr. Rarey. with, a mare, although he had never had his head through a collar before; and he went as quietly as the best-broken carriage-horse in Paris. Mr Rarey concluded by firing a six-chambered revolver fron his back."- ~*Pwris lllustrated Journal*

" Mr. Rarey succeeded on the first attempt in putting him in harness

having omitted the precautions of gagging this wild beast with the wooden bit, which forms one of the vignettes of this book, he turned round suddenly, while the tamer was soothing his legs, caught his shoulder in his mouth, and would have made an end of the Rarey system if assistance had not been at hand in the shape of Mr. Goodenough and a pitchfork.

---

6 " Stafford is a half-brad carriage stallion, six years old. For three yeans he has formed one of the breeding-stud at Cluny, where he has acquired the character of being a most dangerous animal. He was about to be withdrawn from the stud and destroyed, in consequence of the protests of the breeders—for a whole year he had obstinately refused to be dressed, and was obliged to be closely confined in his box. He rushed at every one who appeared with both fore-feet, and open mouthed. Every means of subduing and restraining him was adopted; he was muzzled, blindfolded, and hobbled. In order to give Mr. Rarey's method a trial, Stafford was sent to Paris, and there a great number of persons, including the principal members of the Jockey Club, had an opportunity of judging of his vicious disposition.

" After being alone with Stafford for an hour and a half, Mr. Rarey rode on him into the Biding School, guiding him with a common snaffle-bridle. The appearance of the horse was completely altered : he was calm and docile. His docility did not seem to be produced by fear or constraint, but the result of perfect confidence. The astonishment of the spectators was increased when Mr. Rarey unbridled him, and guided the late savage animal, with a mere motion of his hands or indication with his leg, as easily as a trained circus-horse. Then, dashing into a gallop, he stopped him short with a single word.

Intense enthusiasm was created in Paris by the conquest of Stafford, but 250 francs was too large a sum to found a long subscription list in a city so little given to private horsemanship, and a French experiment did not produce much effect in England.

In fact, the English list, which started so bravely under distinguished patronage, after touching some 250 names, languished, and in spite of testimonials from great names, only reached 820, when Mr. Rarey, at the pressing recommendation of his English friends, returned from Paris, and fixed the day for commencing his lessons in the private riding-school of the Duke of Wellington, the use of which had been in the kindest manner offered by his Grace as a testimony of his high opinion of the value of the new system.

The course was commenced on the 20th March, by inviting to a private lesson a select party of noblemen and gentlemen, twenty-one in all, including, amongst other accomplished horsemen and horse-breeders, Lord Palmerston, the two ex-masters of the Royal Buck-hounds, Earls Granville and Bessborough, the Marquis of Stafford, Vice-President of the Four-Horse Driving Club, and the Honourable Admiral Rous, the leading .authority of the Jockey Club on all racing matters. The favourable report of these, perhaps, among the most competent judges of anything appertaining to horses in the world, settled the value of Mr. Rarey's lessons, and the list began to fill speedily; many of the subscribers, no doubt, being more influenced by the prevailing fashion and curiosity, than by an inclination to turn horse-tamers.

But early in April, when it became known that Mr. Rarey had tamed Cruiser,[7]

---

7   "Cruiser was the property of Lord Dorchester, and was a good favourite for the Derby in Wild Dayrell's year, but broke down before the race. Like all Venison horses, his temper was not of the mildest kind, and John Day was delighted to get rid of him. "When started for Rawcliffe, he told the man who led him on no account to put him into a stable, as he would never get him out. This injunction was of course disregarded, for when the man wanted some refreshment, he put him into a country public-house stable, and left him, and to get him out, the roof of the building had to be pulled off. At Rawcliffe, he was always exhibited by a groom with a ticket-of-leave bludgeon in his hand, and few were bold enough to venture into his yard. This animal, whose temper has depreciated him perhaps a thousand pounds in value, I think would be e right horse in the right

the most vicious stallion in England, "who could do more fighting in less time than any horse in the world," and that he had brought "Mr. Rarey, when here, first subjugated a two-year old filly, perfectly unbroken. This he accomplished under half an hour, riding on her, opening an umbrella, beating a drum upon her, &c. He then took Cruiser in hand, and in three hours Mr. Rarey and myself mounted him. He had not been ridden for nearly three years, and -was so vicious that it was impossible even to dress him, and it was necessary to keep him muzzled constantly. The following morning Mr. Rarey led him behind an open carriage, on his road to London. This horse was returned to me by the Rawcliffe and Stud Company on. account of his vice, it being considered as much as a man's life was worth to attend to him.

" Greywell, April 7.'     "DOBCHESTER.""

him to London on the very day after, that he first backed him and had ridden him within three hours after the first interview, slow conviction swelled to enthusiasm. The list filled up rapidly.

The school in Kinnerton Street, to which Mr. Rarey was obliged to remove, was crowded, the excitement increasing with each lesson. On the day that Cruiser was exhibited for the first time, long before the doors were open, the little back street was filled with a fashionable mob, including ladies of the highest rank. An admission by noble non-subscribers with notes, gold, and cheques in hands, was begged for with a polite insinuating humility that was quite edifying. A hatful of ten-guinea subscriptions was thrust upon the unwilling secretary at the door with as much eagerness as if he had been the allotter of shares in a ten per cent, railway in the day of Hudsonian guarantees. And it must be observed that this crowd included among the mere fashion-mongers almost every distinguished horseman and hunting-man in the three kingdoms.

It is quite too late now to attempt to depreciate a system the value of which has been repeatedly and openly acknowledged by authorities above question. As to the place' for Mr. Rarey. Phlegon and Vatican would also be good patients. I am sorry to hear that the latter has been blinded: if leathern blinds had been put on his eyes, the same effect would have been produced."—*Morning Post*, March 2, 1858.

" secret," the subscribers must have known that it was impossible that a system that required so much space, and involved so much noise, could long remain a secret.

The Earl of Jersey, so celebrated in this century as a breeder of race-horses, in the last century as a rider to hounds, stood through a long lesson, and was as much delighted as his son the Honourable Frederick Villiers, Master of the Pytchley Hounds. Sir Tatton Sykes of Sledmere, perhaps the finest amateur horseman that ever rode a race, whose equestrian performances on the course and in the hunting-field date back more than sixty years, was as enthusiastic in his approval as the young Guardsman who, fortified by Mr. Rarey's lessons, mastered a mare that had defied the efforts of all the farriers of the Household Cavalry.

In a word, the five-hundred list was filled, and overflowed, the subscribers were satisfied, and the responsibility of Messrs. Tattersall as stakeholders for the public ceased, and the Secretary and Treasurer to the fund, having wound up the accounts and retired, tho connection between Mr. Rarey and the Messrs. Tattersall resolved itself into the use of an office at Hyde Park Corner.

The London subscription list had passed eleven hundred names, and, in conjunction with the subscription received in Yorkshire, Liverpool, 'Manchester, Dublin, and Paris, besides private lessons at £25 each, had realised upwards of £20,000 for Mr. Rarey and his partner, when the five-hundred secrecy agreement was extinguished by the re-publication of the little American pamphlet already mentioned.

It was high time that it should, for, while Mr. Rarey had been handsomely paid for his instruction, the more scrupulous of his subscribers were unable to practise his lessons for want of a place where they could work in secrecy.

But although the re-publication of Mr. Rarey'g American pamphlet virtually absolved his subscribers from the agreement which he gave up formally a few days later in his letter to the Times, it is quite absurd to assert that the little pamphlet teaches the Art of Horse-Taming as now practised by Mr. Rarey. Certainly no one but a horseman skilled in the equitation of schools could do much with a horse without great danger of injuring the animal and himself; if he had no other instruction than that contained in Mr. Rarey's clever, original, but vague chapters.

In the following work I shall endeavour to fill up the blanks in Mr. Rarey's sketch, and with the help of pictures and diagrams, show how a cool determined man or boy may break in any colt, and make him a docile hack, harness horse, or hunter; stand still, follow, and obey the voice almost as much as the reins.

To say that written or oral instructions will teach evey man how to grapple with savages like Stafford, Cruiser, Phlegon, or Mr. Gurney's gray colt, would be shere humbug—that must depend on the man; but we have an instance of what can be done that is encouraging. "When Mr. Rarey was so ill that he was unable to sit Mr. Gurney's gray colt, the boasting Mr. Good-enough tried his hand, and was beaten pale and trembling out of the circus by that equine tiger; but Mr. Thomas Rice, the jobmaster of Motcombe Street, who had had the charge of Cruiser in Mr. Rarey's absence up to that time, although he had never before tried his hand at Rareyrfying a horse, stuck to the gray colt, laid down, made him fast, and completely conquered 1dm in one evening, so that he was fit to be exhibited the next day, when Mr. Goodenough, *more suo*, claimed the benefit of tho victory.

Several ladies have succeeded famously in horse-taming ; but they have been ladies accustomed to horses and to exercise, and always with gentlemen by, in case a customer proved too tough.

Before concluding this desultory but necessary introductory sketch of the rise, progress, and success of the Rarey system,it will be as well, perhaps, for the benefit of lady readers, to give a personal sketch of Mr. Rarey, who is by no means the athletic giant that many imagine.

Mr. Rarey is about thirty years of age, of middle height, and well-proportioned figure, wiry and active rather than muscular—his complexion is almost effeminately fair, with more colour than is usually found in those of his countrymen who live in the cities of the sea-coast. And his fair hair, large gray eyes, which only light up and flash fire when he has an awkward customer to tackle, give him altogether the appearance of a Saxon Englishman. • His walk is remarkably light and springy, yet regular, as he turns round his horse; something between the set-up of a soldier and the light step of a sportsman. Altogether his appearance and manners are eminently gentlemanly. Although a self-educated and not a book-educated man, his conversation, when he cares to talk, for he is rather reserved, always displays a good deal of thoughtful originality, relieved by flashes of playful humour. This may be seen in his writing.

It may easily be imagined that he is extremely popular with all these with whom he has been brought in contact, and Las acquired the personal friendship of some of the most accomplished noblemen and gentlemen of the day.

Mr. Rarey's system of horse-training will infallibly supersede all others for both civil and military purposes, and his name will take rank among the great social reformers of the nineteenth century. May we have many more such importations from America !

# CHAPTER II.

## Mr. Rarey's Pamphlet.—Introduction,

MR. RAREY'S American Pamphlet would make about fifty pages of this type, if given in fall; but, in revising my Illustrated Edition, I have decided on omitting six pages of Introduction, which, copied from Mr. Hollo Springfield, an American author, do not contain any reliable facts or useful inferences.

The speculations of the American author, as to the early history of the horse, wee mitten without sufficient information. So far from the " polished Greeks " having, as he states, "ridden without bridles," we have the best authority in the frieze of the Parthenon for knowing that, although they rode barebacked on their compact cobby ponies, they used reins and handled them skilfully and elegantly.

To go still further back, the bas-reliefs in the British Museum, discovered by Mr. Layard in the Assyrian Palace of Nimroud, contain spirited representation of horses with bridles, ridden in hunting and in pursuit of enemies, as well as driven in war-chariots. These horses are Arabs, while those of the Elgin Marbles more resemble the cream-coloured Hanoverians which draw the state carriage of our sovereigns. In one of the Nimroud bas-reliefs, we have cavalry soldiers standing with the bridles of their horses in their hands, " waiting," as Mr. Bonomi tells us, " for the orders to mount;" but, as they stand on the left side, with the bridles in their left hands, it is difficult to understand how they could obey such an order with reasonable celerity.

The Arabian stories, as to the performances of Arab horses and their owners, must be received with considerable hesitation, for the horse is one of the subjects on which Orientals love to found their poetical fireside stories. This is certain, that the Arab horse being highly bred, is very intelligent, being reared from its birth in the family of its master, extremely docile, and, being always in the open air and fed on a moderate quantity of dry food, very hardy.

If we lived with our horses, as we do with our dogs, they would be equally affectionate and tractable.

In Norway, in consequence of the severity of the climate, the ponies are all housed during the winter, and thus become so familiar with their owner that there is scarcely any difficulty in putting them into harness, even the first time.

English thoroughbred horses, when once acclimatized and bred in the open air on the dry pastures of Australia and South Africa, are found, if not put to work too early, as enduring as the Arab. Experiments in the Indian artillery have proved that the Australian horse and the Cape[8] horse, which has also been improved by

---

8  The Cape horse has recently come into notice, in consequence of the publication of " Papers relating to the Purchase of Horses at the Gape for the Army of India." It seems that not less than 3300 have been purchased for that purpose; that Cape horses purchased by Colonel Havelock ar-

judicious crosses with English blood, are superior for strength and endurance to the Eastern horses bred in the stud establishments of the East India Company.

The exaggerated idea that long prevailed of the value of the Arab horse, as compared with the English thorough-bred, which is an Eastern horse improved by long years of care and ample food, has been to a great extent dissipated by the large importation of Arabs that took place after the Crimean war—in fact, they are on the average pretty ponies of great endurance, but of very little use in this country, where size is indispensable for profit. In the East they are of great value for cavalry; they are hardy and full of fire and spirit. " But," says Captain Nolan, " no horse can compare with the English—no horse is more easily broken in to anything and everything—there is no quality in which the English horse does not excel—no performance in which he cannot beat all competition; " and Nolan was as familiar with the Eastern, Hungarian, and German crosses with the Arab as with the English thorough-bred.

We spoil our horses, first by pampering them in hot stables under warm clothing; next, by working them too young; and, lastly, by entrusting their training to rude, ignorant men, who rely for leading colt the way he should go on mere force, harsh words, a sharp whip, .and the worrying use of the longeing rein. Rarey has shown how easily, quietly, and safely horses may be tamed; but we must also train men before we can obtain full benefit from our admirable breeds of horses.

---

rived from India in the Crimea in better con-dition than any other horses in the regiment; and that in the Caffre War Cape horses condemned by the martinets of a Remount Com-mittee, carried the 7th Dragoons, averaging, in marching order, over nineteen stone, and no privation or fatigue could make General Cath-cart's horses succumb, These horses are bred between the Arabs introduced by the Dutch and the English thoroughbred. I confess I Bee with surprise that Colonel Apperley, the remount agent, recommends crosses with Norfolk trotting and Cleveland stallions. No such cross has ever answered in this country. Had he recommended thoroughbred weight-carrying stallions in preference to Arabs, I could have understood his condemnation of the latter. I should have hesitated to set my opinion against Colonel Apperley, had I not found that he differs entirely from the late General Sir Walter Gilbert, the greatest horseman, take him for all in all, as a cavalry officer, as a flat and steeple-chase rider, and rider to hounds of his day.—*See Napier's Indian Misgovernment*, p. 286 et seq

Proof that our horses have become feeble from pampering may be found in Devonshire. There the common hacks of the county breed on the moors, and, crossed with native ponies, are usually undersized and coarse and heavy about the shoulders, like most wild horses, and all the inferior breeds of Arabs, but they are hardy and enduring to a degree that a Yorkshire breeder would scarcely believe. Mean-looking Galloways will draw a heavy dog-cart over the Devonshire hills fifty miles a-day for many days in succession.

A little common sense has been introduced into the management of our cavalry, since the real experience of the Crimean war. General Sir Charles Napier was not noticed when, nearly ten years ago, he wrote, " The cavalry charger, on a Hounslow Heath parade, well fed, well groomed, goes through a field-day without injury, although carrying more than twenty stone weight; he and his rider presenting together a kind of alderman centaur. But if in the field, half starved, they have, at the end of a forced march, to charge an enemy! The biped full of fire and courage, transformed by war-work to a wiry muscular dragoon, is able and willing, but the overloaded quadruped cannot gallop—he staggers."

Our poor horses thus loaded, are expected to bound to hand and spur, while the riders wield their swords worthily. They cannot; and both man and horse appear inferior to their Indian opponents. The Eastern warrior's eye is quick, but not quicker than the European's ; his heart is big, yet not bigger than the European's ; his arm is strong, but not so strong as the European's; the swing of his razor-like scimetar is terrible, but an English trooper's downright blow splits the skull. Why then does the latter fail? The light-weighted horse of the dark swordsman carries him round his foe with elastic bounds, and the strong European, unable to deal the cleaving blow, falls under the activity of an inferior adversary!

Since the war, light men with broad chests have been enlisted for Indian service. The next step, originally suggested by Nolan, that every cavalry soldier should train his own horse, will be made easy by the introduction of the Rarey system. Country horse-breakers are too ignorant, too prejudiced, and too much interested in keeping up a mystery that gives them three months employment, instead of three weeks, to adopt it. The reform will probably commence in the army and in racing stables.

In the following pages, I have given the text of the American edition of Mr. Rarey's pamphlet, and added the information I have derived from hearing his lectures, seeing his operations on " Cruiser," and other difficult horses, and from the experience of my friends and self in taming horses. Thus, in Chap. VI. to Mr. Rarey's five pages I have added sixteen, and nine woodcut illustrations. In Chap. VII. the directions for the drum, umbrella, and riding habit are in print for the first time, as well as the directions for mounting with slack girths. Chap3. VIII. to XIV. have been added, in order to make this little work a complete manual for those who wish to benefit in riding as well as training horses from the experience of others.

In my opinion, the Rarey system is invaluable for training colts, breaking horses into harness, and curing kickers and jibbers. I do not profess to be a horse-tamer, my pursuits are too sedentary during the greater part of the year, but I have succeeded with even colts. I tried my hand on two of them wild from the Devonshire moors, in August last, and succeeded perfectly in an hour. I made them as affectionate as pet ponies, ready to follow me everywhere, as well as to submit to be mounted and ridden.

As to curing vicious horses, all that can be safely said is, that it puts it into the power of a *courageous, calm-tempered horseman* to conquer any horse. " Cruiser " was quiet in the hands of Mr. Rarey and Mr. Rice, but when insulted in the circus of Leicester Square by a violent jerk, he rushed at his tormentor with such ferocity that he cleared the ring of all the spangled troope, yet, in the midst of his rage, he halted and ran up on being called by Rarey.

From this we learn that such a horse wont be bullied and must not be feared. But such vicious horses are rare exceptions, It is curious, that Mr. Rarey should have made his reputation by the least useful exercise of his art.

# CHAPTER III

The three fundamental principles of the Rarey Theory.—Heads of the
Rarey Lectures.—Editor's paraphrase.—That any horse may be taught
docility.—That a horse should be so handled and tied as to feel inferior
to man.—That a horse should be allowed to see, smell, and feel all fearful
objects.—Key note of the Rarey system.

FIRST.—That he is so constituted by nature that he will not offer resistance to
any demand made of him which he fully comprehends, if made in a way consistent
with the laws of his nature.

SECOND.—That he has no consciousness of his strength beyond his experience, and can be handled according to our will without force.

THIRD.—That we can, in compliance with the laws of his nature, by which he
examines all things new to him, take any object, however frightful, around, over, or
on him, that does not inflict pain—without causing him to fear.

To take these assertions in order, I will first give you some of the reasons why
I think he is naturally obedient, and will not offer resistance to anything fully com-
prehended. The horse, though possessed of some faculties superior to man's, being
deficient in reasoning powers, has no knowledge of right or wrong, of free will and
independent government, and knows not of any imposition practised upon him,
however unreasonable these impositions may be. Consequently, he cannot come to
any decision as to what he should or should not do, because he has not the reasoning faculties of man to argue the justice of the thing demanded of him. If he had,
taking into consideration his superior strength, he would be useless to man as a
servant. *Give him mind* in proportion to his strength, and he will demand of us the
green fields for his inheritance, where he will roam at leisure, denying the right of
servitude at all. God has wisely formed his nature so that it can be operated upon

by the knowledge of man according to the dictates of his will; and he might well be termed an unconscious, submissive servant. This truth we can see verified in every day's experience by the abuses practised upon him. Any one who chooses to be so cruel can mount the noble steed and run him till he drops with fatigue, or, as is often the case with the more spirited, falls dead beneath his rider. If he had the power to reason, would he not rear and pitch his rider, rather than suffer him to run him to death? Or would he condescend to carry at all the vain impostor, who, with but equal intellect, was trying to impose on his equal rights and equally independent spirit? But, happily for us, he has no consciousness of imposition, no thought of disobedience except by impulse caused by the violation of the law of his nature. Consequently, when disobedient, it is the fault of man.

Then, we can but come to the conclusion that, if a horse is not taken in a way at variance with the laws of his nature, he will do anything that he fully comprehends, without making any offer of resistance.

Second—The fact of the horse being unconscious of the amount of his strength can be proven to the satisfaction of any one. For instance, such remarks as these are common, and perhaps familiar to your recollection. One person says to another, " If that wild horse there was conscious of the amount of his strength, his owner would have no business with him in thai vehicle: such light reins and harness, too—if he knew, he could snap them asunder in a minute, and be as free as the air we breathe;" and, " That horse yonder, that is pawing and fretting to follow the company that is fast leaving him— if he knew his strength, he would not remain long fastened to that hitching post so much against his will, by. a strap that would no more resist his powerful weight and strength than a cotton thread would bind a strong man." Yet these facts, made common by every-day occurrence, are not thought of as anything wonderful. Like the ignorant man who looks at the different phases of the moon, you look at these things as he looks at her different changes, without troubling your mind with the question, " Why are these things so ? " What would be the condition of the world if all our minds lay dormant? If men did not think, reason, and act, our undisturbed, slumbering intellects would not excel the imbecility of the brute; we should live in chaos, hardly aware of our existence. And yet, with all our activity of mind, we daily pass by unobserved that which would be wonderful if philosophized and reasoned upon; and with the same inconsistency wonder at that which a little consideration, reason, and philosophy, would make but a simple affair.

Third—He will allow any object, however frightful in appearance, to come around, over, or on him, that does not inflict pain.

We know, from a natural course of reasoning, that there has never been an effect without a cause; and we infer from this that there can be no action, either in animate or inanimate matter, without there first being some cause to produce it. And from this self-evident fact we know that there is some cause for every impulse or movement of either mind or matter, and that this law governs every action or movement of the animal kingdom. Then, according to this theory, there must be some cause before fear can exist; and if fear exists from the effect of imagination, and not from the infliction of real pain, it can be removed by complying with those laws of nature by which the horse examines an object, and determines upon its innocence or harm.

A log or stump by the road-side may be, in the imagination of the horse, some great beast about to pounce upon him; but after you take him up to it, and let him stand by it a little while, and touch it with his nose, and go through his process of examination, he will not care anything more about it. And the same principle and process will have the same effect with any other object, however frightful in appearance, in which there is no harm. Take a boy that has been frightened by a false face, or any other object that he could not comprehend at once; but let him take that face or object in his hands and examine it, and he will not care anything more about it. This is a demonstration of the same principle.

With this introduction to the principles of my theory, I shall next attempt to teach you how to put it into practice ; and whatever instructions may follow, you can rely on as having been proven practically by my own experiments. And knowing, from experience, just what obstacles I have met with in handling bad horses, I shall try to anticipate them for you, and assist you in surmounting them, by commencing with the first steps to be taken with the colt, and accompanying you through the whole task of breaking.

These three principles have been enlarged upon and, explained in a fuller and more familiar manner by Mr. Rarey in his Lectures, of which the following are the heads.

" Principles on which horses should be treated and educated —not by fear or force—By an intelligent application of skill with firmness and patience—How to approach a colt—How to halter—How teach to lead in twenty minutes—How to subdue and cause to lie down in fifteen minutes—How to tame and cure fear and-nervousness—How to saddle and bridle—How to accustom to be mounted and ridden—How to accustom to a drum—to an umbrella—to a lady's habit, or any other object, in a few minutes—How to harness a horse for the first time—How to drive a horse unbroken to harness, and make go steady, single or double, in a couple of hours—How to make any horse stand still until called —How to make a horse follow his owner."

In plain language, Mr. Rarey means, that—
1st. That any horse may be taught to do anything that a horse can do if taught in a proper manner.
'

2nd. That a horse is not conscious of his own strength until he has resisted and conquered a man, and that by Taking advantage of man's reasoning powers a horse can-be handled in such a manner that he shall not find out his strength.

3rd. That by enabling a horse to examine every object with which we desire to make him familiar, with the organs naturally used for that purpose, viz. *seeing, smelling,* and *feeling,* you may take any object around, over, and on him that does not actually hurt him.

Thus, for example, the objects which affright horses are the feel of saddles, riding-habits, harness, and wheeled carriages; the sight of umbrellas and flags; loaded

waggons, troops, or a crowd; the sound of wheels, of drums, of musketry. There
are thousands of horses that by degrees learn to bear all these things; others, under
our old imperfect system, never improve, and continue nervous or vicious to the
end of their lives. Every year good sound horses are drafted from the cavalry, or
from hunters' barbs and carriage-horses, into omnibuses and Hansom cabs, because
they cannot be made to bear the sound of drums and firearms, or will not submit
Jo be shod, and be safe and steady in crowded cities, or at covert side. Nothing is
more common than to hear that such a horse would be invaluable if he would go
in harness, or carry a lady, or that a racehorse of great swiftness is almost valueless
because his temper is so bad, or his nervousness in a crowd so great that he cannot
be depended on to start or to run his best.

All these varieties of nervous and vicious animals are deteriorated in value,
because they have not been educated to confide in and implicitly obey man.

The whole object of the Rarey system is, to give the horse full confidence in
his rider, to make him obedient to his voice and gestures, and to impress the animal
with the belief that he could not successfully resist him.

Lord Pembroke, in his treatise on Horsemanship, says, "His hand is the best
whose indications are so clear that his horse cannot mistake them, *and whose gentleness and fearlessness* alike induce obedience to them." " The noblest animal," says
Colonel Greenwood, " will obey such a rider; and it is ever the noblest, most intelligent horses, that rebel the most. In riding a colt or a restive horse we should never
forget that he has the right to resist, and that as far as he can judg we have not the
right to insist. The great thing in horsemanship is to get the horse to be your party,
not to obey only, but to obey willingly. For this reason the lessons cannot be begun
too early, or be too progressive."

The key-note to the Rarey system is to be found in the opening sentence of his
early lectures in England: "Man has reason in addition to his senses. A horse judges
everything by SEEING, SMELLING, and FEELING." It must be the business of every one who undertakes to train colts that they shall see, smell, and feel everything

that they are to wear or to bear.

# CHAPTER IV.

How to drive a colt from pasture.—How to drive into a stable.—The kind of hatter.—Experiment with a robe or cloak.—HorM-tamatg drugs.—The Editors remarks.—Importance of patience.—Best kind of head-stall.—Danger of approaching some colts.—Hints from' a Colonel of the Life Guards.

## HOW TO DB1VE A COLT FROM PASTUBE.

Go to the pasture and walk around the whole herd quietly, and at such a distance as not to cause them to scare and run. Then approach them very slowly, and if they stick up their heads and seem to be frightened, stand still until they become quiet, so as not to make them run before you are close enough to drive them in the direction you want them to go. And when you begin to drive, do not flourish your arms or halloo, but gently follow them off, leaving the direction open that you wish them to take. Thus taking advantage of their ignorance, you will be able to get them into the pound as easily as the hunter drives the quails into his net. For, if they have always run in the pasture uncared for (as many horses do in prairie countries and on large plantations), there is no reason why they should not be as wild as the sportsman's birds, and require the same gentle treatment, if you want to get them without trouble; for the horse, in his natural state, is as wild as a stag, or any of the undomesticated animals, though more easily tamed.

## HOW TO STABLE A COLT WITHOUT TROUBLE.

The next step will be, to get the horse into a stable or shed. This should be done as quietly as possible, so as not to excite any suspicion in the horse of any danger befalling him. The best way to do this, is to lead a broken horse into the stable first and hitch (tie) him, then quietly walk around the colt and let him go in of his own accord. It is almost impossible to get men who have never practised on this principle to go slowly and considerately enough about it. They do not know that in handling a wild horse, above all other things, is that good old aSage true, that " haste makes waste;" that is, waste of time—for the gain of trouble and perplexity.

One wrong move may frighten your horse, and make him think it necessary to escape at all hazards for the safety of his life—and thus make two hours' work of a ten minutes' job ; and this would be all your own fault, and entirely unnecessary— for *he will not run unless you run after him, and that would not be good policy unless you knew that you could outrun him, for you will have to let him stop of his own accord after a*ll. But he will not try to break away unless you attempt to force him into measures. If he does not see the way at once, and is a little fretful about going in, do not undertake to drive him, but give him a little less room outside, by gently closing in around him. Do not raise your arms, but let them hang at your side, for you might as well raise a club: *the horse has never studied anatomy, and does not. know but that they will unhinge themselves and fly at him.* If he attempts to turn back, walk before him, but do not run; and if he gets past you, encircle him again in the same quiet manner, and he will soon find that you are not going to hurt him ; and then you can walk so close around him that he will go into the stable for more room, and to get farther from you. As soon as he is in, remove the quiet horse and shut the door. This will be his first notion of confinement—not knowing how he got into such a place, nor how to get out of it. That he may take it as quietly at possible, see that the shed is entirely free from dogs, chickens, or anything that would annoy him. Then give him a few ears of corn, and let him remain alone fifteen or twenty minutes, until he has examined his apartment, and has become reconciled to his confinement

TIME TO REFLECT.

And now, while your horse is eating those few ears of corn, is the proper time to see that your halter is ready and all right, and to reflect on the best mode of operations ; for in horse-breaking it is highly important that you should be governed by some system. And you should know, before you attempt to do anything, just what you are going to do, and how you are going to do it And, if you are experienced in the art of taming wild horses, you ought to be able to tell, within a few minutes, the length of time it would take you to halter the colt, and teach him to lead.

THE KIND OF HALTER.

Always use a leather halter, and be sure to have it made so that it will not draw tight around his nose if he pulls on it It should be of the right size to fit his head easily and nicely; so that the nose-band will not be too tight or too low. Never put a rope halter on an unbroken colt, under any circumstances whatever. Hope halters have caused more horses to hurt or kill them-< selves than would pay for twice the cost of all the leather halters that have ever been needed for the purpose of halter- ing colts. It is almost impossible to break a colt that is very wild with a rope halter, without having him pull, rear, and throw himself, and thus endanger his life; and I will tell you why. It is just as natural for a horse to try to get his head out of any- thing that hurts it, or feels unpleasant, at it would be for you to try to get your hand out of a fire. The cords of the rope are hard and cutting; this makes him raise his head and draw on it, and as soon as he pulls, the slip noose (the way rope halters are always made) tightens, and pinches his nose, and then he will struggle for life, until, perchance, he throws himself; and who would have his horse throw himself, and run the risk of breaking his neck, rather than pay the price of a leather halter ? But this is not the worst. *A horse that has once pulled on his halter can never be a well broken as one that has never pulled at all.*

But before we attempt to do anything more with the colt, I will give you some of the characteristics of his nature, that you may better understand his motions. Every one that has ever paid any attention to the horse, has noticed his natural inclination to smell everything which to him looks new and frightful. This is their strange mode of examining everything. And when they are frightened at anything, though they look at it sharply, they seem to have no confidence in their eyesight alone, but must touch it with their nose before they are entirely satisfied; and, as soon as they have done that, all seems right.

EXPERIMENT WITH THE KOBE.

If you want to satisfy yourself of this characteristic of the horse, and to learn something of importance concerning the peculiarities of his nature, &c, turn him into the barn-yard, or a large stable will do, and then gather up something that you know will frighten him—a red blanket, buffalo robe, or something of that kind. Hold it up so that he can see it, he will stick up his head and snort Then throw it down somewhere in the centre of the lot or bam, and walk off to one side. Watch his motions, and study his nature. If he is frightened at the object, he will not rest until he has touched it with his nose. You will see him begin to walk around the robe and snort, all the time getting a little closer, as if drawn up by some magic spell, until he finally gets within reach of it. He will then very cautiously stretch out his neck as far as he can reach, merely touching it with his nose, as though he thought it was ready to fly at him. But after he has repeated these touches a few times, for the first time (though he has been looking at it all the while) he seems to have an idea what it is. But now he has found, by the sense of feeling, that it is nothing that will do him any harm, and he is ready to play with it. And if you watch him closely, you will see him take hold of it with his teeth, and raise it up and pull at it. And in a few minutes you can see that he has not that same wild look about his eye, but stands like a horse biting at some familiar stump.

Yet the horse is never so well satisfied when he is about anything that has frightened him, as when he is standing with his nose to it. And, in nine cases out of ten, you will see some of that same wild look about him again, as he turns to alk from it. And you will, probably, see him looking back very suspiciously as he walks away, as though he thought it might come after him yet. And in all probability, he will have to go back and make another examination before he is satisfied. But he will familiarize himself with it, and, if he should run in that field a few days, the robe that frightened him so much at first will be no more to him than a familiar stump.

We might very naturally suppose from the fact of the horse's applying his nose to everything new to him, that he always does so for the purpose of smelling these objects. But I believe that it is as much or more for the purpose of feeling, and that he makes use of his nose, or muzzle (as it is sometimes called), as we would of our hands; because it is the only organ by which he can touch or feel anything with much susceptibility.

I believe that he invariably makes use of the four senses, SEEING, HEARING, SMELLING, and FEELING, in all of his examinations, of which the sense of feeling is, perhaps, the most important. And I think that in the experiment with the robe, his gradual approach and final touch with his nose was as much for the purpose of feeling as anything else, his sense of smell being so keen that it would not be necessary for him to touch his nose against anything in order to get the proper scent; for it is said that a horse can smell a man at a distance of a mile. And if the scent of the robe was all that was necessary he could get that several rods off. But we know from experience, that if a horse sees and smells a robe a short distance from him he is very much frightened (unless he is used to it) until he touches or feels it with his nose; which is a positive proof that feeling is the controlling sense in this case.

HORSE-TAMING DRUGS (?).

It is a prevailing opinion among horsemen generally that the sense of smell is the governing sense of the horse. And Baucher, as well as others, has with that view got up receipts of strong smelling oils, &c, to tame the horse, sometimes using the chestnut of his leg, which they dry, grind into powder, and blow into his nostrils, sometimes using the oils of rhodium, origanum, &c, that are noted for their strong smell; and sometimes they scent the hand with the sweat from under the arm, or blow their breath into his nostrils, &c, &c. All of which, as far as the scent goes, have no effect whatever in gentling the horse, or conveying any idea to his mind; though the acts that accompany these efforts—handling him, touching him about the nose and head, and pat ting him, as they direct you should, after administering the articles, may have a very great effect, which they mistake for the effect of the ingredients used; And Baueher, in his work, entitled " The Arabian Art of Taming Horses," page 17, tells us how to accustom a horse to a robe, by administering certain articles to his nose; and goes on to say that these articles must first be applied to the horse's nose, before you attempt to break him, in order to operate successfully.

Now, reader, can you, or any one else, give one single reason how scent can convey any idea to the horse's mind of what we want him to do ? If not, then of course strong scents of any kind can be of no use in taming the unbroken horse. For, everything that we get him to do of his own accord, without force, must be accomplished by conveying our ideas to his mind. I say to my horse, "Go-long!" and he goes; "Ho!" and he stops, because these two words, of which he has learned the meaning by the tap of the whip and the pull of the rein that first accompanied them, convey the two ideas to his mind of *go and stop*.

It is impossible to teach the horse a single thing by the means of scent alone; and as for affection, that can be better created by other means.

How long do you suppose a horse would have to stand and smell a bottle of oil, before he would learn to bend his knee and make a bow at your bidding, " Go yonder and bring my hat," or " Gome here and lie down ? " The absurdity of trying to break or tame the horse by the means of receipts for articles to smell at, or of medicine to swallow, is self-evident.

The only science that has ever existed in the world, relative to the breaking of horses, that has been of any value, is that method which, taking them in their native state, improves their intelligence.

EDITOR'S REMABKS.

The directions for driving colts from the pasture are of less importance in this country where fields are enclosed, and the most valuable colts wear headstalls, and are handled, or ought to be, from their earliest infancy; but in Wales, and on wastes like Exmoor or Dartmoor, the advice may be found useful.

Under all circumstances it is important that the whole training of a colt (and training of the boy who is to manage horses) should be conducted from first to last on consistent principles; for, in the mere process of driving a colt from the field to the fold-yard, ideas of terror may be instilled into the timid animal, for instance, by idle drumming on a hat, which it will take weeks or months to eradicate.

The next step is to get the colt into a stable, barn, or other building sufficiently large for the early operations, and secluded from those sights and sounds so common in a farmyard, which would be likely to distract his attention. In training a colt the squeaking of a litter of pigs has lost me the work of three hours. An outfield, empty barn, or bullock- shed, is better than any place near the homestead.

It is a good plan to keep an intelligent old horse expressly for the purpose of helping to train and lead the young colts. I have known horses that seemed to take a positive pleasure in helping to subdue a wild colt when first put in double harness.

The great point is not to force or frighten a colt into the stable, but to edge him into it quietly, and cause him to glide in of his own accord. In this simple operation, the horse-trainer will test himself the indispensable quality of a horse trainer— patience. A word I shall have to repeat until my readers are almost heartily sick of the "*damnable iteration*" There is a world of equestrian wisdom in two sentences of the chapter just quoted, " he will not run unless you run after him," and " the horse has not studied anatomy."

The observations about rope halters are very sound, and in addition I may add, that the mouths of hundreds of horses are spoiled by the practice of passing a looped rope round the lower jaw of a fiery horse, which the rider often makes the stay for keeping himself in his seat.

The best kind of head-stall for training colts is that delineated at the head of this chapter[9], called the Bush Bridle, to which any kind of bit may be attached, and by unbuckling the bit it is converted into a capital halter, with a rope for leading a colt or picketing a horse at night

The long rope is exactly what Mr. Rarey recommends for teaching a colt to lead. Every one of any experience will agree that " a horse that has once pulled on his halter can never be so well broken as one that has never pulled at all."

9   Made by Stokey, North Street, Little Moorfields, London.

The directions for stroking and patting the body and limbs of a colt are curious, as pro@ring that an operatio n which we have been in the habit of performing as a matter of course without attaching any particular virtue to it, has really a sort of mesmeric effect in soothing and conciliating a nervous animal. The directions in Chapter V. for approaching a colt deserve to be studied very minutely, remembering always the maxim printed at p. 57—*Fear and anger, a good horseman should never feel,*

It took Mr. Rarey himself two hours to halter a savage half-broken colt in Liverpool, but then he had the disadvantage of being surrounded by an impatient whispering circle of spectators. At Lord Poltimore's seat in Devonshire, in February last (1858), Lord Rivers was two hours alone with a very sulky biting colt, but finally succeeded in haltering and saddling him. Yet his lordship had only seen one lesson illustrated on a very difficult horse at the Duke of Wellington's school. But this operation is much more easily described than executed, because some colts will smell at your hand one moment, and turn round as quick as lightning, and plant their heels in your ribs if you are not very active, and don't stand very close to them. On the directions for using the whip, p. 55, with colts of a stubborn disposition, I can say nothing, never having seen it so employed; but it is evident, that it must be employed with very great discretion.

The directions for haltering are very complete, but to execute them with a colt or horse that paws violently, even in play, with his fore-feet, requires no common agility. But I may mention that I saw Mr. Rarey alone put a bridle on a horse seventeen hands high that was notoriously difficult to bridle even with two men assisting in the operation.

In reference to the hints for treating a colt in a little work from which I have already quoted, a colonel in the Life Guards says, " The great thing in horsemanship is to get your horse to be of your party; not only to obey, but to obey willingly. For this reason, a young horse cannot be begun with too early, and his lessons cannot be too gradually progressive. He should wear a headstall from the beginning, be accustomed to be held and made fast by the head, to give up all four feet, to bear the girthing of a roller, to be led, &c." But if all this useful preliminary education, in which climbing through gaps after an old hunter, and taking little jumps, be omitted, then the Rarey system comes in to shorten your domesticating labours.

" A wild horse, until tamed, is just as wild and fearful as a wild stag taken for the first time in the toils.

" When a horse hangs back and leads unwillingly, the eommon error is to get in front of him and pull him. This may answer when the man is stronger than the horse, but not otherwise.

" In leading you should never be further forward than your horse's shoulder: with your right-hand hold his head in front of you by the bridle close to his mouth or the head-stall, and with your left hand touch him with a whip as far back as you can; if you have not a whip you can use a stirrup-leather."

# CHAPTER V.

Powell's system of approaching & colt.—Rarey's remarks on.—Lively high-spirited horses tamed easily.—Stubborn sulky ones more dif-ficult.—Motto, " Fear, love and obey."—Use of a whalebone gig-whip. —How to frighten and then approach.—Use kind words. —How to halter and lead a colt.— By the side of a horse.—To lead into a stable.—To tie up to a manger.— Editor's remarks.—Longeing. Use and abuse of.—On bitting.—Sort of bit for a colt.—Dick Christian's bit.—The wooden gag bit

BUT, before we go further, I will give you Willis J. Powell's system of approaching a wild colt, as given by him in, a work published in Europe, about the year 1814, on the " Art of Taming Wild Horses."[10]He says, " A horse is gentled by my secret in from two to sixteen hours." The time I have most commonly employed

---

10    Is there such a work ? I cannot find it in any English catalogue.-Itraroa.

has ' been from four to six hours. He goes on to say, " Cause your horse to be put in a small yard, stable, or room. If In a stable or room, it ought to be large, in order to give him some exercise with the halter" before you lead him out. If the horse belongs to that class which appears only to fear man, you must introduce yourself gently into the stable, room, or yard, where the horse is. He will naturally run from you, and frequently turn his head from you; for you must walk about extremely slow and softly, so that he can see you whenever he turns his head towards you, which he never fails to do in a short time, say in a quarter Or half an hour. I never knew one to be much longer without turning towards me,

" At the very moment he turns his head, hold out your left hand towards him, and stand perfectly still, keeping your eyes upon the horse, watching his motions, if he makes any. If the horse does not stir for ten or fifteen minutes, advance as slowly as possible, and without making tho least noise, always holding out your left hand, without any other ingredient in it than what nature put in it." He says, " I have made use of certain ingredients before people, such as the sweat under my arm, &c, to disguise the real secret, and many believed that the docility to which the horse arrived in so short a time was owing to these ingredients: but you see from this explanation that they were of no use whatever. The implicit faith placed in these ingredients, though innocent of themselves, becomes ' faith without works.' And thus men remained always in doubt concerning the secret. If the horse makes the least motion when you advance towards him, stop, and remain perfectly still until he is quiet. Remain a few moments in this condition, and then advance again in the same slow and almost imperceptible manner. Take notice—if the horse stirs, stop, without changing your position. It is very uncommon for the horse to stir more than once after you begin to advance, yet there are exceptions. He generally keeps his eyes steadfast on you, until you get near enough to touch him on the forehead. When you are thus near to him, raise slowly and by degrees your hand, and let it come in contact with that part just above the nostrils, as lightly as possible. If the horse flinches (as many will), repeat with great rapidity these light strokes upon the forehead, going a little farther up towards his ears by degrees, and descending with the same rapidity until he will let you handle his forehead all over. Now let the strokes be repeated with more force over all his forehead, descending by lighter strokes to each side of his head, until you can handle that part·with equal facility. Then touch in the same light manner, making your hands and fingers play around, the lower part of the horse's ears, coming down now and then to his forehead, which may be looked upon as the helm that governs all the rest.

" Having succeeded in handling his ears, advance towards the neck, with the same precautions, and in the same manner; observing always to augment the force of the strokes whenever the horse will permit it. Perform the same on both sides of the neck, until he lets you take it in your arms without flinching.

" Proceed in the same progressive manner to the sides, and then to the back of the horse. Every time the horse shows any nervousness, return immediately to the forehead, as the true standard, patting him with your hands, and thence rapidly to where you had already arrived, always gaining ground a considerable distance farther on every time this happens. The head, ears, neck, and body being thus gentled, proceed from the back to the root of the tail.

" This must be managed with dexterity, as a horse is never to be depended on that is skittish about the tail. Let your hand fall lightly and rapidly on that part next to the body a minute or two, and then you will begin to give it a slight pull upwards every quarter of a minute. At the same time you continue this handling of him, augment the force of the strokes as well as the raising of the tail, until you can raise it and handle it with the greatest ease, which commonly happens in a quarter of an hour in most horses, in others almost immediately, and in some much longer. It now remains to handle all his legs; from the tail come back again to the head, handle it well, as likewise the ears, breast, neck, &c., speaking now and then to the horse. Begin by degrees to descend to the legs, always ascending and descending, gaining ground every time you descend, until you get to his feet

" Talk to the horse in Latin, Greek, French, English, or Spanish, or in any other language you please; but let him hear the sound of your voice, which at the beginning of the operation is not quite so necessary, but which I have always done in making him lift up his feet 'Hold up your foot'—'Leve le pied'—'Aha el pie'—' Aran ton poda,' &c.; at the same time lift his foot with your hand. He soon becomes familiar with the sounds, and will hold up his foot at command. Then proceed to the hind feet, and go on in the same man-ner ; and in a short time the horse will let you lift them, and even take them up in your arms.

" All this operation is no magnetism, no galvanism; it is merely taking away the fear a horse generally has of a man, and familiarizing the animal with his master. As the horse .doubtless experiences a certain pleasure from this handling, he will soon become gentle under it, and show a, very marked attachment to his keeper."

### RAREY'S REXABKS ON POWELL'S TREATMENT,

These instructions are very good, but not quite sufficient for horses of all kinds, and for haltering and leading the colt; but I have inserted them here because they give some of the true philosophy of approaching the horse, and of establishing confidence between man and horse. He speaks only of the kind that fear man.

To those who understand the philosophy of horsemanship, these are the easiest trained; for when we have a horse that is wild and lively, we can train him to oar will in a very short time—for they are generally quick to learn, and always ready to obey. But there is another kind that are of a stubborn or vicious disposition ; and although they are not wild, and do not require taming, in the sense it is generally understood, they are just as ignorant as a wild horse, if not more so, and need to be taught just as much: and in order to have them obey quickly, it is very necessary that they should be made to fear their master; for, in order to obtain perfect obedience from any horse, we must first have him fear us, for our motto is, " Fear, love and obey;" and we must have the fulfilment of the first two before we Can expect the latter; for it is by our philosophy of creating fear, love, and confidence, that we govern to our will every kind of horse whatever.

Then, in order to take horses as we find them, of all kinds, and to train them to our liking, we should always take with us, when we go into a stable to train a colt, a long switch whip (whalebone buggy-whips are the best), with a good silk cracker, so as to cut keenly and make a sharp report. This, if handled with dexterity, and rightly applied, accompanied with a sharp, fierce word, will be sufficient to enliven the spirits of any horse. With this whip in your right hand, with the lash pointing backward, enter the stable alone. It is a great disadvantage, in training a horse, to have any one in the Stable with you; you should be entireiy alone, so as to have nothing but yourself to attract his attention, if he is wild, you will soon see him on the opposite side of the stable from you; and now is the time to use a little judgment. I should not require, myself, more than half or three-quarters of an hour to handle any kind of colt, and have him running about in the stable after me; though I would advise a new beginner to take more time, and not be in too much of a hurry. If you have but one colt to gentle, and are not particular about the length of time you spend, and have not had any experience in handling colts, I would advise you to take Mr. Powell's method at first, till you gentle him, which, he says, takes from two to six hours. But as I want to accomplish the same, and, what is more, teach the horse to lead, in less than one hour, I shall give you a much quicker process of accomplishing the same end. Accordingly, when you have entered the stable, stand still, and let your horse look at you a minute or two, and as soon as he is settled in one place, approach him slowly, with both arms stationary, your right hanging by your side, holding the whip as directed, and the left bent at the elbow, with your hand projecting. As you approach him, go not too much towards his head or croup, so as not to make him move either forward or backward, thus keeping your horse stationary; if he does move a little either forward or backward, step a little to the right or left very cautiously; this will keep him in one place. As you get very near him, draw a little to his shoulder, and stop a few seconds. If you are in his reach he will turn his head and smell your hand, not that he has any preference for your hand, but because that is projecting, and is the nearest portion of your body to the horse. This all colts will do, and they will smell your naked hand just as quickly as they will 6f anything that you can put in it, and with just as good an effect, however much some men have preached the doctrine of taming horses by giving them the scent of articles from the hand. I have already proved that to be a mistake. As soon as he touches your hand with his nose, caress him as before directed, always using a very light, soft hand, merely touching the horse, always rubbing the way the hair lies, so that your hand will pass along as smoothly as possible. As you stand by his side, you may find it more convenient to rub his neck or the side of his head, which will answer the same purpose as rubbing his forehead. Favour every inclination of the horse to smell or touch you with his nose. *Always follow each touch or communication of this kind with the most tender and affectionate caresses, accompanied with a kind look, and pleasant word of some sort*, such as, " Ho! my little boy—ho ! my little boy!" " Pretty boy ! " " " Nice lady ! " or something of that kind, constantly repeating the same words, with the same kind, steady tone of voice; for the horse soon learns to read the expression of the face and voice, and will know as well when fear, love, or anger prevails, as you know your own feelings; two of which, FEAR AND

ANGER, A GOOD HORSEMAN SHOULD NEVER FEEL.

IF TOUR HORSE IS OF A STUBBORN DISPOSITION.

If your horse, instead of being wild, seems to be of a stubborn or mulish disposition; if he lays back his ears as you approach him, or turns his heels to kick you, he has not that regard or fear of man that he should have, to enable you to handle him quickly and easily; and it might be well to give him a few sharp cuts with the whip, about the legs, pretty close to the body. It will crack keenly as it plies around his legs, and the crack of the whip will affect him as much as the stroke ; besides on6 sharp cut about his legs will affect him more than two or three over his back, the skin on the inner part of his legs or about his flank being thinner, more tender, than on his back. But do not whip him much—just enough to frighten him; it *is not because we want to hurt the horse that we whip him*—we only do it to frighten vice and stubbornness out of him. But whatever you do, do quickly, sharply, and with a good deal of fire, but always without anger. If you are going to frighten him at all, you must do it at once. Never go into a pitched battle with your horse, and whip him until he is mad and will fight you; it would be better not to touch him at all, for you will establish, instead of fear and respect, feelings of resentment, hatred, and ill-will. It will do him no good, but harm, to strike him, unless you can frighten him; but if you can succeed in frightening him, you can whip him without making him mad; *for fear and anger never exist together in the horse*, and as soon as one is visible, you will find that the other has disappeared. As soon as you have frightened him, so that he will stand up straight and pay some attention to you, approach him again, and caress him a good deal more than you whipped him; thus you will excite the two controlling passions of his nature, love and fear; he will love and fear you, too; and, as soon as he learns what you require, will obey quickly.

### HOW TO HALTER AND LEAD A COLT.

As soon as you have gentled the colt a little, take the halter in your left hand, and approach him as before, and on the same side that you have gentled him. If he ' is very timid about your approaching closely to him, you can get up to him quicker by making the whip a part of your arm, and reaching out very gently with the butt end of it, rubbing him lightly on the neck, all the time getting a little closer, shortening the whip by taking it up in your hand, until you finally get close enough to put your hands on him. If he is inclined to hold his head from you, put the end of the halter-strap around his neck, drop your whip, and draw very gently; he will let his neck give, and you can pull his head to you. Then take hold of that part of the halter which buckles over the top of his head, and pass the long side, or that part which goes into the buckle, under his neck, grasping it on the opposite side with your right hand, letting the first strap loose—the latter will be sufficient to hold his head to you. Lower the halter a little, just enough to get his nose into that part which goes around it; then raise it somewhat, and fasten the top buckle, and you will have it all right. The first time you halter a colt you should stand on the left side, pretty well back to his shoulder, only taking hold of that part of the halter that goes around his neck; then with your two hands about his neck you can hold his head to you, and raise the halter on it without making him dodge by putting your hands about his nose. You should have a long rope or strap ready, and as soon as you have the halter on, attach this to it, so that you can let him walk the length of the stable without letting go of the strap, or without making him pull on the halter, for if you only let him feel the weight of your hand an the halter, and give him rope when he runs from you, he will never rear, pull, or throw himself, yet you will be holding him all the time, and doing more towards gentling him than if you had the power to snub him right up, and hold him to one spot; because he does not know anything about his strength, and if you don't do anything to make him pull, he will never know that he can. In a few minutes you can begin to control him with the halter, then shorten the distance between yourself and the horse by taking up the strap in your hand.

As soon as he will allow you to hold him by a tolerably short strap, and to step up to him without flying back, you can begin to give him some idea about leading. But to do this, do not go before and attempt to pull him after you, but commence by pulling him very quietly to one side. He has nothing to brace either side of his neck, and will soon yield to a steady, gradual pull of the halter; and as soon as you have pulled him a step or two to one side, step up to him and caress him, and then pull him again, repeating this operation until you can pull him around in every direction, and walk about the stable with him, which you can do in a few minutes, for he will soon think when you have made him step to the right or left a few times, that he is compelled to follow the pull of the halter, not knowing that he has the power to resist your pulling; besides, you have handled him so gently that he is not afraid of you, and you always caress him when he comes up to you, and he likes that, and would just as lief follow you as not. And after he has had a few lessons of that kind, if you turn him out in a field, he will come up to you every opportunity he gets.

You should lead him about in the stable some time before you take him out, opening the door, so that he can see out, leading him up to it and back again, and past it

See that there is nothing on the outside to make him jump when you take him out, and as you go out with him, try to make him go very slowly, catching hold of the halter close to the jaw with your left hand, while the right is resting on the top of the neck, holding to his

mane- After you are out with him a little while, you can lead him about as you please.

Don't let any second person come up to you when you first take him out; a stranger taking hold of the halter would frighten him, and make him run. There should not even be any one standing near him, to attract his attention or scare him*

If you are alone, and manage him rightly, it will not require any more force to lead or hold him than it would to manage a broken horse.

HOW TO LEAD A COLT BY THE SIDE OP A BROKEN HORSE.

If you should want to lead your colt by the side of another horse, as is often the case, I would advise you to take your horse into the stable, attach a second strap to the colt's halter, and lead your horse up alongside of him. Then get on the broken horse and take one strap around his breast, under his martingale (if he has any on), holding it in your left hand. This will prevent the colt from getting back too far; besides, you will have more power to hold him with the strap pulling against the horse's breast. The other strap take up in your right hand to prevent him from running ahead; then turn him about a few times in the stable, and if the door is wide enough, ride out with him in that position; if not, take the broken horse out first, and stand his breast up against the door, then lead the colt to the same spot, and take the straps as before directed, one on each side of his neck, then let some one start the colt out, and as he comes out, turn your horse to the left, and you will have them all right. This is the best way to lead a colt; you can manage any kind of colt in this way, without any trouble; for if he tries to run ahead, or pull back, the two straps wilt bring the horses facing each other, so that you can very easily follow up his movements without doing nmeh holding, and as soon as he stops running backward you are right with him, and all ready to go ahead; and if he gets stubborn and does not want to go, you can remove all his stubbornness by riding your horse against his neck, thus compelling him to turn to the right; and as soon as you have turned him about a few times, he will be willing to. go along The next thing after you have got through leading him, will be to take him into a stable, and hitch him in such a way as not to have him pull on the halter; and as they are often troublesome to get into a stable the first few times, I will give you some instructions about getting him in.

TO LEAD INTO A STABLE,

You should lead the broken horse into the stable first, and get the colt, if you can, to follow in after him. If he refuses to go, step unto him, taking a little stick or switch in your right hand; then take hold of the halter close to his head with your left hand, at the same time reaching over his back with your right arm so that you can tap him on the opposite side with your switch ; bring him up facing the door, tap him slightly with your switch, reaching as far back with it as you can. This tapping, by being pretty well back, and on the opposite side, will drive him ahead, and keep him close to you; then by giving him the right direction with your left hand you can walk into the stable with him. I have walked colts into the stable this way in less than a minute, after men had worked at them half an hour, trying to pull them in. If you cannot walk him in at once in this way, turn him about and walk him around in every direction, until you can get him up to the door without pulling at him. Then let him stand a few minutes, keeping his head in the right direction with the halter, and he will walk in in less than ten minutes; Never attempt to pull the colt into the stable; that would make him think at once that it was a dangerous place, and if he was not afraid of it before he would be then. Besides, we do not want him to know anything about pulling on the halter. Colts are often hurt and sometimes killed, by trying to force them into the stable; and those who attempt to do it in that way go into an up-hill business, when a plain smooth road is before them.

If you want to tie up your colt, put him in a tolerably wide stall, which should not be too long, and should be connected by a bar or something of that kind to the partition behind it; so that, after the colt is in he cannot go far enough back to take a straight, backward pull on the halter; then by tying him in the centre of the stall, it would be impossible for him to pull on the halter, the partition behind preventing him from going back, and the halter in the centre checking him every time he turns to the right or left. In a stall of this kind you can break any horse to stand tied with a light strap, anywhere, without his ever knowing anything about pulling. For if you have broken your horse to lead, and have taught him the use of the halter (which you should always do before you hitch him to anything), you can hitch him in any kind of a stall, and if you give him something to eat to keep him up to his place for a few minutes at first, there is not one colt in fifty that will pull on his halter.

EDITOR S REMARKS.

Mr. Rarey says nothing about "longeing," which is the first step of European and Eastern training. Perhaps he considers his plan of pulling up the leg to be sufficient ; but be that as it may, we think it well to give the common sense of a much-abused practice.

Ignorant horse-breakers will tell you that they *longe* a colt to supple him. That is ridiculous nonsense. A colt unbroken will bend himself with most extraordinary flexibility. Look at a lot of two-years before starting for a run; observe the agility of their antics: or watch a colt scratching his head with his hind foot, and you will never believe that such animals can require supple-ing. But it is an easy way of teaching a horse simple acts of obedience—of getting him to go and stop at your orders: but in brutal hands more horses are spoiled and lamed by the longe than any other horse-breaking operation. A stupid fellow drags a horse's head and shoulders into the circle with the cord, while his hind-quarters are driven out by the whip.

" *A colt should, he longed at a walk only, until he circles without force,*

" He should never be compelled to canter in the longe, though he may be permitted to do it of himself.

" He must not be stopped by pulling the cord, which would pull him across, but by meeting him, so that he stops himself straight. A skilful person will, single-handed, longe, and, by heading him with the whip, change him without stopping, and longe him in the figure of 8. No man is fit to be trusted with such powerful implements as the longe-cord and whip who cannot do this.

" The snaffle may be added when he goes freely in the head-stall."

A colt should never he buckled to the pillar reins by his bit, but by the head-stall; for if tightly buckled to the bit, he will bear heavily—even go to sleep: raw. lip, which, when cured, becomes callous, is the result. Yet nothing is more common than to see colts standing for hours on the bit, with reins tightly buckled to the demi-jockey, under the ignorant notion of giving him a mouth, or setting up his head in the right place. The latter, if not done by nature, can only be done, if ever, by delicate, skilful hands.

A colt's bit should be large and smooth snaffle, with players to keep his mouth moist.

Dick Christian liked a bit for young horses as thick as his thumb—we don't know how thick that was—and four and a half inches between the cheeks; and there was no better judge than Dick.

The Germans use a wooden bit to make a horse's mouth, and good judges think they are right, as it may not be so unpleasant as metal to begin with; but wood or iron, the bridle should be properly put on, a point often neglected, and a fertile source of restiveness. There is as much need to fit a bridle to the length of a horse's head, as to buckle the girths of the saddle.

For conquering a vicious, biting horse, there is nothing equal to the large wooden gag-bit, which Mr. Rarey first exhibited in public on the zebra. A muzzle only prevents a horse from biting; a gag, properly used, cures; for when he finds he cannot bite, and that you caress him and rub his ears kindly with perfect confidence, he by degrees abandons this most dangerous vice. Stafford was driven in a wooden gag the first time. Colts inclined to crib-bite, should be dressed with one on.

Our woodcut is taken from the improved model produced by Mr. Stokey; no doubt Mr. Rarey took the idea of his gag-bit from the wooden gag, which has been in use among country farriers from time immemorial, to keep a horse's mouth while they are performing the cruel and useless operation of firing for lampas.

# CHAPTER VII

The Drum. —The Umbrella. —Riding-habit.—How to bit a colt.— How to saddle.—To mount.—To ride.—To break.—To harness.— To make a horse follow and stand without holding.—Baucher's plan.—Nolan's plan.

It is an excellent practice to accustom all horses to strange sounds and sights, and of very great importance to young horses which are to be ridden or driven in large towns, or used as chargers. Although some horses are very much more timid and nervous than others, the very worst can be very much improved by acting on the first principles laid down in the introduction to this book—that is, by proving that the strange sights and sounds will do them no harm.

When a railway is first opened, the sheep, the cattle, and especially the horses, grazing in the neighbouring fields, are terribly alarmed at the sight of the swift, dark, moving trains, and the terrible snorting and hissing of the steam-engines. They start away—they gallop in circles—and when they stop, gaze with head and tail erect, until the monsters have disappeared. But from day to day the live stock become more accustomed to the sight and sound of the steam horse, and after a while they do not even cease grazing when the train passes. They have learned that it will do them no harm. The same result may be observed with respect to young horses when first they are brought to a large town, and have to meet great loads of hay, omnibuses down." It is essential to unite these sections, because, if you put a well-bred horse in harness with his leg up, without first putting him down, it is ten to one but that he throws himself down violently, breaks the shafts of the vehicle, and his own knees.

The following are the sections verbatim, of which I shall afterwards give a paraphrase, with illustrative woodcuts :—

" Take up one fore-foot and bend his knee till his hoof is bottom upwards, and nearly touching his body; then slip a loop over his knee, and up until it comes above the pastern-joint, to keep it up, being careful to draw the loop together between the hoof and pastern-joint with a second strap of some kind to prevent the loop from slipping down and coming off. This will leave the horse standing on three legs; you can now handle him as you wish, for it is utterly impossible for him to kick in this position. There is something in this operation of taking up one foot, that conquers a horse quicker and better than anything else you can do to him. There is no process in the world equal to it to break a kicking horse, for several reasons. First, there is a principle of this kind in the nature of the horse; that by conquering one member, you conquer, to a great extent, the whole horse.

" You have perhaps seen men operate upon this principle, by sewing a horse's ears together to prevent him from kicking. I once saw a plan given in a newspaper to make a bad horse stand to be shod, which was to fasten down one ear. There were no reasons given why you should do so; but I tried it several times, and thought that it had a good effect—though I would not recommend its use, especially stitching his ears together. The only benefit arising from this process is, ihat by disarranging his ears we draw his attention to them, and he is not so apt to resist the shoeing. By tying up one foot we operate on the same principle to a much better effect. When you first fasten up a horse's foot, he will sometimes get very mad, and strike with his knee, and try every possible way to get it down; but he cannot do that, and will soon give up.

" This will conquer him better than anything you could do, and without any possible danger of hurting himself or you either, for you can tie up his foot and sit down and look at him until he gives up. When you find that he is conquered, go to him, let down his foot, rub his leg with your hand, caress him, and let him rest a little; then put it up again. Repeat this a few times, always putting up the same foot, and he will soon learn to travel on three legs, so that you can drive him some distance. As soon as he gets a little used to this way of travelling, put on your harness, and hitch him to a sulky. If he is the worst kicking horse that ever raised a foot, you need not be fearful of his doing any damage while he has one foot up, for he cannot kick, neither can he run fast enough to do any harm. And if he is the wildest horse that ever had harness on, and has run away every time he has been hitched, you can now hitch him in a sulky, and drive him as you please. If he wants to run, you can let him have the lines, and the whip too, with perfect safety, for he can go but a slow gait on three legs, and will soon be tired, and willing to stop ; only hold him enough to guide him in the right direction, and he will soon be tired and willing to stop at the word. Thus you will effectually cure him at once of any further notion of running off. Kicking horses have always been the dread of everybody; you always hear men say, when they speak about a bad horse, 'I don't care what he does, so he don't kiek.' This new method is an effectual cure for this worst of all habits. There are plenty of ways by which you can hitch a kicking horse, and force him to go, though he kicks all the time; but this doesn't have any good effect towards breaking him, for we know that horses kick because they are afraid of what is behind them, and when they kick against it and it hurts them, they will only kick the harder; and this will hurt them still more and make them remember the scrape much longer, and make it still more difficult to persuade them to have any confidence in anything dragging behind them ever after.

" But by this new method you can harness them to a rattling sulky, plough, waggon, or anything else in its worst shape. They may be frightened at first, but cannot kick or do anything to hurt themselves, and will soon find that you do not intend to hurt them, and then they will not care anything more about it. You can then let down the leg and drive along gently without any further trouble. By this new process a bad kicking horse can be learned to go gentle in harness in a few hours' time."[11]

" HOW TO MASK A HORSE LIE DOWN.

" Everything that we want to teach the horse must be commenced in such a way as to give him an idea of what you want him to do, and then be repeated till he learns it perfectly. To make a horse lie down, bend his left fore-leg and slip a loop over it, so that he cannot get it down. Then put a surcingle around his Body, and fasten one end of a long strap around the other fore-leg, just above the hoof. Place

---

11    I should not recommend this plan with a well-bred horse without first laying him down, as he would be likely to throw himself down. —EDITOR.

the other end under the before-described surcingle, so as to keep the strap in the right direction; take a short hold of it with your right hand; stand on the left side of the horse, grasp the bit in your left hand, pull steadily on the strap with your right; bear against his shoulder till you cause him to move. As soon as he lifts his weight, your pulling will raise the other foot, and he will have to come on his knees. Keep the strap tight in your hand, so that he cannot straighten his leg if he rises up. Hold him in this position, and turn his head towards you; bear against his side with your shoulder, not hard, but with a steady, equal pressure, and in about ten minutes he will lie down. As soon as he lies down, he will be completely conquered, and you can handle him as you please. Take off the straps, and straighten out his legs; rub him lightly about the face and neck with your hand the way the hair lies; handle all his legs, and after he has lain ten or twenty minutes, let him get up again. After resting him a short time, make him lie down as before. Repeat the operation three or four times, which will be sufficient for one lesson. Give him two lessons a day, and when you have given him four lessons, he will lie down by taking hold of one foot. As soon as he is well broken to lie down in this way, tap him on the opposite leg with a stick when you take hold of his foot, and in a few days he will lie down from the mere motion of the stick."

EDITOR'S DETAILED EXPLANATIONS.

Although, as I before observed, the tying up of the fore-leg is not a new expedient, or even the putting a horse down single-handed, the two operations, as taught and performed by Mr. Rarey, not only subdue and render docile the most violent horses, but, most strange of all, inspire them with a positive confidence and affection after two or three lessons from the horse-tamer. " How this is or why this is," Mr. Langworthy, the veterinary surgeon to Her Majesty's stables, observed, " I cannot say or explain, but I am convinced, by repeated observation on many horses, that it is a fact."

If, however, a man, however clever with horses, were to attempt to perform the operations without other instruction than that contained in the American pamphlet, he would infallibly break his horse's knees, and probably get his toes trodden on, his eyes blacked, and his arm dislocated—for all these accidents have happened within my own knowledge to rash experimentalists; while under proper instructions, not only have stout and gouty noblemen succeeded perfectly, but the slight-built, professional horsewoman, Miss Gilbert, has conquered thorough-bred colts and fighting Arabs, and a young and beautiful peeress has taken off her bonnet before going to a morning féte, and in ten minutes laid a full-sized horse prostrate and helpless as a sheep in the hands of the shearer.

Having, then, in your mind Mr. Rarey's maxim that a horseman should know neither fear nor anger, and having laid in a good stock of patience, you must make your approach to the colt or stallion in the mode prescribed in

the preceding chapters. In dealing with a colt, except upon an emergency, he should be first accustomed to be handled and taught to lead; this, first-rate horse-tamers will accomplish with the wildest colt in three hours, but it is better to give at least one day up to these first important steps in education. It will also be as well to have a colt cleaned and his hoof trimmed by the blacksmith. If this cannot be done the operation will be found very dirty and disagreeable.

In approaching a spiteful stallion you had better make your first advances with a half-door between you and him, as Mr. Rarey did in his first interview with Cruiser: gradually make his acquaintance, and teach him that you do not care for his open mouth; but a regular biter must be gagged in the manner which will presently be described.

Of course there is no difficulty in handling the leg of a quiet horse or colt, and by constantly working from the neck down to the fetlock you may do what you please. But many horses and even colts have a most dangerous trick of striking out with their fore-legs. There is no better protection against this than a cart-wheel. Thewheel may either be used loose, or the animal may be led up to a cart loaded with hay, when the horse-tamer can work under the cart through one of the wheels, while the colt is nibbling the load.

Having, then, so far soothed a colt that he will permit you to take up his legs without resistance, take the strap No. 1[12]—pass the tongue through the loop under the buckle so as to form a noose, slip it over the near foreleg and draw it close up to the pastern-joint, then take up the leg as if you were going to shoe him, and passing the strap over the fore-arm, put it through the buckle, and buckle the lower limb as close as you can to the arm without hurting the animal.

Take care that your buckle is of the very best quality, and the leather sound. It is a good plan to stretch it before using it. The tongues of buckles used for this purpose, if not of the very best quality, are very likely to come out, when all your labour will have to be gone over again. Sometimes you may find it better to lay the loop open on the ground, and let the horse step into it. It is better the buckle should be inside the leg if you mean the horse to fall toward you, because then it is easier to unbuckle when he is on the ground.

In those instances in which you have had no opportunity of previously taming and soothing a eolt, it will frequently take you an hour of quiet, patient, silent perseverance before he will allow you to buckle up his leg—if he resists you have nothing for it but patience. You must stroke him, you must fondle him, until he lets you enthral him. Mr, Rarey always works alone, and disdains assistance, and so do some of his best pupils, Lord B., the Marquis of S and Captain S. In travelling in foreign countries you may have occasion to tame a colt or wild horse alone, but there is no reason why you should not have assistance if you can get it, and in that case the process is of course much easier. But it must never be forgotten that to tame a horse properly no unnecessary force must be employed; it is better that he should put down his foot six times that he may yield it willingly at last, and under no circumstances must the trainer lose patience, or give way to temper.

The near fore-leg being securely strapped, and the horse, if so inclined, secured from biting by a wooden bit, the next step is to make him hop about on three legs.

---

12    All these straps may "be obtained from Mr. Stokey, saddler, North
      Street, Little Moorfields, who supplied Mr. Rarey, and has patterns of
      the improvements by Lord B and Colonel R   .

This is comparatively easy if the animal has been taught to read, but it is difficult with one which has not. The trainer must take care to keep behind his horse's shoulder and walk in a circle, or he will be likely to be struck by the horse's head or strapped-up leg.

Mr. Rarey is so skilful that he seldom considers it necessary to make his horses hop about; but there is no doubt that it saves much after-trouble by fatiguing the animal; and that it is a useful preparation before putting a colt or kicking horse into harness. Like every other operation it must be done very gently, and accompanied by soothing words—" Come along "—" Come along, old fellow," &c.

A horse can hop on three legs, if not severely pressed, for two or three miles; and no plan is more successful for curing a kicker or jibber.

"When the horse has hopped for as long as you think necessary to tire him, buckle a common single strap roller or surcingle on his body tolerably tight. A single strap surcingle is the best.

It is as well, if possible, to teach colts from a very early age to bear a surcingle. At any rate it will require & little management the first time.

You have now advanced your colt so far that he is not afraid of a man, he likes being patted and caressed, led, but Mr. Rarey always makes him hop alone. The moment he lifts up his off fore-foot you must draw up strap No. 2 tightly and steadily. The motion will draw up the off leg into the same position as the near leg, and the horse will go down on his knees. Your object is to hold the strap so firmly that he will not be able to stretch his foot out again. Those who are very con-fident in their skill are content to hold the strap only with a twist round their hand, but others take the opportunity of the horse's first surprise to give the strap a double turn round the surcingle.

Another way of performing this operation is to use with difficult violent horses the strap invented by Lord Bh, which consists first of the loop for the off fore-leg shown in our cut. A surcingle strap, at least seven feet long, with a buckle, is thrown across the horse's back; the buckle end is passed through the ring; the tongue is passed through the buckle, and the moment the horse moves the Tamer draws the strap tight round the body of the horse, and in buckling it makes the leg so safe that he has no need to use any force in holding it up.

As soon as a horse recovers from his astonishment at being brought to his knees, he begins to resist; that is, he rears up on his hind4egs, and springs about in a manner that is truly alarming for the spectators to behold, and which in the case of a well-bred horse in good condition requires a certain degree of activity in the Trainer. (See page of Horse Struggling.)

You must remember that your business is not to set your strength against the horse's strength, but merely to follow him about, holding the strap just tight enough to prevent him from putting out his off fore-leg. As long as you keep *close to him and behind his shoulders* you are in very little danger. The bridle in the left hand must be used like steering lines: by pulling to the right or left as occasion requires, the horse, turning on his hind-legs, may be guided just as a boat is steered by the rudder lines; or pulling straight, the horse may be fatigued by being forced to walk backwards. The strap passing through the surcingle keeps, or ought

to keep, the Trainer in bis right place—he is not to pull or in any way fatigue himself more than he can help, but, standing up right, simply follow the horse about, guiding him with the bridle away from the walls of the training school when needful. It must be admitted that to do this well requires considerable nerve, coolness, patience, and at times agility; for although a grass-fed colt will soon give in, a corn-fed colt, and, above all, a high-couraged hunter in condition, will make a very stout fight; and I have known one instance in which a horse with both fore-legs fast has jumped sideways.

The proof that the danger is more apparent than real lies in the fact that no serious accidents have as yet happened; and that, as I before observed, many noblemen, and some noble ladies, and some boys, have succeeded perfectly. But it would be untrue to assert that there is no danger. When held and guided properly, few horses resist more than ten minutes; and it is believed that a quarter of an hour is the utmost time that any horse has ever fought before sinking exhausted to the earth. But the time seems extremely long to an inexperienced performer; and it is a great comfort to get your assistant to be time-keeper, if there is no clock in a conspicuous situation, and tell you how you are getting on. Usually at the end of eight minutes' violent struggles, the animal sinks forward on his knees, sweating profusely, with heaving flanks and shaking tail, as if at the end of a thirty minutes' burst with foxhounds over a stiff country.

Then is the time to get him into a comfortable position for lying down; if he is still stout, he may be forced by the bit to walk backwards. Then, too, by pushing gently at his shoulder, or by pulling steadily the off-rein, you can get him to fail, in the one case on the near side, on the other on the off side; but this assistance should be so slight that the horse must not be able to resist it. The horse will often make a final spring when you think he is quite beaten; but, at any rate, at length lie slides over, and lies down, panting and ex-hausted, on his side. If he is full of corn and well bred, take advantage of the moment to tie up the off fore-leg to the surcingle, as securely as the other, in a slip loop knot.

Now let your horse recover his wind, and then encourage him to make a second fight. It will often be more stubborn and more fierce than the first. The object of this tying-up operation is, that he shall thoroughly exhaust without hurting himself, and that he shall come to the conclusion that it is you who, by your superior strength, have conquered him, and that you are always able to conquer him.

Under the old rough-riding system, the most vicious horses were occasionally conquered by daring men with firm seats and strong arms, who rode and flogged them into subjection; but these conquests were temporary, and usually *personal*; with every stranger, the animal would begin his game again.

One advantage of this Rarey system is, that the horse is allowed to exhaust himself under circumstances that render it impossible for him to struggle long enough to do himself any harm. It has been suggested that a blood-vessel would be likely to be broken, or apoplexy produced by the exertion of leaping from the hind legs; but, up to the present time, no accident of any kind has been reported.

When the horse lies down for the second or third time thoroughly beaten, the time has arrived for teaching him a few more of the practical parts of horse-training.

When you have done all you desire to the horse tied up,—smoothed his ears, if fidgety about the ears—the hind-legs, if a kicker—shown him a saddle, and allowed him to smell it, and then placed it on his back—mounted him yourself, and pulled him all over—take off all the straps. In moving round him for the purpose of gentling him, walk slowly always from the head round the tail, and again to the head: scrape the sweat off him with a scraper; rub him down with a wisp ; smooth the hair of his legs, and draw the fore one straight out. If he has fought hard, he will lie like a dead horse, and scarcely stir. You must now again go over him as conscien tiously as if you were a mesmeric doctor or shampooer: every limb must be *gentled,*" to use Mr. Rarey's expressive phrase; and with that operation you have completed your *first* and most important lesson.

You may now mount en the back of an unbroken colt, and teach him that you do not hurt him in that attitude: if he were standing upright he might resist, and throw you from fright; but as he is exhausted and powerless, he has time to find out that you mean him no harm. You can lay a saddle or harness on him, if he has previously shown aversion to them, or any part of them: his head and his tail and his legs are all safe for your friendly caresses; don't spare them, and speak to him all the time.

If he has hitherto resisted shoeing, now is the time for handling his fore and hind legs; kindly, yet, if he attempts to resist, with a voice of authority. If he is a violent, savage, confirmed kicker, like Cruiser, or Mr. Gurney's gray colt, or the zebra, as soon as he is down put a pair of hobbles on his hind-legs, like those-used for mares during covering. (Frontispiece of Zebra.) These must be held by an assistant on whom you can depend; and passed through the rings of the surcingle. With his fore-legs tied, you may usefully Spend an hour, in handling his legs, tapping the hoofs with your hand or hammer—all this to he done in a firm, measured, soothing manner; only now and then, if he resist, crying, as you paralyze him with the ropes, " Wo ho !" in a determined manner. It is by this continual soothing and handling that you establish confidence between the horse and yourself. After patting him as much as you deem needful, say for ten minutes or a quarter of an hour, you may encourage him to rise. Borne horses will require a good deal of helping, and their fore-legs drawing out before them.

It may be as well to remark, that the handling the limbs, of colts particularly, requires caution. A cart colt, tormented by flies, will kick forward nearly up to the fore-legs.

If a horse, unstrapped, attempts to rise, you may easily stop him by taking hold of a fore-leg and doubling it back to the strapped position. If by chance he should be too quick, don't resist; it is an essential principle in the Rarey system, never to enter into a contest with a horse unless you are certain to be victorious.

In all these operations, you must be calm, and not in a hurry.

Thus, under the Rarey system, all indications are so direct, that the horse must understand them. You place him in a position, and under such restraint, that he cannot resist anything that you chose to do to him; and then you proceed to caress him when he assents, to reprove him when he thinks of resisting—resist, with all his legs tied, he cannot—repeated lessons end by persuading the most vicious horse that it is useless to try to resist, and that acquiescence will be followed by the ca-resses that horses evidently like.

The last instance of Mr. Rarey's power was a beautiful gray mare, which had been fourteen years in the band of one of the Life Guards regiments, and conse-quently at least seventeen years old; during all that time she would never submit quietly to have her hind-legs shod; the farriers had to put a twitch on her nose and ears, and tie her tail down: even then she resisted violently. In three days Mr. Rarey was able to shoe her with her head loose. And this was not done by a trick, but by proving to, her that she could not resist even to (he extent of an inch, and that no harm was meant her; her lessons were repeated many times a day for three days. Such continual impressive perseverance is an essential part of the system.

When you have to deal with a horse as savage a kicker as Cruiser, or the zebra, a horse that can kick from one leg as fiercely as others can from two, in that case, to subdue and compel him to lie down, have a leather surcingle with a ring sewed on the belly part, and when the hobbles are buckled on the hind-legs, pass the ropes through ' the rings, and when the horse rises again, by buckling up one fore-leg, and pulling steadily, when needful, at the hind-legs, or tying the hobble-ropes to a collar, you reduce him to perfect helplessness; he finds that he cannot rear, for you pull his hind-legs—or kick, for you can pull at all three legs, and after a few lessons he gives in in despair.

These were the methods by which Cruiser and the zebra were subdued. They seem, and are, very simple; properly carried out they are effective for subduing the most spirited colt, and curing the most vicious horse. But still in difficult and exceptional cases it cannot be too often repeated that a MAN is required, as well as a method. Without nerve nothing can be attempted; without patience and perseverance mere nerve will be of little use; all the quackery and nonsense that has been talked and written under the inspiration of the Barnum who has had an interest in the success of the silent, reserved, practical Rarey, must be dismissed. Horse-training is not a conjuror's trick. The principles may certainly be learned by once reading this book; a few persons specially organised, accustomed to horses all their lives, may succeed in their first attempts with even difficult horses. The success of Lord Burghersh, after one lesson from Rarey, with a very difficult mare; of Lord Rivers, Lord Vivian, the Hon. Frederick Vil-liers, and the Marquess of Stafford, with colts, is well known in the sporting world. Mr. Thomas Bice, of Motcombe Street, who has studied everything connected with the horse, on the Continent as well as in England, and who is thoroughly acquainted with the Spanish school, as well as the English cross-country style of horsemanship, succeeded, as I have already mentioned, the very first time he took the straps in hand in subduing Mr. Gurney's gray colt—the most vicious animal, next to Cruiser, that Mr. Rarey tackled in England. This brute tore off the flaps of the saddle with his teeth.

But it is sheer humbug to pretend that a person who knows no more of horses than is to be learned by riding a perfectly-trained animal now and then for an hour or two, can acquire the whole art of horse-taming, or can even safely tackle a violent horse, without a previous preparation and practice.

As you must not be nervous or angry, so you must not be in a hurry.

Many ladies have attended Mr. Rarey's lessons, and studied his art, but very few have tried, and still fewer l:ave succeeded. It is just one of those things that all ladies fond of horses should know, as well as those who are likely to visit India, or the Colonies, although it is not exactly a feminine occupation; crinoline would be sadly in the way—
"

 Those little hands were never made
To hold a leather strap."

But it may be useful as an emergency, as it will enable any lady to instruct a friend, or groom, or sailor, or peasant, how to do what she is not able to do herself, and to argue effectively that straps will do more than whips and spurs.

At the Practice Club of noblemen and gentlemen held at Miss Gilbert's stables, it has been observed that every week some horse more determined than the average has been too much for the wind, or the patience, of most of the subscribers. One only has never been

beaten, the Marquess of S
 , but then he was always in

condition; a dab hand at every athletic sport, extremely active, and gifted with a " calmness," as well as a nerve, which few men of his position enjoy.

In a word, the average horse may be subdued by the average horseman, and colts usually come within the average; but a fierce, determined, vicious horse requires a man above the average in temper, courage, and activity; activity and skill in *steering* being of more importance than strength. It is seldom necessary to lay a colt down more than twice.

Perhaps the best way is to begin practising the strap movements with a donkey, or a quiet horse full of grass or water, and so go on from day to day with as much perseverance as if you were practising skating or walking on a tight rope; until you can approach, halter, lead, strap up, and lay down a colt with as much calmness as a huntsman takes his fences with his eye on his hounds, you are not perfect.

Remember you must not hurry, and you must not chatter. "When you feel impatient you had better leave off, and begin again another day. And the same with your horse: you must not tire him with one lesson, but you must give him at least one lesson every day, and two or three to a nervous customer; we have a striking example of patience and perseverance in Mr. Rarey's first evening with Cruiser. He had gone through the labour of securing him, and bringing him up forty miles behind a dog-cart, yet he did not lose a moment but set to work the same night to tame him limb by limb, and inch by inch, and from that day until he produced him in public, he never missed a day without spending twice a day from two to three hours with him, first rendering him helpless by gag-bit, straps and hobbles, then caressing him, then forcing him to lie down, then caressing him again, stroking every limb, talking to him in soothing tones, and now and then, if he turned vicious, taking up his helpless head, giving it a good shake, while scolding him as you would a naughty boy. And then again taking off the gag and rewarding submission with a lock of sweet hay and a drink of water, most grateful after a tempest of passion, then making him rise, and riding him—making him stop at a word.

I mention these facts, because an idea has gone abroad that any man with Mr. Rarey's straps can manage any horse. It would be just as sensible to assert that any boy could learn to steer a yacht by taking the tiller for an hour under the care of an

" old salt"

The most curious and important feet of all in connection with this strapping up and laying down process, is, that the moment the horse rises *he seems to have contracted a personal friendship for the operator,* and with a very little encouragement will generally follow him round the box or circus; this feeling may as well be encouraged by a little bit of carrot or bread and sugar.

PLACE AND PREPARATIONS FOB TRAINING A COLT.

It is almost impossible to train or tame a horse quickly in an open space. As his falls are violent, the floor must be very soft. The best place is a space boarded off with partitions six or seven feet high, and on the floor a deep layer of tan or sand or saw-dust, on which a thick layer of straw has been spread; but the floor must not be too soft; if it is, the horse will sink on his knees without fighting, and without the lesson of exhaustion, which is so important. To throw a horse for a surgical operation, the floor cannot be too soft: the enclosure should be about thirty feet from side to side, of a square or octagonal shape; but not round if possible, because it is of great advantage to have a corner into which a colt may turn when you are teaching him the first haltering lesson. A barn may be converted into a training-school, if the floor be made soft enough with straw. But in every case, it is extremely dangerous to have pillars, posts, or any projections against which the horse in rearing might strike; as when the legs are tied, a horse is apt to miscalculate his distance. And if the space is too narrow, the trainer, in dealing with a violent horse, may get crushed or kicked. It'is of great advantage that the training-school should be roofed, and if possible, every living thing, that might distract the horse's attention by sight or sound, should be removed. Other horses, cattle, pigs, and even dogs or fowls moving about or making a noise, will spoil the effect of a good lesson.

In an emergency, the first lesson may be given in an open straw-yard. Lord Burghersh trained his first pupil on a small space in the middle of a thick wood; Cruiser was laid down the first time in a bullock-yard. But if you have many colts to train, it is well worth while to dig out a pit two feet deep, fill it with tan and straw, and build round it a shed of rough poles, filled in with gorse plastered with clay, on the same plan as a bullock feeding-box. The floor should not be too deep or soft, because if it is, the colt will sink at once without fighting, and a good lesson in obedience is lost:

This may be done for from 30s. to 2l. on a farm. In a riding-school it is very easy to have lofty temporary partitions. It is probable that in future every riding-school will have a Rarey box for training hacks, as well as to enable pupils to practise the art.

It is quite out of the question to attempt to do anything with a difficult horse while other horses can be seen or heard, or while a party of lookers-on are chattering and laughing.

As to the costume of the trainer, I recommend a close cap, a stout pair of boots, short trousers or breeches of stout tweed or corduroy, a short jacket with pockets outside, one to hold the straps and gloves, the other a few pieces of carrot to reward the pupil, A pocket-handkerchief should be handy to wipe your perspiring brow. A trainer should not be without a knife and a piece of string, for emergencies. Spare straps, bridles, a surcingle, a long wholebone whip, and a saddle, should be hung up outside the training inclosure, where they can be handed, when required, to the operator as quickly and with as little delay and fuss as possible. A sort of dumb-waiter, with hooks instead of trays, could be contrived for a man who worked alone.

If a lady determines to become a horse-trainer, she had better adopt a Bloomer costume, without any stiff petticoats, as long robes would be sure to bring her to grief. To hold the long strap No. 2, it is necessary to wear a stout glove, which will be all the more useful if the tips of the fingers are cut off at the first joint, so as to make it a sort of mitten.

# CHAPTER VI

Taming a colt or horse.—Rarey's directions for strapping up and laying down detailed.—Explanations by Editor.—Tc approach a Vicions horse with half door.—Cartwheel.—No. 1 strap applied.— No. 2 strap applied.—Woodcuts of.—How to hop about.—Knot up bridle.—Struggle described.—Lord B.'s improved No. 2 strap. —Not much danger.—How to steer a horse.—Laid down, how to gentle.—To mount, tied up.—Place and preparations for training described.

IN this chapter I change the arrangement of the original work, and unite two sections which Mr. Rarey has divided, either because when he wrote them he was not aware of the importance of what is really the cardinal point, the mainstay, the foundation of his system, or be-cause he wished to conceal it from the uninitiated. The Rarey system substitutes for severe longeing, for whipping and spurring, blinkers, physic, starving, the twitch, tying the tail down, sewing the ears together, putting shot in the ears, and all the cruelties hitherto resorted to for subduing high-spirited and vicious animals (and very often the high-spirited become, from injudicious treatment, the most vicious), a method of laying a horse down, tying up his limbs, and gagging, if necessary, his mouth, which makes him soon feel that man is his superior, and yet neither excites his terror or his hatred. These two sections are to be found at pp. 48 and 51 and at pp. 59 and 60, orig. edit., under the titles of " How to drive a Horse that is very wild, and has any vicious Habits," and "How to make a Horse lie crowded with passengers, and other strange or noisy objects—if judiciously treated, not flogged and ill-used, they lose their fears without losing their high courage. Nothing is more astonishing in London than the steadiness of the high-bred and highly-fed horses in the streets and in Hyde Park

But until Mr. Rarey went to first principles, and taught " the reason why " there were horses that could not be brought to bear the beating of a drum, the rustling of an umbrella, or the flapping of a riding-habit against their legs—and all attempts to compel them by force to submit to these objects of their terror failed and made them furious. Mr. Rarey, in his lectures, often told a story of a horse which shied at buffalo-robes—the owner tied him up fast and laid a robe on him—the poor animal died instantly with fright. And yet nothing can be more simple.

*To accustom a horse to a drum.*—Place it near him on the ground, and, without forcing him, induce him to smell it again and again until he is thoroughly accustomed to it. Then lift it up, and slowly place it on the side of his neck, where he can see it, and tap it gently with a stick or your finger. If he starts, pause, and let him carefully examine it Then re-commence, gradually moving it backwards until it rests upon his withers, by degrees playing louder and louder, pausing always when he seems alarmed, to let him look at it and smell, if needful. In a very few minutes you may play with all your force, without his taking any notice. When this practice has been repeated a few times, your horse, however spirited, will rest his nose unmoved on the big drum while the most thundering piece is played.

*To teach a horse to bear an umbrella, go through the same cautious* forms, let him see it, and smell it, open it by degrees—gain your point inch by inch, passing it always from his eyes to his neck, and from his neck to his back and tail; and so with a riding-habit, in half an hour any horse may be taught that it will not hurt him, and then the difficult is over.

*To fire off a, horse's back.*—Begin with caps, and, by degrees, as with the drum, instead of lengthening the reins, stretch the bridle hand to the front, and raise it for the carbine to rest on, with the muzzle clear of the horse's head, a little to one side. Lean the body forward without rising in the stirrups. Avoid interfering with the horse's mouthy or exciting his fears by suddenly closing your legs either before or after firing—be quiet yourself and your horse will be quiet. The colt can learn, as I have already observed, to bear a rider on his bare back during his first lessons, when prostrate and powerless, fast bound by straps. The surcingle has accustomed him to girths—he leads well, and has learned that when the right rein is pulled he must go to the right, and when the left rein to the left. You may now teach him to bear the BIT and the SADDLE—if you have not placed it upon his back while on the ground, and for this operation I cannot do better than return, and quote literally from Mr. Rarey.

"HOW TO ACCUSTOM A HORSE TO A BIT.

" You should use a large, smooth, snaffle bit, so as not to hurt his mouth, with a bar to each side, to prevent the bit from pulling through either way. This you should attach to the head-stall of your bridle, and put it on your colt without any reins to it, and let him run loose in a large stable or shed some time, until he becomes a little used to the bit, and will bear it without trying to get it out of lis mouth. It would be well, if convenient, to repeat this several times, before you do anything more . with the colt; as soon as he will bear the bit, attach a single rein to it. You should also have a halter on your colt, or a bridle made after the fashion of a halter, with a strap to it, so that you can hold or lead him about without pulling on the bit much. (See Woodcut, p. 39.) He is now ready for the saddle.

" THE PROPER WAT TO BIT A COLT.

" Farmers often put bitting harness on a colt the first thing they do to him, buckling up the bitting as tight as they can draw it, to make him carry his head high, and then turn him out in a field to run a half-day at a time. This is one of the worst of punishments that they could inflict on the colt, and very injurious to a young horse that has been used to running in pasture with his head down. I have seen colts so injured in this way that they never got over it.

" A horse should be well accustomed to the bit before • you put on the bitting harness, and when you first bit him you should only rein his head up to that point where he naturally holds it, let that be high or low; he will soon learn that he can- not lower his head, and that raising it a little will loosen the bit in his mouth. This will give him the idea of raising his head to loosen the bit, and then you can draw the bitting a little tighter every time you put it on, and he will still raise his head to loosen it; by this means you will gradually get his head and neck in the position you want him to carry it, and give him a nice and graceful carriage without hurting him, making him mad, or causing his mouth to get sore.

" If you put the bitting on very tight the first time, ha cannot raise his head enough to loosen it, but will bear on it all the time, and paw, sweat, and throw himself. Many horses have been killed by falling backward with the bitting on; their heads being drawn up strike the ground with the whole weight of the body. Horses that have their heads drawn up tightly should not have the bitting on more than fifteen or twenty minutes at a time.

HOW TO SADDLE A COLT.

"The first thing will be to tie each stirrup-strap into a loose knot to make them short, and prevent the stirrups from flying about and hitting him. Then double up the skirts and take the saddle under your right arm, so as not to frighten him with it as you approach. When you get to him rub him gently a few times with your hand, and then raise the saddle very slowly, until he can see it, and smell and feel it with his nose. Then let the skirt loose, and rub it very gently against his neck the way the hair lies, letting him hear the rattle of the skirts as he feels them against him; each time getting a little farther backward, and finally slipping it over his shoulders on his back. Shake it a little with your hand, and in less than five minutes you can rattle it about over his back as much as you please, and pull it off and throw it on again, without his paying much attention to it.

" As soon as you have accustomed him to the saddle, fasten the girth. Be careful how you do this. It often frightens the colt when he feels the girth binding him, and making the saddle fit tight on his back. You should bring up the girth very gently, and not draw it too tight at first, just enough to hold the saddle on. Move him a little, and then girth it as tight as you choose, and he will not mind it.

" You should see that the pad of your saddle is all right before you put it on, and that there is nothing to make it hurt him, or feel unpleasant to his back. It should not have any loose straps on the back part of it, to flap about and scare him. After you have saddled him in this way, take a switch in your right hand to tap him up with, and walk about in the stable a few times with your right arm over your saddle, taking hold of the reins on each side of his neck with your right and left hands, thus marching him about in the stable until you teach him the use of the bridle and can turn him about in any direction, and stop him by a gentle pull of the rein. Always caress him, and loose the reins a little every time you stop him.

" You should always be alone, and have your colt in some light stable or shed, the first time you ride him; the loft should be high, so that you can sit on his back without endangering your head. You can teach him more in two hours' time in a stable of this kind, than you could in two weeks in the common way of breaking colts, out in an open place. If you follow my course of treatment, you need not run any risk, or have any trouble in riding the worst kind of horse. You take him a step at a time, until you get up a mutual confidence and trust between yourself and horse. First teach him to lead and stand hitched; next acquaint him with the saddle, and the use of the bit; and then all that remains is to get on him without scaring him, and you can ride him as well as any horse

"HOW TO MOUNT THE COLT.

"First gentle him well on both sides, about the saddle, and all over until he will stand still without holding, and is not afraid to see you anywhere about him.

" As soon as you have him thus gentled, get a small block, about one foot or eighteen inches in height, and set it down by the side of him, about where you want to stand to mount him; step up on this, raising yourself very gently: horses notice every change of position very closely, and, if you were to step up suddenly on the block, it would be very apt to scare him; but, by raising yourself gradually on it, he will see you, without being frightened, in a position very nearly the same as when you are on his back.

" As soon as he will bear this without alarm, untie the stirrup-strap next to you, and put your left foot into the stirrup, and stand square over it, holding your knee against the horse, and your toe out, so as not to touch him under the shoulder with the toe of your boot. Place your right hand on the front of the saddle, and on the opposite side of you, taking hold of a portion of the mane and the reins, as they hang loosely over his neck, with your left hand; then gradually bear your weight on the stirrup, and on your right hand, until the horse feels your whole weight on the saddle: repeat this several times, each time raising yourself a little higher from the block, until he will allow you to raise your leg over his croup and place yourself in the saddle.

" There are three great advantages in having a block to mount from. First, a sudden change of position is very apt to frighten a young horse who has never been handled: He will allow you to walk up to him, and stand by his side without scaring at you, because you have gentled him to that position; but if you get down on your hands and knees and crawl towards him, he will be very much frightened; and upon the same principle, he would be frightened at your new position if you had the power to hold yourself over his back without touching him. Then the first great advantage of the block is to gradually gentle him to that new position in which he will see you when you ride him.

" Secondly, by the process of leaning your weight in the stirrups, and on your hand, you can gradually accustom him to your weight, so as not to frighten him by having him feel it all at once. And, in the third place, the block elevates you so that you will not have to make a spring in order to get on the horse's back, but from it you can gradually raise yourself into the saddle. When you take these precautions, there is no horse so wild but what you can mount him without making him jump. I have tried it on the worst horses that could be found, and have never failed in any case. When mounting, your horse should always stand without being held. *A horse is never well broken when he has to be held with a tight rein when mounting*; and a colt is never so safe to mount as when you see that assurance of confidence, and absence of fear, which cause him to stand without holding." [Mr. Rarey's improved plan is to press the palm of the right hand on the off-side of the saddle, and as you rise lean your weight on it; by this means you can mount with the girths loose, or without any girths at all.—EDITOR.]

" HOW TO RIDE THE COLT.

" When you want him to start do not touch him on the side with your heel, or do anything to frighten him and make him jump. But speak to him kindly, and if he does not start pull him a little to the left until he starts, and then let him walk off slowly with the reins loose. Walk him around in the stable a few times until he gets used to the bit, and you can turn him about in every direction and stop him as you please. It would be well to get on and off a good many times until he gets perfectly used to it before you take him out of the stable.

" After you hare trained him in this way, which should not take you more than one or two hours, you can ride him anywhere you choose without ever having him jump or make any effort to throw you.

" When you first take him out of the stable be very gentle with him, as he will feel a little more at liberty to jump or run, and be a little easier frightened than he was while in the stable. But after handling him so much in the stable he will be pretty well broken, and you will be able to manage him without trouble or danger.

" When you first mount him take a little the shortest hold on the left rein, so that if anything frightens him you can prevent him from jumping by pulling his head round to you. This operation of pulling a horse's head round against his side will prevent any horse from jumping ahead, rearing up, or running away. If he is stubborn and will not go, you can make him move by pulling his head round to one side, when whipping would have no effect. And turning him round a few times will make him dizzy, and then by letting him have his head straight, and giving him a little touch with the whip, he will go along without any trouble.

" Never use martingales on a colt when you first ride him; every movement of the hand should go right to the bit in the direction in which it is applied to the reins, without a martingale to change the direction of the force applied. You can guide the colt much better without it, and teach him the use of the bit in much less time. Besides, martingales would prevent you from pulling his head round if he should try to jump.

n After your colt has been ridden until he is gentle and well accustomed to the bit, you may find it an advantage, if he carries his head too high or his nose too far out, to put martingales on him.

" *You should be careful not to ride your colt so for at first as to heat, worry*, or tire him. Get off as soon as you see he is a little fatigued; gentle him and let him rest; this will make him kind to you, and prevent him from getting stubborn or mad.

"TO BREAK A HORSE TO HARNESS.

"Take him in a light stable, as you did to ride him; take the harness and go through the same process that you did with the saddle, until you get him familiar with it, so that you can put it on him and rattle it about without his caring for it As soon as he will bear this, put on the lines, earess him as you draw them over him, and drive him about in the stable till he will bear them over his hips. The lines are a great aggravation to some colts, and often frighten them as much as if you were to raise a whip over them. As soon as he is familiar? waft, the harness and lines, take him out and put him by to comprehend all at once. The shafts, the lines, the harness, and the rattling of the sulky, all tend to scare him, and he must be made familiar with them by degrees. If your horse is very wild, I would advise you to put up one foot the first time you drive him.'*

With the leg strapped up, the lighter the break or gig the better, and four wheels are better than two.

TO MAKE A HORSE FOLLOW YOU.

The directions make simple what have hitherto been among the mysteries of the circus. I can assert from personal observation that by the means described by Mr. Rarey a very nervous thorough-bred mare, the property of the Earl of Derby, was taught to stand, answer to her name, and follow one of his pupils in less than a week.

No hack, and certainly no lady's horse, is, perfect until he has been taught to stand still, and no hunter is complete until he has learned to follow his master. Huntsmen may spend a few hours in the summer very usefully in teaching their old favourites to wait outside cover until wanted.

Turn him into a large stable or shed, where there is no chance to get out, with a halter or bridal on. Go to him and gentle him a little, take hold of his halter, and turn him towards you, at the same time touching him lightly over the hips with a long whip. Lead him the length of the stable, rubbing him on the neck, saying in a steady tone of voice as you lead him, " Come along, boy!" or use his name instead of " boy," if you choose. Every time you turn, touch him slightly with the whip, to make him step up close to you, and then caress him with your hand. He will soon learn to hurry up to escape the whip .and be caressed, and you can make him follow you around without taking hold of the halter. if he should stop and turn from you, give him a few sharp cuts about the hind legs, and he will soon turn his head towards you, when you must always caress him. A few lessons of this kind will make him rum after you, when he sees the motion of the whip—in twenty or thirty minutes he will follow you about the stable. After you have given him two or three lessons in the stable, take him out into a small field and train him; and from thence yon can take him into the road and make him follow you anywhere, and run after you.

To make a horse stand without holding, after you have him well broken to follow you, place him in the centre of the stable—begin at hie head to caress him, gradually working backwards. If he move, give him a cut with the whip, and put him back to the same spot from which he started. If he stands, caress him as before, and continue gentling him in this way until you can get round him without making him move, Keep walking around him, increasing your pace, and only touch him occasionally. Enlarge your circle as you walk around, and if he then moves, give him another cut with the whip, and put him back to his place. If he stands, go to him frequently and caress him, and then walk around him again. Do not keep him in one position too long at a time, but make him come to you occasionally, and follow you around the stable. Then make him stand in another place, and proceed as before. You should not train your horse more than half an hour at a time.

The following is Baucher's method of making a horse stand to be mounted, which, he says, may be taught in two lessons, of half an hour each. I do not. know any one who has tried, but it is worth trying.

"Go up to him, pat him on the neck (i. e. gentle him), and speak to him; then taking the curb reins a few inches from the rings with the left hand, place yourself so as to offer as much resistance as possible to him when he tries to break away. Take the whip in the right hand with the point down, raise it quietly and tap the horse on the chest; he will rein back -to avoid punishment; resist and follow him, continuing the tapping of the whip, but without anger or haste. The horse, soon tired of running back, will endeavour to avoid the infliction by rushing forward; then stop and make much of him. This repeated once or twice will teach the horse that, to stand still, is to avoid punishment, and will move up to you on a slight motion of the whip."

I doubt whether high-spirited horses would stand this treatment.

*To teach a horse to stand in the field.*—Nolan's plan was, to draw the reins over the horse's head and fasten them to the ground with a peg, walk away, return in a few minutes and reward him with bread, salt, or carrot; in a short time the horse will fancy himself fast whenever the reins are drawn over his bead. It may be doubted whether, in the excitement of the hunting-field, either Rarey's or Nolan's plan would avail to make a huntsman's horse stand while hounds were running. • Scrutator gives another method which is not within everyone's means to execute.

" In my father's time we had a; large field, enclosed by a high wall, round which the lads used to exercise their horses, with a thick rug only, doubled, to sit upon. A single snaffle and a sharp curb-bit were placed in the horse's mouth; the former to ride and guide by. To the curb was attached a long single rein, which was placed in the boy's hand, or attached to his wrist. "When the horse was in motion, either walking, trotting, or cantering, the lad would throw himself off, holding only the long rein attached to the curb, the sudden pull upon which, when the lad was on the ground, would cause the horse's head to be turned round, and stop him in his career. The boy would then gradually shorten the rein, until the horse was brought up to him, then patting and caressing him, he would again mount. After a very few lessons of this kind, the horse would always stop the instant the boy fell, and remain stationary beside him. The lads, as well as the horses, were rewarded by my father for their proper performance of this rather singular manoeuvre, but I never saw or knew any accident occur. The horses thus trained proved excellent hunters, and would never run away from their riders when thrown, always standing by them until re-mounted. From the lads constantly rubbing and pulling their legs about, we had no kickers. When a boy of only fifteen, I was allowed to ride a fine mare which has been thus broken in, in company with the hounds. Being nearly sixteen hands high, I had some difficulty in clambering up and down; but when dislodged from my seat, she would stand quietly by until re-mounted, and appeared as anxious for me to get up again as I was myself.

" It may be said that all this was time and trouble thrown away, and that the present plan of riding a young four-year-old, straight across country at once, will answer the same purpose. My reply is, that a good education, either upon man, horse, or dog, will never be thrown away; and, notwithstanding the number of horses now brought into the hunting-field, there are still few well-trained hunters to be met with. The horse, the most beautiful and useful of animals to man is seldom sufficiently instructed or familiarised, although certainly capable of the greatest attachment to his master when well used, and deserving to be treated more as a friend than a slave. It is a general remark how quiet some high-spirited horses will become when ridden by ladies. The cause of this is, that they are more quietly handled, patted, and caressed by them, and become soon sensible of this difference of treatment, from the rough whip-and-spur system, too generally adopted by men."

ON BAULKING OB JIBBING HOUSES.

Horses are taught the dangerous vice of baulking, or jibbing, as it is called in England, by improper management. When a horse jibs in harness, it is generally from some mismanagement, excitement, confusion, or from not knowing how to pull, but seldom from any unwillingness to perform all that he understands. High-spirited free-going horses are the most subject to baulking, and only so because drivers do not properly understand how to manage this kind. A free horse in a team may be so anxious to go, that when he hears the word he will start with a jump, which will not move the load, but give him such a severe jerk on the shoulders that he will fly back and stop the other horse. The teamster will continue his driving without any cessation, and by the time he has the slow horse started again, he will find that the free horse has made another jump, and again flown back. And now he has them both badly baulked, and so confused that neither of them knows what is the matter, or how to start the load. Next will come the slashing and cracking of the whip, and hallooing of "the driver, till something is broken, or he is through with his coarse of treatment. But what a mistake the driver commits by whipping his horse for this act! Reason and common sense should teach him that the horse was willing and anxious to go, but did not know how to start the load. And should he whip him for that? If so, he should whip him again for not knowing how to talk. A man that wants to act with reason should not fly into a passion, hut should always think before he strikes. It takes a steady pressure against the collar to move a load, and you cannot expect him to act with a steady, determined purpose while you are whipping him. There is hardly one baulking horse in five hundred that will pull truly from whipping: it is Only adding fuel to fire, and will make him more liable to baulk another time. You always see horses that hare been baulked a few times turn their heads and look back as soon as they are a little frustrated. This is because they have been whipped, and are afraid of what is behind them. This is an invariable rule with baulked horses, just as much as it is for them to look around at their sides when they have the bots[13]. In either case they are deserving of the same sympathy and the same kind, rational treatment.

13   A much more severe disease in America than in England.—Bras.

When your horse baulks, or is a little excited, if he wants to start quickly, or looks around and doesn't want to go, there is something wrong, and he needs kind treatment immediately. Caress him kindly, and if he doesn't understand at once what you want him to do, he will not be so much excited as to jump and break things, and do everything wrong through fear. As long AS you are calm, and keep down the excitement of the horse, there are ten chances that you will make him understand you, where these would not be one under harsh treatment; and then the little flare up will not carry with it any unfavourable recollections, and he will soon forget all about it, and learn to pull truly. Almost every wrong act the horse commits is from mismanagement, fear, or excitement: one harsh word will so excite a nervous horse as to increase his pulse ten beats in a minute.

When we remember that we are dealing with dumb brutes, and reflect how difficult it must be for them to understand our motions, signs, and language, we should never get out of patience with them because they don't understand us, or wonder at their doing things wrong. With all our intellect, if we were placed in the horse's situation, it would be difficult for us to understand the driving of some foreigner, of foreign ways and foreign language. We should always recollect that our ways and language are just as foreign and unknown to the horse as any language in the world is to us, and should try to practise what we could understand were we the horse, endeavouring by some simple means to work on his understanding rather than on the different parts of his body. All baulked horses can be started true and steady in a few minutes' time: they are all willing to pull as soon as they know how, and X never yet found a baulked horse that I could not teach to start his load in fifteen, and often less than three, minutes' time.

Almost any team, when first baulked, will start kindly if you let them stand five or ten minutes as though there was nothing wrong, and then speak to them with a steady voice, and turn them a little to the right or left, so as to get them both in motion before they feel the pinch of the load. But if you want to start a team that you are not driving yourself, that has been baulked, fooled, and whipped for some time, go to them and hang the lines on their hames, or fasten them to the waggon, so that they will be perfectly loose; make the driver and spectators (if there are any) stand off some distance to one side, so as not to attract the attention of the horses; unloose their check-reins, so that they can get their heads down if they choose; let them stand a few minutes in this condition until you can see that they are a little composed. While they are standing, you should be about their heads, gentling them: it will make them a little more kind, and the spectators will think that you are doing something that they do not understand, and will not learn the secret. When you have them ready to start, stand before them, and, as you seldom have but one baulky horse in a team, get as near' in front of him as you can, and, if he is too fast for the other horse, let his nose come against your breast: this will keep him steady, for he will go slow rather than run on you. Turn them gently to the right, without letting them pull on the traces as far as the tongue will let them go: stop them with a kind word, gentle them a little, and then turn them back to the left, by the same process. You will then have them under your control by this time; and as you turn them again to the right, steady them in the collar, and you can take them where you please.

There is a quicker process that will generally start a baulky horse, but not so sure. Stand him a little ahead, so that his shoulders will be against the collar, and then take up one of his fore feet in your hand, and let the driver start them, and when the weight comes against his shoulders he will try to step: then let him have his foot, and he will go right along. If you want to break a horse from baulking that has long been in that habit, you ought to set apart a half-day for that purpose. Put him by the side of some steady horse; have driving reins on them; tie up all the traces and straps, so that there will be nothing to excite them; do not rein them up, but let them have their heads loose. Walk them . about together for some time as slowly and lazily as possible ; stop often, and go up to your baulky horse and gentle him. Do not take any whip about him, or do anything to excite him, but keep him just as quiet as you can. He will soon learn to start off at the word, and stop whenever you tell him.

As soon, as he performs rightly, hitch him in an empty waggon; have it standing in a favourable position for starting. It would be well to shorten the trace-chain behind the steady horse, so that, if it is necessary, he can take the weight of the waggon the first time you start them. Do not drive more than a few rods at first; watch your jibbing horse closely, and if you see that he is getting excited, stop him before he stops of his own accord, caress him a little, and start again. As soon as they go well, drive them over a small hill a few times, and then over a larger one, occasionally adding a little load. This process will make any horse true to pull.

The following anecdote from Scrutator's " Horses and Hounds," illustrates the soundness of Mr. Rarey's system :—" A gentleman in our neighbourhood having purchased a very fine carriage horse, at a high price, was not a little annoyed, upon trial, to 'find that he would not pull an ounce, and when the whip was applied he began plunging and kicking. After one or two trials the coachman declared he could do nothing with him, and our neighbour, meeting my father, expressed his grievances at being thus taken in, and asked what he had better do. The reply was ' Send the horse to me to morrow morning, and I will return him a good puller within a week/ The horse being brought, was put into the shafts of a wagon, in a field, with the hind wheels tied, and being reined up so that he could not get his head between his legs, was there left, with a man to watch him for five or six hours, and, of course, without any food. When my father thought he had enough of standing still, he went up to him with a handful of sweet hay, let down the bearing rein, and had the wheels of the wagon released. After patting the horse on the neck, when he had taken a mouthful or two of hay, he took hold of the bridle and led him away—the wagon followed—thus proving stratagem to be better than force. Another lesson was scarcely required, but, to make sure, it was repeated, and, after that, the horse was sent back to the owner. There was no complaint ever made of his jibbing again. The wagon to which he was attached was both light and empty, and the ground inclined rather towards the stable."

# CHAPTER VIII.

Value of good horsemanship to both sexes.—On teaching children.—
Anecdote.—Havelock's opinion.—Rarey's plan to train ponieB.— The
use of books.—Necessicty of regular teaching for girls, hoys can he self-
taught.—Commence -without a bridle.—Ride with one pair of reins and
two hands.—Ad7antage of hunting-horn on side-saddle.—On the best plan
for mounting.—Rarey's plan.—On a man's seat.—Nolan's opinion.—Military style.—Hunting style.— Two examples in Lord Cardigan.—The Prussian style.—Anecdote by Mr. Gould, Blucher, and the Prince Regent.—
Hints for men learning to ride.—How to use the reins.—Pull right for right,
and left for left.—How to collect your horse.

You cannot learn to ride from a book, but you may learn how to do some things
and how to avoid many things of importance. Those who know all about horses and
horsemanship, or fancy they do, will not read this chapter. But as there are riding-
schools in the City of London, where an excellent business is done in teaching well-
grown men how to ride for health or fashion, and as papas who know their own
bump-bump style very well often desire to teach their daughters, I have collected
the following instructions from my own experience, now extending over full thirty
years, on horses of all kinds, including the worst, and from the best books on the
subject, some of the best being anonymous contributions by distinguished horsemen, printed for private circulation. Everyman and woman, girl and boy, who has
the opportunity, should learn to ride on horseback. It is almost an additional sense—
it is one of the healthiest exercises—it affords amusement when other amusements
fail—relaxation from the most severe toil, and often, in colonies or wild countries,
the only means of travelling or trading.

A man feels twice a man on horseback. The student and the farmer meet, when
mounted, the Cabinet Minister and the landlord on even terms—good horsemanship is a passport to acquaintances in all ranks of life, and to make acquaintances is

one of the arts of civilised life; to ripen them into use or friendship is another art. On horseback you can call with less ceremony, and meet or leave a superior with less form than on foot. Rotten Row is the ride of idleness and pleasure, but there is a great deal of business done in sober walks and slow canters, commercial, political, and matrimonial.

For a young lady not to be able to ride with a lover is a great loss; not to be able to ride with a young husband a serious privation.

The first element for enjoying horse exercise is good horsemanship. Colonel Greenwood says very truly:— " Good riding is worth acquiring by those whose pleasure or business it is to ride, because it is soon and easily acquired, and, when acquired, it becomes habitual; and it is as easy, nay, much more easy, and infinitely more safe, than bad riding." " Good riding will last through age, sickness, and decrepitude, but bad riding will last only as long as youth, health, and strength supply courage; *for good riding is an affair of skill, but bad riding is an affair of courage.*"

A bold bad rider must not be merely brave; he must be fool-hardy; for he is perpetually in as much danger as a blind man among precipices.

In riding, as in most other things, danger is for the timid and the unskilful. The skilful rider, when apparently Courting danger in the field, deserves no more credit for courage than for sitting in an arm-chair, and the un-skilful no more the imputation of timidity for backwardness than if without practice he declined to perform on the tight-rope. Depend upon it, the bold bad rider is the hero.

There is nothing heroic in good riding, when dissected. The whole thing is a matter of detail—a collection of trifles—and its principles are so simple in-theory and so easy in practice that they are despised.

It is an accomplishment that may, to a certain extent, be acquired late in life. I know instances in both sexes of a fair firm seat, hairing been acquired under the pres sure of necessity after forty years- of: age (I could name lawyers, sculptors, architects, and sailors), but it may be acquired with ease and perfection in youth, and it is most important that no awkward habits should be acquired.

Children who have courage may be taught to ride almost as soon as they can walk. On the Pampas of South America you may see a boy seven years old on horseback, driving a herd of horses; and carrying a baby in his arms!

I began my own lessons at four, when I sat upon an old mare in the stall while the groom polished harness or blacked his boots Mr, Nathaniel Gould, who, at upwards of seventy years, and sixteen stone weight, can still ride hunting for seven or eight hours at a stretch, mentions in his observations on horses and hunting[14], that a nephew of his followed the Cheshire fox-hounds at seven years of age. " His manner' of gathering up his reins was most singular, and his power of keeping his seat, with his little legs stretched horizontally along the saddle, quite surprising." The hero Havelock, writing to his little, boy, says, " You are now seven years old, and ought to learn to ride. I hope to hear soon that you have made progress in that important part of your education. Your uncle William (a boy-hero in the Peninsula) rode well before he was seven years old." The proper commencement for a boy is a pony in which he can interest himself, and on which he may learn to sit as a horseman should.

I particularly warn parents against those broad-backed animals which, however suitable for carrying heavy old gentlemen, or sacks to market, are certainly very uncomfortable for the short legs of little boys, and likely to induce rupture. On a narrow, well-bred pony, of 11 or 12 hands high, a boy of six can sit like a little man. It is cruel to make children ride with bare legs

Before Rarey introduced his system, there was no satisfactory mode of training those ponies that were too small for a man to mount, unless the owner happened to live near some racing' stable, where he could obtain the services of a " featherweight doll," and then the pony often learned tricks more comic than satisfactory.

---

14   Hints on Horses and Hunting,"by Senex.

By patiently applying the practices explained in the preceding chapters, the smallest and most highly-bred pony may be reduced to perfect docility without impair* ing its spirit, and taught a number of amusing tricks.

Young ladies may learn on full-sized horses quite as well as on ponies, if they are provided with suitable side-saddles.

A man, or rather a boy, may learn to ride by practice and imitation, and go on tumbling about until he has acquired a firm and even elegant seat, but no lady can ever learn to ride as a lady should ride, without a good deal of instruction; because her seat on horseback is so thoroughly artificial, that without some competent person to tell her of her faults, she is sure to fall into a number of awkward ungraceful tricks. Besides, a riding school, with its enclosed walls and trained horses, affords an opportunity of going through the preliminary lessons without any of those accidents which on the road, or in a field, are very likely to occur with a raw pupil on a fresh horse. For a young lad to fall on the grass, is not a serious affair, but a lady should never be allowed to ran the chance of a fall, because it is likely to destroy the nerve, without which no lessons can be taught successfully. All who have noticed the performances of Amazones in London, or at Brighton, must have in remembrance the many examples of ladies who, with great courage, sit in a manner that is at once fearful and ridiculous to behold; entirely dependent on the good behaviour of horses, which they, in reality, have no power of turning, and scarcely of stopping.

Little girls who learn their first lessons by riding with papa, who is either absorbed in other business, or himself a novice in the art of horsemanship, get into poky habits, which it is extremely difficult to eradicate when they reach the age when every real woman wishes to be admired.

Therefore, let everyone interested in the horsemanship of a young lady commence by placing her, as early as possible, under the tuition of a competent professional riding-master, unless he knows enough to teach her himself. There are many riding-schools where a fair seat is acquired by the lady pupils, but in London, at any rate, only two or three where they learn to use the reins, so as to control an unruly horse.

Both sexes are apt to acquire the habit of holding on by the bridle. To avoid this grave error, the first lessons in walking and cantering should be given to the pupil on a led horse, without taking hold of the bridle ; and this should be repeated in learning to leap. The horsemanship of a lady is not complete until she has learned to leap, whether she intends to ride farming or hunting, or to confine herself to Rotten Row canters; for horses will leap and bound at times without per-mission.

I have high authority for recommending lessons without holding the bridle. Lady Mildred H , one of the most accomplished horsewomen of the day, taught her daughter to walk, trot, canter, gallop, and leap, without the steadying assistance of the reins.

A second point is, that every pupil in horsemanship should begin by holding the rein or reins (one is enough to begin with) in both hands, pulling to the right when they want to go to the right, and to the left when they wish to go to the left, that is the proper way of riding every strange horse, every colt, and every hunter, that does not perfectly know his business, for it is the only way in which you have any real command over your horse. But almost all our riding-school rules are military. Soldiers are obliged to carry a sword in one hand, and to rely, to a great extent, on the training of their horses for turning right or left. Ladies and gentlemen have no swords to carry, and neither possess, nor can desire to possess, such machines as troop-horses. Besides other more important advantages which will presently be described by commencing with two-handed riding, a lady is more likely to continue to sit squarely, than when holding the reins with one hand, and pretending to guide a horse who really guides himself. A man has the power of turning a horse, to a certain extent, with his legs and spurs; a woman must depend on her reins, whip, and left leg. As only one rein and the whip can be well held in one hand, double reins, except for hunting, are to a lady merely a perplexing puzzle. The best way for a lady is to knot up the snaffle, and hang it over the pommel, and ride with a light hand on the curb.

In order to give those ladies who may not have instruction at hand an idea of a safe, firm, and elegant seat, I have placed at the head of this chapter a woodcut, which shows how the legs should be placed. The third or hunting-horn pommel must be fitted to the rider, as its situation in the saddle will differ, to some extent, according to the length of the lady's legs. I hope my plain speaking will not offend American friends.

The first step is to sit well down on the saddle, then pass the right leg over the upstanding pommel, and let it hang straight down,—a little back, if leaping; if the foot pokes out, thelady has no firm hold. The stirrup must then be shortened, so as to bring the bent thigh next to the knee of the left leg firmly against the under side of the hunting-horn pommel. If, when this is done, an imaginary line were drawn from the rider's backbone, which would go through the centre of the saddle, close to the cantle, she is in her proper place, and leaning rather back than forward, firm and close from the hips downwards, flexible from her hips upwards, with her hands holding the reins apart, a little above the level of her knee, she is in a position at once powerful and graceful. This is a very imperfect description of a very elegant picture. The originals, few and far between, are to be found for nine months of the year daily in Hot-ten Row. A lady in mounting, should hold the reins in her left hand, and place it on the pommel, the right hand as far over the cantle as she can comfortably reach. If there is no skilful man present to take her foot, make any man kneel down and put out his right knee as a step, and let down the stirrup to be shortened afterwards. Practise on a high chest of drawers !

After all the rules of horsemanship have been perfectly learned, nothing but practice can give the instinct which prepares a rider for the most sudden starts, leaps, and " kickings up behind and before."

The style of a man's seat must, to a certain extent, be settled by his height and shape. A man with short round legs and thighs cannot sit down on his horse like tall thin men, such as Jim Mason, or Tom Oliver, but men of the most unlikely shapes, by dint of practice and pluck, go well in the hunting-field, and don't look ridiculous on the road.

There are certain rules laid down as to -the length of a man's stirrup leathers, but the only good rule is that they should be short enough to give the rider full confidence in his seat, and full power over a pulling horse. For hunting it is generally well to take them up one hole shorter than on the road.

The 'military directions for mounting are absurd for civilians; in the first place, there ought to be no Tight side or wrong side in mounting; in both the street and hunting-field it is often most convenient to mount on what is called the wrong side. In the next place horses trained on the Rarey plan (and very soon all horses will be), will stand without thinking of moving when placed by the rider, so that the military direction to stand before the stirrup becomes unnecessary.

The 'following is Mr. Rarey's plan of mounting for men, which is excellent, but is not described in his book, And indeed is difficult to describe at all.

*To mount with the girths slack without bearing on the stirrup.*—Take up the reins and a lock of the mane, stand behind the withers looking at your horse's head, put your foot in the stirrup, and While holding the reins in one hand on the neck, place the other open and flat on the other side of the saddle as far down as the edge of the little flap, turn your toe out, so as not to touch the horse's belly, and rise by leaning on your fiat hand, thus pressing hard on the side of the saddle opposite to that on which you are mounting. The pressure of your hands will counterbalance your weight, and you will be able to mount without straining 'the girths, or even without any girths at all. If you are not tall enough to put your foot fairly in the stirrup, use a horse-block, or, better still, a piece of solid wood about eighteen inches high, that can be moved about anywhere.

Young men should learn to leap into the saddle by placing both hands on the cantle, as the horse moves. I have seen Daly, the steeplechaser, who was a little man, do this often in the hunting-field, before he broke his thigh.

With respect to the best model for a seat, I recommend the very large class who form the best customers of riding-school masters in the great towns of England, I mean the gentlemen from eighteen to eight-and-twenty, who begin to ride as soon as they have the means and the opportunity, to study the style of the first-class steeplechase jockeys and gentlemen riders in the hunting-field whenever they have the opportunity. Almost all riding-masters are old dragoons, and what they teach is good as far as it goes, as to general appearance and carriage of the body, but generally the military notions about the use of a rider's arms and legs are utterly wrong.

On this point we cannot have a better authority than that of the late Captain Nolan, who served in the Austrian, Hungarian, and in the English cavalry in India, and who studied horsemanship in Russia, and all other European countries celebrated for their cavalry. He says—

"

The difference between a school (viz. an ordinary military horseman) and a real horseman is this, the first depends upon guiding and managing his horse for maintaining his seat; the second depends upon his seat for controlling and guiding his horse. At a trot the school rider, instead of lightly rising to the action of the horse, bumps up and down, falling heavily on the horse's loins, and hanging on the reins to prevent the animal slipping from under him, whilst he is thrown up in his seat."

It is a curious circumstance that the English alone have two styles of horsemanship. The one, natural and useful, formed in the hunting-field; the other, artificial and military, imported from the Continent. If you go into Rotten Row in the season you may see General the Earl of. Cardigan riding a trained charger in the most approved military style—the toes in the stirrups, long stirrup-leathers, heels down, legs from the knee carefully clear of the horse's side—in fact, the balance seat, handed down by tradition from the time when knights wore complete armour and could ride in no other way, for the weight of the armour rendered a fall certain if once the balance was lost; a very grand and graceful style it is when performed by a master of the art of the length of limb of the Earl, or his more brilliant predecessor, the late Marquess of Anglesea. But if you go into Northamptonshire in the hunting season, you may see the same Earl of Cardigan in his scarlet coat, looking twice as ,thick in the waist, sailing away in the first flight, sitting down on the part intended by nature for a seat, with his knees well bent, and his calves employed in distributing his weight over the horse's back and sides. In the one case the Earl is a real, in the other a show, horseman.

Therefore, when a riding-master tells you that you must ride by balance, " with your body upright, knee drawn back, and the feet in a perpendicular line with the shoulder, and your legs from the knee downward brought away to prevent what is called clinging" listen to him, learn all you can—do not argue, that would be useless—and then take the first opportunity of studying those who are noted for combining an easy, natural seat with grace—that is, if you are built for gracefulness —some people are not. In Nolan's words, "Let a man have a roomy saddle, and sit close to the horse's back; let the leg be supported by the stirrup, in a natural position, without being so short as to throw back the thigh, and the nearer the whole leg is brought to the horse the better, so long as the foot is not bent below the ankle-joint."

Soon after the battle of Waterloo, by influence of the Prince Regent, who fancied he knew something about cavalry, a Prussian was introduced to teach our cavalry a new style of equitation, which consisted in entirely abandoning the use of that part of the person in which his Royal Highness was so highly gifted, and riding on the fork like a pair of compasses on a rolling pin, with. perfectly straight legs. For a considerable period this ridiculous drill, which deprived the soldiers of all power over their horses, was carried on in the fields where Belgrave Square now stands, and was not abandoned until the number of men who suffered by it was the cause of a serious remonstrance from commanding officers. It is a pity that the reverse system has never been tried, and a regiment of cavalry taught riding on English fox-hunting principles, using the snaffle on the road, and rising in the trot. But it must be admitted that since the war there has been a great improvement in this respect, and there will probably be more as the martinets of the old school die off.

It was not for want, of examples of a better style that the continental military style was forced upon our cavalry. Mr. Nathaniel Gould relates in his little book as an instance of what determined hnntingmen can do, that—

"When, in the year 1616, Blucher arrived in London and drove at once to Carlton House, I was one of a few out of an immense concourse of horsemen who accompanied his carriage from Shooter's Hill, riding on each side; spite of all obstacles we forced ourselves through the Horse Guards gate and the troop of guardsmen, in like maimer through the Light Cavalry and gate at Carlton House, as well as the posse of constables in the court -yard, and drove our horses up the flight of stone steps into the salon, though the guards, beefeaters, and constables arrayed themselves against this irruption of Cossacks, and actually came to the charge. The Prince, however, in the noblest manner waved his hand, and we were allowed to form a circle round the Regent while Blucher had the blue ribbon placed on his shoulders, and was assisted to rise by the Prince in the most dignified manner. His Royal Highness then slightly acknowledged our presence, we backed to the door, and got down the steps again with only one accident, that arising from a horse, which, on being urged forward, took a leap down the whole flight of stairs."

But to return to the subject of a man's seat on horseback. Nolan, quoting Baucher, says, "When first put on horseback, devote a few lessons to making his limbs supple, in the same way that you begin drill on foot with extension motions. Show him how-to close up the thigh and leg to the saddle, and then work the leg backwards and forwards, up and down, *without stirrups; make him swing a weight round in a circle from the shoulder centre*; the other hand placed on the-thigh, thence to the rear, change-the weight to the opposite hand, and same."

*"Placing one hand on the horse's mane*, make him lean down to each side in succession, till he reaches to within a short distance of the ground." " These exercises give a man a firm hold with his leg3, on a horse, and teach him to move his limbs without quitting his seat. Then take him in the circle in the longe, and, by walking and trotting alternately, teach him the necessity of leaning with the body to the side the horse is turning to. This is the necessary balance. Then put him with others, and give him plenty of trotting, to shake him into his seat. By degrees teach him how to

use the reins, then the leg."

These directions for training a full-grown trooper may be of use to civilians.,

HANDS AND REINS.

Presuming that you are in a fair way to obtain a secure seat, the next point is the use of the reins and the employment of your legs, for it is by these that a horseman holds, urges, and turns his horse. To handle a horse in perfection, you must have, besides instruction, " good hands." Good or light hands, like the touch of a first-rate violinist, are a gift, not always to be acquired even by thought and practice. The perfection of riding is to make your horse understand and obey your directions, as conveyed through the reins—to halt, or go fast or slow; to walk, trot, canter, or gallop ; to lead off with right or left leg, to change leg, to turn either way, and to rise in leaping at the exact point you select. No one but a perfect horseman, with naturally fine hands, can do this perfectly, but every young horseman should try.

The golden rule of horsemanship is laid down by Colonel Greenwood, in a sentence that noodles will despise for its " trite simplicity:"—"When you wish to turn to the right, pull the right rein stronger than the left." This is common sense. No horse becomes restive in the colt-breaker's hands. The reason is, that they ride with one bridle and two hands, instead of two bridles and one hand. When they wish to go to the left, they pull the left rein stronger than the right. When they wish to go to the right, they pull the right rein stronger than the left. If the colt does not obey these indications, at least he understands them, even the first time he is mounted, and the most obstinate will not long resist them. Acting on these plain principles, I saw, in August last, a three-year-old colt which, placed absolutely raw and unbridled in Mr. Rarey's hands, within seven days answered every indication of the reins like an old horse—turned right or left, brought his nose to the rider's knee, and backed like an old trooper.

" But it takes a long time to make a colt understand that he is to turn to the right when the left rein is pulled;" and if any horse resists, the rider has no power one-handed, as the reins are usually held, to compel him.

The practice of one-handed riding originated in military schools; for a soldier has to carry a sword or lance, and depends chiefly on his well-trained horse and the pressure of his legs. No one ever attempts to turn a horse in harness with one hand, although there the driver has the assistance of the terrets, and it is equally absurd to attempt it with a colt or horse with a delicate mouth. Of course, with an old-trained hack even the reins are a mere form; any hint is enough.

The advantage of double-handed riding is, that, in a few hours, any colt and any pupils in horsemanship may learn it.

To make the most of a horse, the reins must he held with a smooth, even hearing, not hauling at a horse's mouth, as if it were made of Indian rubber, nor yet leaving the reins slack, but so feeling him. that your can instantaneously direct his course in any direction, " as if," to use old Chifney's phrase, " your rein was a worsted thread." Your legs ace to be used to force your horse forward up to the bit, and also to guide him. That is, when you turn to the right pull the right rein sharpest and press with the left leg; when to the left, vice versâ. Unless a horse rides up to the bit you have no control over; him.

A good horseman chooses his horse's ground and his pace for him. " To avoid a falling leaf a horse will put his foot over a precipice. When a horse has made a stumble, or is in difficulties at a fence, you cannot leave him too much at liberty, or be too quiet with him." Don't believe the nonsense people talk about holding a horse up *after* he has stumbled.

The pupil horseman should remember to drop his hands as low as he can on each side the withers, without stooping, when a horse becomes restive, plunging or attempting to run away. The instinct of a novice is to do exactly what he ought not to do—raise his hands,

By a skilful use of the reins and your own legs, with or without spurs, you collect, ox, as Colonel Greenwood well expresses it, you condense your, horse, at a stand, that is, you make him stand square, yet ready to move in any direction at any pace that you require; this is one use of the curb bit. It is on the same principle that fashionable coachmen "hit and hold" their high-bred horses while they thread the crowded streets of the West end in season, or that you see a ha d rider; when starting with three hundred companions at the joyful sound of Tally-ho, pricking and holding his horse, to have him ready for a great effort the moment he is clear of the crowd.

By a judicious use of the curb rein, you collect a tired horse; tired horses are inclined to sprawl about You draw his hind-legs- under him, throw him upon his haunches, and render him less-liable to fall even on his weary or weak fore-legs But a pull at the reins when a horse is falling may make him hold up his head, but cannot make him hold up his legs..

" When a horse is in movement there should be a constant touch or feeling or play between his mouth and the rider's hands." Not the hold by which riders of the foreign school retain: their horses, at an artificial parade pace, which is inconceivably fatiguing to the animal, and quite contrary to our English notions of natural riding; but a gradual, delicate firm feeling of the mouth and steady indications of the legs, which keep a fiery well-broken horse always, to use a school phrase, " between your hands and legs."

You cannot take too much, pains to acquire this art, for although it is not exercised on an old hack, that you ride with reins held any how, and your legs dangling anywhere, it is called into action and gives additional enjoyment to be striding the finest class of high-couraged delicate-mouthed horses—beautiful creatures that seem to enjoy being ridden by a real horseman or; light-handed Amazone, but which become frantic in igncrant or brutal hands.

" A horse should never be turned without being made to collect himself without being; retained by the hands and urged by the legs, as-well as guided by both; that is in turning to. the right both hands should retain him, and the right hand guide him, by being used the strongest; in turning to the left, both legs should urge him, and the left guide him by being pressed the strongest. Don't turn into the contrary extreme, slackening the left rein, and hauling the horse's head. round to the right.

The same rules should be observed for making a horse canter with the right leg, but the right rein should be only drawn enough to develop his right nostril.

*Reining Back.*—You must collect a horse with your legs before you rein him back, because if you press him back first with the reins he may throw all his weight on his hind legs under him, stick out his nose, hug his tail, and then he cannot stir— you must recover him to his balance, and give him power to step back. This rule is often neglected by carters in trying to make the shaft-horse back.

*Bearing.* — Knot the snaffle rein—loose it when the horse rears — put your right arm round the horse's neck, with the hand well up and close under the horse's gullet; press your left shoulder forward so as to bring your chest to the horse's near side, for, if the horse falls, you will fall clear; the moment he is descending, press him forward, take up the rein, which, being knotted, is short to your hands, and ply the spurs. But a horse, after being laid down and made walk, tied up like the zebra a few times, will seldom persist, because the moment he attempts to rise you pull his off hind leg under him and he is powerless.

*Leaping.*—The riding-school is a bad place to teach a horse to leap. The bar, with its posts, is very apt to frighten him; if a colt has not been trained to leap as it should be by following its dam before it is mounted, take it into the fields and let it follow well-trained horses over easy low fences and little ditches, slowly with- out fuss, and, as part of the ride, not backwards and forwards—always leap on the snaffle. Our cavalry officers learn to leap, not in the school, but "across country." Nolan tells a story that, during some manoeuvres in Italy, an Austrian general, with his staff, gotamongst some enclosures and sent some of his aid-de-camps to find an outlet. They peered over the stone walls, rode about, but could find no gap. The general turned to one of his staff, a Yorkshireman, and said, " See if you can find a way out of this place." Mr. W k, mounted on a good English horse, went

straight at the wall, cleared it, and, while doing so, turned in his saddle and touched his cap and said, " This way, general;" but his way did not suit the rest of the party.

There is a good deal taught in the best military schools, well worth time and study, which, with practice in horse-taming, would fill up the idle time of that numerous class who never read, and find time heavy on their hands, when out of town life.

" But a military riding-school," says Colonel Greenwood, " is too apt to teach you to sit on your horse as stiff as a statue, to let your right hand hang down as useless as if God had never gifted you with one, to-stick your left hand out, with a stiff straight wrist like a boltsprit, and to turn your horse invariably on the wrong rein." I should not venture to say so much on my own authority, but Captain Nolan says further, speaking of the effect of the foreign school (not Baucher's), on horses and men, "The result of this long monotonous course of study is, that on the uninitiated the school rider makes a pleasing impression, his horse turns, prances, and caracoles without any visible aid, or without any motion in the horseman's upright, imposing attitude. But I have lived and served with them. I have myself been a riding-master, and know, from experience, the disadvantages of this foreign seat and system."

There is nothing that requires more patience and firmness than a shying horse. Shying arises from three causes—defective eyesight, skittishness, and fear. If a horse always shies from the same side you may be sure the eye on that side is defective.

You may know that a horse shies from skittishness if he flies one day snorting from what he meets the next with indifference; dark stables also produce this irregular shying.

Nervousness, which is often increased by brutality, as the horse is not only afraid of the object, but of the whipping and spurring he has been accustomed to receive, can be alleviated, to some extent, by the treatment already described in the horse-training chapter. But horses first brought from the country to a large town are likely to be alarmed at a number of objects. You must take time to make them acquainted with each. Tor instance, I brought a mare from the country that everything moving seemed to frighten. I am convinced she had been ill-used, or had had an accident in harness. The first time a railway train passed in her sight over a bridge spanning the road she was travelling, she would turn round and would have run away had I not been able to restrain her; I could feel her heart beat between my legs. Acting on the principles of Xenophon and Mr. Rarey, I allowed her to turn, but compelled her to stand, twenty yards off, while the train passed. She looked back with a fearful eye all the time—it was a very slow luggage train-while I soothed her. After once or twice she consented to face the train, watching it with crested neck and ears erect; by degrees she walked slowly forwards, and in the course of a few days passed under the bridge in the midst of the thunder of a train with perfect indifference.

If you can distinctly ascertain that a horse shies and turns round from mere skittishness, correct him when he turns, not as long as he feces the object: he will soon learn that it is for turning that he is visited with whip and spurs. A few days' practice and patience essentially alter the character of the most nervous horses.

Books contain very elaborate descriptions of what a back or a hunter should be in form, &c To most persons these descriptions convey no practical ideas. The better plan is to take lessons on the proportions and anatomy of a horse from some intelligent judge or veterinary surgeon. You must study, and buy, and lose your money on many horses before you can safely, if ever, depend on your own judg- ment in choosing a horse. And, after all, a natural talent for comparison and eye for proportion are only the gift of a few. Some men have horses all their lives, and yet scarcely know a good animal from a bad one, although they may know what they like to drive, or ride or hunt The safe plan is to distrust your own judgment until you feel you have had experience enough to choose for yourself.

Hacks for long distances are seldom required in England in these railway days. A town hack should be good-looking, sure-footed, not too tall, and active, for you are always in sight, you have to ride over slippery pavement, to turn sharp corners, and to mount and dis-; mount often. Rarey's system of making the horse obey the voice, stand until called, and follow the rider, may easily be taught, and is of great practical value thus applied. A cover or country hack must be fast, but need not be so showy in action or handsome as a town hack —his merit is to get over the ground.

Teach your hack to walk well with the reins loose —no pace is more gentlemanly and useful than a good steady walk. Any well-bred screw can gallop; it is the slow paces that show a gentleman's hack.

If on a long journey, walk a quarter of a mile for every four you trot or canter, choosing the softest bits of road or turf.

Do not permit the saddle to be removed for at least half an hour after arriving with your horse hot. A neglect of this precaution will give a sore back.

A lady's horse, beside other well-known qualifications of beauty and pace, should be up to the lady's weight. It is one of the fictions of society that all ladies eat little and weigh little. Now, a saddle and habit weigh nearly three stone, a very slim lady will weigh nine, so there you reach twelve stone, which, considering how fond young girls are of riding fast and long over hard roads, is no mean weight. The best plan is to put the dear creatures into the scales with their saddles, register the result, and choose a horse calculated to be a good stone over the gross weight. How few ladies remember, as for hours they canter up and down Rotten Row, that that famous promenade is a mile and a quarter in length, so ten turns make twelve miles and a half.

The qualifications of a hunter need not be described, because all those who need these hints will, if they have common sense, only take hunters like servants, with established characters of at least one season.

Remember that a horse for driving requires "courage," for he is always going fast—he never walks. People who only keep one or two horses often make the same mistake, as if they engaged Lord Gourmet's cook for a servant of all work. They see a fiery caprioling animal, sleek as a mole, gentle, but full of fire, come out of a nobleman's stud, where he was nursed like a child, and only ridden or driven in his turn, with half-a-dozen others. Seduced by his lively appearance, they purchase him, and place him under the care of a gardener-groom, or at livery, work him every day, early and late, and are surprised to find his flesh melt, his coat lose its bloom, and his lively pace exchanged for a dull shamble. This is a common case. The wise course is to select for a horse of all work an animal that has been always accustomed to work hard ; he will then improve with care and regular exercise.

Horses under six years' old are seldom equal to very hard work: they are not, full-grown, of much use, where only one or two are kept.

Make a point of caressing your horse, and giving him a carrot or apple whenever he is brought to you, at the same time carefully examine him all over, see to his legs, his shoes, and feet; notice if he is well groomed; see to the condition of his furniture, and see always that he is properly bitted. Grooms are often careless and ignorant.

*As to Shoeing*. In large towns there are always veterinary surgeons' forges, where the art is well understood and so, too, in hunting districts; but where you have to rely on ignorant blacksmiths you cannot do better than rely on the rather exaggerated instructions contained in " Miles on the Horse's Foot," issued at a low price by the Royal Agricultural Society. Good shoeing prolongs the use of a horse for years.

*Stables*.—Most elaborate directions are given for the construction of stables; but most people are obliged to put up with what they find on their premises. Stables should be so ventilated that they never stink, and are never decidedly warm in cold weather, if you wish your horses to be healthy. Grooms will almost always stop up ventilation if they can. Loose boxes are to be preferred to stalls, because in them a tired horse can place himself in the position most easy to him. Sloping stalls are chambers of torture.

Hunters should be placed away from other horses, where, after a fatiguing day, they can lie at length, undisturbed by men or other horses in use. Stables should be as light as living rooms, but with louvers to darken them in summer, in order to keep out the flies. An ample supply of cold and hot water without troubling the cook is essential in a well-managed stable.

Large stables are magnificent, but a mistake. Four or five horses are quite as many as can be comfortably lodged together. I have seen hunters in an old barn in better condition than in the grandest temples of fashionable architects.

It takes an hour to dress a horse well in the morning, and more on return hot from work. From this hint you may calculate what time your servant must devote to his horses if they are to be well dressed.

If you are in the middle class, with a small stud, never take a swell groom from a great stable—-he will despise you and your horses. Hunting farmers and hunting country surgeons train the best class of grooms.

When you find an hone6t, sober man, who thoroughly knows his business, you cannot treat him too well, for half the goodness of a horse depends, like a French dish, on the treatment.

# CHAPTER IX

ON HORSEMAN'S AND HORSEWOMAM'S DRESS, AND HORSE

FURNITURE.

On bits.—The snaffle.—The use of the curb.—The Pelham.—The Hanoverian bit described.—Martingales.—The gentleman's saddle to be
large enough.—Spurs.—Not to be too sharp.—The Somerset saddle for
the timid and aged.—The Nolan saddle without flaps.— Ladies' saddle
described.—Advantages of the hunting-horn crutch. —Ladies' stirrup.—
-ladies' dress.—Hints on.—Habit.—Boots.-—-Whips.—Hunting whips.—
Use of the lash.—Gentleman's riding costume.—Hunting dress.—Poole,
the great authority.—Advantage of cap over hat in hunting.—Boot-tops
and Napoleons.—Quotation from Warburton's ballads.

IF you wish to ride comfortably, you must look as carefully to see that your
horse's furniture fits and suits him as to your own hoots and breeches.

When a farmer buys a team of oxen, if he knows his business he asks their
names, because oxen answer to their names. On the same principle it is well to
inquire what bit a horse has been accustomed to, and if you cannot learn, try several until you find out what suits him. There are rare horses, "that carry their own
heads," in dealers' phrase, safely and elegantly with a plain snaffle bridle; but except
in the hands of a steeplechase jock, few are to be so trusted. Besides, as reins, as well
as snaffles, break, it is not safe to hunt much with one bit and one bridle-rein. The
average of horses go best on a double bridle, that is to say, the common

hard and sharp or curb, with a snaffle. The best way is to ride on the snaffle,
and use the curb only when it is required to stop your horse suddenly, to moderate
his speed when he is pulling too hard, or when he is tired or lazy to collect him, by
drawing his nose down and his hind-legs more under him, for that is the first effect

of taking hold of the curb-rein. There are many horses with good mouths, so far that they can be stopped easily with a plain snaffle, and yet require a

curb-bit, to make them carry their heads in the right place, and this they often seem to do from the mere hint of the curb-chain dangling against their chins, without the rider being obliged to pull at the reins with any perceptible force.

.The Pelham-bit (see cut), which is a sort of snaffle-bit with cheeks and a curb-chain, is a convenient style for this class of horse. A powerful variation of the Pelham, called the Hanoverian, has within the last few years come very much into use. It requires the light hands of a practised horseman to use the curb-reins of the Hanoverian on a delicate-mouthed horse; but when properly used no bit makes a horse bend and display himself more handsomely, and in the hunting-field it will hold a horse when nothing else will, for this bit is a

very powerful snaffle, as well as curb, with rollers or rings, that keep the horse's mouth moist, and prevent it from becoming dead (see cut). For hunting, use the first; if the Hanoverian it should not be too narrow.

The Chifney is a curb with a very powerful leverage and one of the best for a pulling horse, or a lady's use.

A perfect horseman will make shift with any bit Sir Tatton Sykes and Sir Charles Knightley, in their prime, could hold any horse with a plain snaffle; but a lady, or a weak-wristed horseman, should be provided with a bit that can stop the horse on an emergency; and many horses, perfectly quiet coot the road, pull hard in the field at the beginning of a run. But it should be remembered, that when a horse runs away, it is useless to rely on the curb, as, when once he has fully resisted it, the longer he runs the less he cares for it The better plan is to keep the snaffle moving and cawing in his mouth, and from time to time take a sharp pull at the curb,

It is of great importance, especially with a high-spirited horse that the bead-piece should fit him that it is neither too tight nor too low down in his mouth. I have known a violently restive horse to become per-ieetly calm and docile when his -bridle had been altered so as to fit him comfortably. The curb-bit should he placed so low as only just to dearths tushes in a horse's mouth, and one inch Above the corner teeth in a mare's. There should be room for at least one finger between the curb-chain and the chin. If the horse is tender-skinned, the chain may be covered with leather.

When you are learning to ride, you should take pains to learn everything concerning the horse and his equipments. In this country we are so well waited upon, that we often forget that we may at some time or other he abliged to become our own grooms and farriers.

For the colonies, the best bridle is that described in the chapter on training colts, which is a halter, a bridle, and a gag combined.

Bridle reins should be soft, yet tough; so long, and no longer, so that by extending your arms you can shorten them to any desired length; then, if your . horse pokes out his head, or extends himself in leaping, you can, if you hold the reins in each hand, as you ought, let them slip through your fingers, and shorten them in an instant by extending your arms. A very good sportsman of my acquaintance has tabs sewn on the curb-reins, which prevents them from slipping. This is a useful plan for ladies who ride or drive; but, as before observed, in hunting the snaffle-reins should slip through the fingers.

Some horses require martingales to keep their heads down, and in the right place. But imperfect horsemen are not to be trusted with running martingales. Running martingales require tabs on the reins, to prevent the rings getting fixed close to the mouth.

For hacks and ladies' horses on the road, a standing martingale, buckled to the nose-band of the bridle, is the best. It should be fixed, as Mr. Rarey directs, not so short as to bring the horse's head exactly where you want it—your hands must do that—but just short enough to keep his nose down, and prevent him from flinging his poll into your teeth. If his neck is rightly shaped, he will by degrees lower his head, and get into the habit of so arching his neck that the martingale may be dispensed with-; this is very desirable, because you cannot leap with a standing martingale, and a running one requires the hands of a steeplechase jock.

The saddle of a gentleman should be large enough. In racing, a few pounds are of consequence; but in

carrying a heavy man on the road or in the field, to have the weight evenly distributed over the horse's back is of more consequence than three or four pounds. The common general fitting saddle will fit nine horses out of ten. Colonial horses usually .have low shoulders; therefore colonial saddles should be narrow, thickly stuffed, and provided with cruppers, although they have gone out of fashion in this country, because it is presumed that gentlemen will only ride horses that have a place for carrying a saddle properly.

On a journey, see to the stuffing of your saddle, and have it put in a draft, or to the fire, to dry, when saturated with sweat: the neglect of either precaution may give your horse a sore back, one of the most troublesome of horse maladies.

Before hunting, look to the spring bars of the stirrup-leathers, and see that they will work: if they are tight, pull them down and leave them open. Of all accidents, that of being caught, after your horses fall, in the stirrup, is the most dangerous, and not uncommon. I have seen at least six instances of it. When raw to the hunting-field, and of course liable to falls, it is well to use the spring-bar stirrups which open, not at the side, but at the eye holding the stirrup-leather; the same that I recommend for the use of ladies.

Spurs are only to be used by those who have the habit of riding, and will not use them at the wrong time. In most instances, the sharp points of the rowels should be filed or rubbed off, for they are seldom required for more than to rouse a horse at a fence, or turn him suddenly away from a vehicle in the street Sharp spurs may be left to jockeys. Long-legged men can squeeze their horses so hard, that they can dispense with spurs; but short-legged men need them at the close of a run, when a horse begins to lumber carelessly oyer his fences, or with a horse inclined to refuse. Dick Christian broke difficult horses to leaping without the spur ; and when he did, only used one on the left heel. Having myself had falls with horses at the close of a run, which rushed and pulled at the beginning, for want of spurs, I have found the advantage of carrying one in my sandwich-bag, and buckling it on, if needed, at a check. Of course, first-rate horsemen need none of these hints; but I write for novices only of whom, I trust, every prosperous year of Old England will produce a plentiful crop from the fortunate and the sons of the fortunate.

A great many persons in this country learn, or re-learn, to ride after they have reached manhood, either because they can then for the first time afford the dignity and luxury, or because the doctor prescribes horse exercise as the only remedy for weak digestion, disordered liver, trembling nerves—the result of overwork or over-feeding. Thus the lawyer, overwhelmed with briefs; the artist, maintaining his position as a Royal Academician; the philosopher, deep in laborious historical researches; and the young alderman, ex-hausted by his first year's apprenticeship to City feeding, come under the hands of the riding-master.

Now although for the man "to the manner bred," there is no saddle for hard work and long work, whether in the hunting-field or Indian campaign, like a broad seated English hunting saddle, there is no doubt that its smooth slippery surface offers additional difficulties to the middle-aged, the timid, and those crippled by gout, rheumatism or pounds- There can be very little benefit derived from horse exercise as long as the patient travels in mortal fear. Foreigners teach riding on a buff leather demi-pique saddle,—a bad plan far the young, as the English saddle becomes a separate difficulty. But to those who merely aspire to constitutional canters, and who ride only for health, or as a matter of dignity, 1 strongly recommend the Somerset saddle, invented for one of that family of cavaliers who had lost a leg below the knee. This saddle is padded before the knee and behind the thigh to fit the seat of the purchaser, and if provided with a stuffed seat of brown buckskin will give the quartogenarian pupil the comfort and the confidence of an arm-chair. They are, it may be encouraging to mention, fashionable among the more aristocratic middle-aged, and the front roll of stuffing is much used among those who ride and break their own eolts, as it affords a fulcrum against a puller, and a protection against a kicker. Australians use a rolled blanket, strapped over the pommel of the saddle, for the same purpose. To bad horsemen who are too conceited to use a Somerset, I say, in the words of the old proverb, " Pride must have a fall."

The late Captain Nolan had a military saddle improved from an Hungarian model, made for him by Gibson, of Coventry Street, London, without flaps, and with a felt saddle cloth, which had the advantage of being light, while affording the rider a close seat and more complete control over his horse, in consequence of the more direct pressure of the legs on the horse's flanks. It would be worth while to try a saddle of this kind for hunting purposes, and for breaking m colts. Of course it could only be worn with boots, to protect the rider's legs from the sweat of the horse's flanks.

With the hunting-horn crutch the seat of a woman is stronger than that of a man, for she presses her right leg down over the upright pommel, and the left leg up against the hunting-horn, and thra grasps the two pommels between her legs at that angle which gives her the most power.

Ladies' saddles ought invariably to be made with what is called the hunting-horn, or crutch, at the left side. The right-hand pommel has not yet gone out of fashion, but it is of no use, and is injurious to the security of a lady's seat, by preventing the right hand from being put down as low as it ought to be with a restive horse, and by encouraging the bad habit of leaning the right hand on it. A flat projection is quite sufficient. The security of the hunting-horn saddle will be quite clear to you, if, when sitting in your chair, you put a cylinder three or four inches in diameter between your legs, press your two knees together by crossing them, in the position of a woman on a side-saddle; when a man clasps his horse, however firmly, it has a tendency to raise the seat from the saddle. This is not the case with the side-saddle seat: if a man wishes to use a lance and ride at a ring, he will find that he has a firmer seat with this kind of side-saddle than with his own. There is no danger in this side-pommel, since you cannot be thrown on it, and it renders it next to impossible that the rider should be thrown upon the other pommel. In case of a horse leaping suddenly into the air and coming down on all four feet, technically, "bucking" without the leaping-horn there is nothing to prevent a lady from being thrown up. But the leaping-horn holds down the left knee, and makes it a fulcrum to keep the right knee down in its proper place. If the horse in violent action throws himself suddenly to the left, the upper part of the rider's body will tend downwards, to the right, and the lower limbs to the left: nothing can prevent this but the support of the leaping-horn. The fear of over-balancing to the right causes many ladies to get into the bad habit of leaning over their saddles to the left. This fear disappears when the hunting-horn pommel is used. The leaping-horn is also of great use with a hard puller, or in riding down a steep place, for it prevents the lady from sliding forward.

But these advantages render the right-hand pommel quite useless, a slight projection being all sufficient (see woodcut); while this arrangement gives the habit and figure a much better appearance. Every lady ought to be measured for this part of the saddle, as the distance between the two pommels will depend partly on the length of her legs.

When a timid inexperienced lady has to ride a fiery horse it is not a bad plan to attach a strap to the outside girth on the right hand, so that she may hold it and the right hand rein at the same time without disturbing her seat. This little expedient gives confidence, and is particularly useful if a -fresh horse should begin to kick a little. Of course it is not to be continued, but only used to give a timid rider temporary assistance. I have also used for the same purpose a broad tape passed across the knees, and so fastened that in a fall of the horse it would give way.

Colonel Greenwood recommends that for fastening a ladies' saddle-flaps an elastic webbing girth, and not a leather girth, should be used, and this attached, not, as is usually the case, to the small, but to the large flap on the near side. This will leave the near side small flap loose, as in a man's saddle, and allow a spring bar to be used. But I have never seen, either in use or in a saddler's shop, although I have constantly sought, a lady's saddle so arranged with a spring bar for the stirrup-leather. This mode of attaching a web girth to the large flap will render the near side perfectly smooth, with the exception of the stirrup-leather, which he recommends to be a single thin strap as broad as * gentleman's, fastened to the stirrup-leg by a loop or slipknot, and fixed over the spring bar of the saddle by a buckle like that on a man's stirrup-leather. This arrangement, which the Colonel also recommends to gentlemen, presumes that the length of the stirrup-leather never requires altering more than an inch or two. It is a good plan for short men when travelling, and likely to ride strange horses, to carry their stirrup-leathers with them, as nothing is more annoying than to have to alter them in a hurry with the help of a blunt pen-knife.

" The stirrup for ladles should be in all respects like a man's, large and heavy, and open at the side, or the eyelet hole, with a spring." The stirrups made small and padded out of compliment to ladies' small feet are very dangerous. If any padding be required to protect the front of the ankle-joint, it had better be a fixture cm the boot.

It is a mistake to imagine that people are dragged owing to the stirrup being too large, and the foot passing through it; such accidents arise from the stirrup being too small, and the foot clasped by the pressure of the upper part on the toe and the lower part on the sole.

Few ladies know how to dress for horse exercise, although there has been a great improvement, so far as taste is concerned, of late years. As to the head-dress, it may be whatever is in fashion, provided it so fits the head as not to require continual adjustment, often needed when the hands would be better employed with the reins and whip. It should shade from the sun, and if used in hunting protect the nape of the neck from rain. The recent fashions of wearing the plumes or feathers of the ostrich, the cock, the capercailzie, the pheasant, the peacock, and the kingfisher, in the ridingfeats of young ladies, in my bumble opinion, are highly to be commended.

As to the riding-habit, it may be of any colour and material suitable to the wearer and the season of year, but the sleeves must fit rather closely; nothing can be more out of place, inconvenient, and ridiculous, than the wide, hanging sleeves which look so well in a drawing. room. For country use the skirt of a habit may be short, and bordered at the bottom a foot deep with leather. The fashion of a waistcoat of light material for summer, revived from the fashion of last century, is a decided improvement, and so is the over-jacket of cloth, or sealskin, for rough weather. There is no reason why pretty young girls should not indulge in pictur-esque riding costume so long as it is appropriate,

Many ladies entirely spoil the sit of the skirts by retaining the usual impedi-menta of petticoats[16]. The best-dressed horsewomen wear nothing more than a flannel chemise with long coloured sleeves, under their trousers.

Ladies' trousers should be of the same material and colour -as the habit, and if full flowing like a Turk's, and fastened with an elastic band round the ankle, they will not be distinguished from the skirt. In this costume, which may be made amply warm by the folds of the trousers, plaited like a Highlander's kilt (fastened with an elastic band at the waist), a lady can sit down in a manner impossible for one en-cumbered by two or three short petticoats. It is the chest and back which require double folds of protection during, and after, strong exercise.

There is a prejudice against ladies wearing long Wellington boots; but it is quite absurd, for they need

[16] At an inquest on a young lady killed at Totnes in September last, it ap-peared that she lost her seat and hang by a *crinoline petticoat form the right hand pommel*

never be seen, and are a great comfort and protection in riding long distances, when worn with the trousers tucked inside. They should, for obvious reasons, be large enough for warm woollen stockings, and easy to get on and off. It would not look well to see a lady struggling out of a pair of wet boots with the help of a boot-jack and a couple of chambermaids. The heels of riding-boots, whether for ladies or gentlemen, should be low, but *long*, to keep the stirrup in its place.

The yellow patent leather recently introduced seems a suitable thing for the "

Napoleons" of hunting ladies. And I have often thought that the long leather gaiters of the Zouave would suit them.

Whips require consideration. By gentlemen on the road or in the park they are rather for ornament than use. A jockey whip is the most punishing, but on the Rarey system it is seldom necessary to use the whip except to a slug, and then spurs are more effective.

A lady's whip is intended to supply the place of a man's right leg and spur; it should therefore, however ornamental and thin, be stiff and real. Messrs. Callow, of Park Lane, make some very pretty ones, pink, green and amber, from the skin of the hippopotamus, light but severe. A loop to hang it from the wrist may bo made ornamental in colours and gold, and is useful, for a lady may require all the power of her little hand to grasp the right rein without the encumbrance of the whip, which on this plan will still be ready if required at a moment's notice. Hunting-whips must vary according to the country. In some districts the formidable metal hammers are still required to break intractable horses, but such whips and jobs should be left to the servants and hard-riding farmers.

As a general rule the hunting-whip of a man who has nothing to do with the hounds may be light, but it should have a good crook and be stiff enough to stop a gate. A small steel stud outside the crook prevents the gate from slipping; flat lashes of a brown colour have recently come into fashion, but they are mere matters of fashion like the colour of top boots, points to which only snobs pay any attention— that is, those asses who pin their faith in externals, and who, in the days of pigtails, were ready to die in defence of those absurd excrescences.

The stock of a whip made by Callow for a hunting nobleman to present to a steeple-chasing and fox-hunting professional, was of oak, a yard long, with a buck-horn crook, and a steel stud; but then the presentee is six feet high.

Every hunting-whip should have a lash, but it need not be long. The lash may be required to rouse a hound under your horse's feet, or turn the pack; as for whipping off the pack from the fox in the absence of the huntsman, the whips and the master, that is an event that happens to one per cent, of the field once in a life-time, although it is a common and favourite anecdote after dinner. But then Saint Munchausen presides over the mahogany where fox-hunting feats are' discussed. One use of a lash is to lead a horse by putting it through the rings of the snaffle, and to flip him up as you stand on the bank when he gets stuck fast, or dead beat in a ditch or brook. I once owed the extrication of my horse from a brook with a deep clay bottom entirely to having a long lash to my whip; for when he had plumped in close enough to the opposite bank for me to escape over his head, I was able first to guide him to a shelving spot, and then make him try one effort more by adroit flicks on his rump at amoment when he seemed prepared to give in and Le drowned. In leading a horse, always pass the reins through the ring of the snaffle, so that if he pulls he is held by the mouth, not by the top of his head.

The riding costume of a gentleman should be suitable without being groomish. It is a feet that does not seem universally known, that a man does not ride any better for dressing like a groom.

It has lately been the fashion to discard straps. This is all very well if the horse and the rider can keep th© trousers down, which can only be done by keeping the legs, away from the horse's sides; but when the trousers rise to the top of the boot, and the stocking or bare leg appears, the sooner straps or knee-breeches are adopted the better.

For hunting, nothing will do but boots and breeches, unless you condescend to gaiters—*for* trousers wet, draggled and torn, are uncomfortable and expensive wear. Leathers are pleasant, except in wet weather, and economical wear if you have a man who can clean them; but if they have to go weekly to the breeches -maker they become expensive, and are not. to be had when wanted; besides, wet leather breeches are troublesome things to travel with. White cord breeches have one great convenience; they wash well, although not so elastic, warm, and comfortable as woollen cords. It is essential for comfort that hunting-breeches should be built by a tailor who knows that particular branch of business, *and tried on sitting down* if not on horseback, for half your comfort depends, on their fit. Many Schneiders who are first-rate at ordinary garments, have no idea of riding clothes. Poole, of Saville Row, makes hunting-dress a special study, and supplies more hunting-men and masters of hounds than any tailor in London, but bis customers must be prepared to pay for per lection.

In the coats, since the modern shooting jacket fashion came in, there is great scope for variety. The fashion does not much matter so long as it is fit for riding—ample enough, to cover the chest and stomach in wet weather, easy enough to allow full play for the arms and shoulders, and not so long as to catch in hedgerows and brambles. Our forefathers in some counties rode in coats like scarlet dressing-gowns. There is one still to be seen in Surrey. For appearance, for wear, and as a universal passport to civility in a strange country, there is nothing like scarlet, provided the horseman can afford to wear it without offending the prejudices of valuable-patrons, Mends or landlords. In Lincolnshire, farmers are expected to appear in pink. In Northamptonshire a yeoman farming his own 400 acres would be thought presumptuous if he followed the Lincolnshire example. Near London you may see the " pals " of fighting men and hell-keepers in pink and velvet. A scarlet coat should never be assumed until the riders experience in the field is such that he is in no danger of becoming at once conspicuous and ridiculous.

A cap is to be preferred to a hat because it fits closer, is less in the way when riding through, cover, protects the head better from a bough or a fall, and will wear out two or three hats. It should be ventilated by a good bole at the top.

Top-boots are very pretty wear for men of the right height and right sort of kg when they fit perfectly—that is difficult on fat calves—and are cleaned to perfection, which is also difficult unless you have a more than ordinarily clever groom;

for men of moderate means, the patent black leather Napoleon, which costs from 3l. 10., to 4l. 4s., and can be cleaned with a wet sponge in five minutes, is the neatest and most economical boot—one in which travelling does not put you under any obligation to your host's servants.

I have often found the convenience of patent leather boots when staying with a party at the house of a master of hounds, while others, as the hounds were coming out of the kennel, were in an agony for tops entrusted two or three days previously to a not-to-be-found servant. In this point of the boots I differ from the author of " A Word ere we Start;" but then, squires of ten thousand a-year are not supposed to understand the shifts of those who on a twentieth part of that income manage to enjoy a good deal of sport with all sorts of hounds and all sorts of horses.

There is a certain class of sporting snobs who endeavour to enhance their own consequence or indulge their cynical humour by talking with the utmost contempt of any variation from the kind of hunting-dress in use, in their own particular district. The best com-mentary on the supercilious tailoring criticism of these gents is to be found in the fact that within a century every variety of hunting clothes has been in and out of fashion, and that the dress in fashion with the Quorn hunt in its most palmy days was not only the exact reverse of the present fashion in that flying country, but, if comfort and convenience are to be regarded, as ridiculous as brass helmets, tight stocks, and but-toned-up red jackets for Indian warfare. It consisted, as may be seen in old Aiken's and Sir John Dean Paul's hunting sketches, of a high-crowned hat, a high tight stock, a tight dress coat, with narrow skirts that could protect neither the chest, stomach, or thighs, long tight white cord breeches, and pale top-boots thrust low down the leg, the tops being supposed to be cleaned with champagne. Leather breeches, caps, and brown top-boots were voted slow in those days. But the men went well as they do in every dress.

> " Old wiseheads, complacently smoothing the brim,
> May jeer at my velvet, and call it a whim ;
> They may think in a cap little wisdom there dwells;
> They may say he who wears it should wear it with bells;
> But when Broadbrim lies flat,
> I will answer him pat,
> Oh ! who but a crackskull would ride in a hat ?"

SQUIBB WARBURTON.

# CHAPTER X.

# ON HUNTING.

" The sailor who rides on the ocean,
Delights when the stormy winds blow:
Wind and steam, what are they to horse motion ?
Sea cheers to a land Tally-ho ?
The canvas, the screw, and the paddle,
The stride of the thorough-bred hack,
 When, fastened like glue to the saddle,
We gallop astern of the pack."
TARPORLEY HUNT SONG, 1855.

> Advantage of hunting.—Libels on.—Great men who have hunted.— Popular notion unlike reality.—Dick Christian and the Marquis of Hastings.—Fallacy of "lifting" a horse refuted.—Hints on riding at fences.—Harriers discussed.—Stag-hunting a necessity and use where time an object.—Hints for novices.—Tally-ho! expounded.— To feed a horse after a hard ride.—Expenses of horse keep.—Song by Squire Warburton, " A word ere we start."

EVERY man who can ride, and, living within a couple of hours' distance of a pack of hounds, can 'spare a day now and then, should hunt. It will improve his horsemanship, enlarge his circle of acquaintance, as well as his tastes and sympathies, and make, as Shakspeare hath it—

" Good digestion wait on appetite, and health on both."

Not that I mean that every horseman should attempt to follow the hounds in the first flight, or even the second; because age, nerves, weight, or other good reasons may forbid: but every man who keeps a good hack may meet his friends at cover side, enjoy the morning air, with a little pleasant chat, and follow the hounds, if not in the front, in the rear, galloping across pastures, trotting through bridle gates, creeping through gaps, and cantering along the green rides of a wood, thus causing a healthy excitement, with no painful reaction; and if, unhappily, soured or overpressed by work and anxious thoughts, drinking in such draughts of Lethe as can no otherwise be drained.

Hunting has suffered as much from overpraise as from the traditionary libels of the fribbles and fops of the time of the first Georges, when a fool, a sot, and a fox-hunter were considered synonymous terms. Of late years it has pleased a sports-man, with a wonderful talent for picturesquely describing the events of a fox-hunt, to write two sporting novels, in which all the leading cha-racters are either fools or rogues.

" In England all conditions of men, except bishops, from ratcatchers to Royalty, are to be found in the hunting-field—equalised by horsemanship, and frater-nising under the influence of a genial sport. Among fox-hunters we can trace a long line of statesmen, from William of Orange to Pitt and Fox. Lord Althorp was a master of hounds ; and Lord Palmerston we have seen, within the last few years, going—as he goes everywhere —in the first flight." This was before the French fall of the late Premier. Cromwell's Ironsides were hunting men; Pope, the poet, writes in raptures of a gallop with the Wiltshire Harriers; and Gladstone, theologian, politician, and editor of Homer, bestrides his celebrated! white mare in Nottinghamshire, and scar-ries along by the side of the ex-War Minister, the Duke of Newcastle.

" The progress of agriculture is indelibly associated with fox-hunting ; for the three great landlords, who did more to turn sand and heath into corn and wool, and make popular the best breeds of stock and best course of cultivation—Francis, Duke of Bedford; Coke, Earl of Leicester; and the first Lord Yarborough—were all masters of hounds.

"When indecency formed the staple of our plays, and a drunken debauch formed the inevitable sequence of every dinner-party, a fool and a fox-hunter were synonymous. Squire Western was the representative of a class, which, however, was not more ridiculous than the patched, perfumed Sir Plumes, whom Hogarth painted, and Pope satirised. Fox-hunters are not a class now—roads, newspapers, and manufacturing emigration have equalised the condition of the whole kingdom; and fox-hunters are just like any other people, who wear clean shirts, and can afford to keep one or more horses. "

It is safe to assert that hunting-men, as a class, are temperate. No man can ride well across a difficult country who is not. We must, however, admit that the birds who have most fouled their own nest have been broken-down sportsmen, chiefly racing men, who have turned writers to turn a penny. These unfortunate people, with the fatal example of ' Noctes Ambrosiansd' before them, fill up a page, whenever their memory or their industry fails them, in describing in detail a breakfast, a luncheon, a dinner, and a supper. And this has been repeated so often, that the uninitiated are led to believe that every fox-hunter must, as a matter of course, keep a French cook, and consume an immense cellar of port, sherry, madeira, hock, champagne, with gallons of strong ale, and all manner of liqueurs.

" The popular notion of a fox-hunt is as unlike the reality as a girl's notion of war—a grand charge and a splendid victory.

"Pictures always represent exciting scenes—hounds flying away with a burning scent; horses taking at a bound, or tumbling neck and crop over, frightful fences. Such lucky days, such bruising horsemen, such burning scents and flying foxes are the exception.

" At least two-thirds of those who go out, even in the most fashionable counties, never attempt brooks or five barred gates, or anything difficult or dangerous; but, by help of open gates and bridle-roads, which are plen tiful, parallel lanes, and gaps, which are conveniently made by the first rush of the straight riders and the dealers with horses to sell, helped by the curves that hounds generally make, and a

fair knowledge of the country, manage to be as near the hounds as the most thrusting horseman. Among this crowd of skirters and road-riders are to be found some
very good sportsmen, who, from some cause or other, have lost their nerve; others,
who live in the county, like the excitement and society, but never took a jump in
their lives; young ladies with their papas; boys on ponies; farmers educating four-
year-olds; surgeons and lawyers, who are looking for professional practice as well
as sport. On cold scenting days, with a ringing fox, this crowd keeps on until nearly
dark, and heads many a fox. Many a beginner, in his first season, has been cheated
by a succession of these easy days over an easy part of the county into the idea that
there was no difficulty in riding to hounds. But a straight fox and a burning scent
over a grass country has undeceived him, and left him in the third or fourth field
with his horse half on a hedge and half in a ditch, or pounded before a 'bul-finch,'
feeling very ridiculous. There are men who cut a very respectable figure in the
hunting-field who never saw a pack of hounds until they were past thirty. The city
of London turns oat many such; so does every great town where money is made by
men of pluck, bred, perhaps, as ploughboys in the country. We could name three—
one an M.P.—under these conditions, who would pass muster in Leicestershire, if
necessary. But a good seat on horseback, pluck, and a love of the sport, are essential.
A few years ago a scientific manufacturer, a very moderate horseman, was ordered
horse exercise as a remedy for mind and body prostrated by over-anxiety. He found
that, riding along the road, his mind was as busy and wretched as ever. A friend
prescribed hunting, purchased for him a couple of made hunters, and gave him the
needful elementary instruction. The first result was, that he obtained such sound,
refreshing sleep as he had not enjoyed since boyhood; the next, that in less than two
seasons he made himself quite at home with a provincial pack, and now rides so as
to enjoy himself without attracting any more notice than one who had been a fox-
hunter from his youth upwards."

    The illustration at the commencement of this chapter gives a very fair idea of
the seat of good horsemen going at a fence and broad ditch, where pace is essential,
A novice may advantageously study the seats of the riders in Herring's " Steeple-
chase Cracks," painted by an artist who was a sportsman in his day.

A few invaluable hints on riding to hounds are to be found in the Druid's account of Dick Christian.

The late Marquis of Hastings, father of the present Marquis, was one of the best and keenest fox-hunters of his day; he died young, and here is Dick's account of his " first fence," for which all fox-hunters are under deep obligations to the Druid.

" The Marquis of Hastings was one of my pupils I was two months at his place before he came of age. He sent for me to Donnington, and I broke all his horses. I had never seen him before. He had seven rare nice horses, and very handy I got them. The first meet I went out with him was Wartnaby Stone Pits. 1 rode by his side, and I says, ' My lord, well save a bit of distance if we take this fence.' So he looked at me and he laughed, and says, 'Why, Christian, I was never over a fence in my life.' ' God bless me, my lord i you don't say so ?' And I seemed quite took aback at hearing him say it. 'Its true enough, Christian, I really mean it.' ' Well, my lord,' says I, ' you're on a beautiful fencer, hell walk up to it and jump it. Now TH go over the fence first. *Put your hands well down on his withers and let him come.*' It was a bit of a low-staked hedge and a ditch; he got over as nice as possible, and he gave quite a hurrah like. He says, 'There, I'm over my first fence—that 's a blessing!' Then I got him over a great many little places, and he quite took to it and went on uncommonly well. Hewas a nice gentleman to teach— he'd just do anything you told him. That's the way to get on!"

In another place Dick says, "A quick and safe jumper always goes from hind-legs to fore-legs. I never rode a steeple-chase yet but I steadied my horse on to his hind-legs twenty yards from his fence, and I was always over and away before the rushers. Lots of the young riders think horses can jump anything if they can only drive them at it fast enough. They force them too much at their fences. If you don't feel your horse's mouth, you can tell nothing about him. You hold him, he can make a second effort; if you drop him, ho won't."

Now, Dick does not mean by this that you are to go slowly at every kind of fence. He tells you that he " sent him with some powder at a bullfinch; " but whatever the pace, you so hold your horse in the last fifty yards up to the taking-off point, that instead of spreading himself out all abroad at every stroke, he feels the bit and gets his hind-legs well under him. If you stand to see Jim Mason or Tom Oliver in the hunting-field going at water, even at what they call " forty miles an hour," you will find the stride of their horses a mea-sured beat, and while they spur and urge them they collect them. This is the art no book can teach; *but it can teach that it ought to be learned.* Thousands of falls have been caused by a common and most absurd phrase, which is constantly repeated in every description of the leaps of a great race or run. " *He took his horse by the head and lifted him,*" &c.

No man in the world ever lifted a horse over anything —it is a mechanical impossibility—but a horseman of the first order can at a critical moment so rouse a horse, and so accurately place his head and hind-legs in the right position, that he can make an extraordinary effort and achieve a miraculous leap. This in metaphori-cal language is called lifting a horse, because, to a bye-stander, it looks like it. But when a novice, or even an average horseman, attempts this sort of tour de force, he only worries his horse, and, ten to one, throws him into the fence. Those who are wise will content themselves with keeping a horse well in hand until he is about to rise for his effort, and to collecting him the moment he lands. The right hold brings his hind legs under him," too hard a pull brings him into the ditch, if there is one. By holding your hands with the reins in each rather wide apart as you come to-wards your fence, and closing them and dropping them near his withers as he rises, you give him room to extend himself; and if you stretch your arms as he descends, you have him in hand. But the perfect hunter, as long as he is fresh, does his work perfectly, so the less you meddle with him when he is rising the better.

Young sportsmen generally err by being too bold and too fast. Instead of study-ing the art in the way the best men out perform, they are hiding their nervousness by going full speed at everything, or trying to rival tho whips in daring. Any hard-headed fool can ride boldly. To go well when hounds are running hard — to savo your horse as much as possible while keeping well forward, for the end, the difficult part of a long run—-these are the acts a good sportsman seeks to acquire by observa-tion and experience.

For this reason young sportsmen should commence their studies with harriers, where the runs are usually circling and a good deal of hunting is done slowly. If a young fellow can ride well in a close, enclosed hedge, bank, and ditch country, with occasional practice at stiles and gates, pluck will carry him through a flying country, if properly mounted.

Any horse that is formed for jumping, with good loins, hocks, and thighs, can be taught to jump timber; but it is madness to ride at a gate or a stile with a doubtful horse. A deer always slacks his pace to a trot to jump a wall or park rails, and it is better to slacken to a trot or canter where there is no ditch on either side to be cleared, unless you expect a fall, and then go fast, that your horse may not tumble on you.

A rushing horse is generally a dangerous fencer; but it is a trick that can only be cured in private lessons, and it is more dangerous to try to make a rusher go slowly than to let him have his own way.

The great error of young beginners is to select young horses under their weight.

It was the saying of a Judge of the old school, that all kinds of wine were good, but the best wine of all was " two bottles of port!" In the same style, one may venture to say that all kinds of hunting are good, but that the best of all is fox-hunting, in a grass scent-holding country, divided into large fields, with fences that may be taken in the stride of a thorough-bred, and coverts that comprise good gorse and open woods—that is, for men of the weight, with the nerve, and with the horse that can shine in such a country. But it is not given to all to have or retain the nerve or to afford a stud of the style of horses required for going across the best part of Leicestershire and Northamptonshire. In this world, the way to be happy is to put up with what you can get. The majority of my readers will be obliged to ride with the hounds that happen to live nearest their dwelling; it is only given to the few to be able to choose their hunting country and change their stud whenever the maggot bites them. After hard brain-work and gray hairs have told on the pulse, or when the opening of the nursery-door has almost shut the stable, a couple of hours or so once a week may be made pleasant and profitable on a thirty-pound hack for the quartogenarian, whom time has not handicapped with weight for age. I can say, from the experience of many years, that as long as you are under twelve stone, you may enjoy very good spor; with such packs as the Bramham Moor in Yorkshire, the Brocklesby in Lincolnshire, the Heythrope in Oxfordshire, the Berkley or the Beaufort in Gloucestershire, without any enormous outlay for horses, for the simple reason that the average runs do not present the difficulties of grass countries, where formers are obliged to make strong fences and deep ditches to keep the bullocks they fatten within bounds. Good-looking little horses, clever jumpers, equal to moderate weights, are to be had, by a man who has not too much money, at moderate prices; but the sixteen hands, well-bred flyer, that can gallop and go straight in such countries as the Vale of Aylesbury, is an expensive luxury. Of course I am speaking of sound horses. There is scarcely ever a remarkable run in which some well-ridden screw does not figure in the first flight among the two hundred guinea nags.

When an old sportsman of my acquaintance heard any of the thousand-amd-one tales of extraordinary rune with fox-hounds, " after dinner," he used to ask—" Were any of the boys or ponies up at the kill?" If the answer was " Yes," he would say, " Then it was not a severe thing;" and he was generally right Men of moderate means had better choose a hunting county where the boys can live with the hounds.

"As to harriers, the people who sneer at them are ludicrously ignorant of the history of modern fox-hunting, which is altogether founded on the experience and maxims of hare-hunters. The two oldest foxhound packs in England—the Brocklesby and the Cheshire—were originally formed for hare-hunting. The best book ever written on hounds and hunting, a text-book to every master of hounds to this day, is by Beckford, who learned all he knew as master of a pack of harriers.

" The great Meynell and Warwickshire Corbett both entered their young hounds to hare, a practice which cannot, however, be approved. The late Parson Froude, in North Devon, than whom a keener sportsman never holloaed to hounds, and the breeder of one of the best packs for showing sport ever seen, hunted hare, fox, deer, and even polecats, sooner than not keep his darlings doing something; and, while his hounds would puzzle out the faintest scent, there were among the leaders several that, with admirable dash, jumped every gate, disdaining to creep. Some of this stock are still hunting on Exmoor. There are at present several very good M.F.H. who began with hare-hounds.

" The intense pretentious snobbishness of the age has something to do with the mysterious manner in which many men, blushing, own that they have been out with harriers. In the first place, as a rule, harriers are slow; although there are days when, with a stout, well-fed, straight-running hare, the best men will have enough to do to keep their place in the field: over the dinner-table that is always an easy task; but in this fast, competitive age, the man who can contrive to stick on a good horse can show in front without having the least idea of the meaning of hunting. To such, harriers afford no amusement. Then again, harrier packs are of all degrees, from the perfection of the Blackmoor Vale, the Brookside, and some Devon or Welsh packs with unpronounceable names, down to the little scratch packs of six or seven couple kept among . jovial farmers in out-of-the-way places, or for the amusement of Sheffield cutlers running afoot. The same failing that makes a considerable class reverently worship an alderman or a city baronet until they can get on speaking terms with a peer, leads others. to boast of foxhunting when the Brighton harriers are more than they . can comfortably manage."

The greater number of what are called harriers now-a-days are dwarf foxhounds, or partake largely of foxhound blood.

If Leicestershire is the county for " swells," Devonshire is the county of sportsmen; for although there is very little riding to hounds as compared with the midland counties, there is a great deal of hunting. Every village has its little pack; every man, woman, and child, from the highest to the humblest, takes an interest in the sport; and the science of hunting is better understood than in the hard-riding, horse-dealing counties. To produce a finished fox-hunter, I would have him commence his studies in Devonshire, and finish his practice in Northamptonshire. On the whole, I should say that a student of the noble science, whose early education has been neglected, cannot do better than go through a course of fox-hunting near Oxford, in the winter vacation, where plenty of perfect hunters are to be hired, and hounds meet within easy reach of the University City, six days in the week, hunting over a country where you may usually be with them at the finish without doing anything desperate, if content to come in with the ruck, the ponies, and the old farmers; or where, if so inclined, you may have more than an average number of fast and furious runs, and study the admirable style of some of the best horsemen in the world among the Oxfordshire and Berkshire squires.

Stag-hunting from a cart is a pursuit very generally contemned in print, and very ardently followed by many hundred hard-riding gentlemen every hunting day in the year. A man who can ride up to stag-hounds on a straight running day must have a perfect hunter, in first-rate condition, and be, in the strongest sense of the term, " a horseman." But it wants the uncertainties which give so great a charm to fox-hunting, where there are any foxes. There is no find, and no finish; and the checks generally consist in whipping off the too eager hounds. As a compensation, when the deer does not run cunning, or along roads, the pace is tremendous.

The Surrey stag-hounds, in the season of 1857, had seme runs with the Ketton Hind equal in every respect to the best fox-hunts on record; for she repeatedly beat them, was loose in the woods for days, was drawn for like a wild deer, and then, with a burning scent, ran clear away from the hounds, while the hounds ran away from the horsemen. But, according to the usual order of the day, the deer begins in a cart, and ends in a barn.

But stag-hunting may he defended as the very best mode of obtaining a constitutional gallop for those whose time is too valuable to be expended in looking for a fox. It is suited to punctual, commercial, military, or political duties. You may read your letters, dictate replies, breakfast deliberately, order your dinner, and invite a party to discuss it, and set off to hunt with the Queen's, the Baron's, or any other stag-hound pack within reach of rail, almost certain of two hours' galloping, and a return by the train you fixed in the morning.

There are a few hints to which pupils in the art of hunting may do well to attend.

" Don't go into the field until you can sit a horse over any reasonable fence. But practice at real fences, for at the leaping-bar only the rudiments of feneing are to fee learned by either man or horse. The hunting-field is not the place for practising the rudiments of the art. Buy a perfect hunter; no matter how blemished or how ugly, so that he has legs, eyes, and wind to carry him and his rider across the country. It is essential that one of the two should perfectly understand the business in hand. Have nothing to say to a puller, a rusher, or a kicker, even if you fancy you are competent; a colt should only be ridden by a man who is paid to risk his bones. An amateur endangers himself, his neighbours, and the pack, by attempting rough-riding. The best plan for a man of moderate means—those who can afford to spend hundreds on experiments can pick and choose in the best stables—is to hire a hack hunter; and, if he suits, buy him, to teach you how to go.

" Never take a jump when an open gate or gap is handy, unless the hounds are going fast. Don't attempt to show in front, unless you feel you can keep there. Beginners, who try to make a display, even if lucky at first, are sure to make some horrid blunder. Go slowly at your fences, except water and wide ditches, and don't pull at the curb when your horse is rising. In ninety-nine cases out of a hundred, the horse will be better without your assistance than with it. Don't wear spurs until you are quite sure that you won't spur at the wrong time. Never lose your temper with your horse, and never strike him with the whip when going at a fence; it is almost sure to make him swerve. Pick out the firmest ground; hold your horse together across ploughed land; if you want a pilot, choose not a scarlet and cap, but some well-mounted old farmer, who has not got a horse to sell: if he has, ten to one but he leads you into grief.

" In going from cover to cover, keep in the same field as the hounds, unless you know the country—then you. can't be left behind without a struggle. To keep in the same field as the hounds when they are running, is more than any man can undertake to do. Make your commencement in an easy country, and defer trying the pasture counties until you are sure of yourself and your horse.

"If you should have a cold-scenting day, and any first-rate steeplechase rider be in the field, breaking in a young one, watch him; you may learn more from seeing what he does, than from hours of advice, or pages of reading.

" Above all, hold your tongue until you have learnt your lesson; and talk neither of your triumphs nor your failures. Any fool can boast; and though to ride boldly and with judgment is very pleasant, there is nothing for a gentleman to be specially proud of, considering that two hundred huntsmen, or whips, do it better than most gentlemen every hunting day in the season."

When you meet the pack with a strange horse, don't go near it until sure that he will not kick at hounds, as some ill-educated horses will do.

Before the hounds begin to draw, you may get some useful information as to a strange country from a talkative farmer.

When hounds are drawing a large cover, and when you cannot see them, keep down wind, so as to hear the huntsman, who, in large woodlands, must keep on cheering his hounds. When a fox breaks cover near you, or you think he does, don't be in a hurry to give the " Tally-a-e-o!" for, in the first place, if you are not experienced and quick-eyed, it may not be a fox at all, but a dog, or a hare. The mistake is common to people who are always in a hurry, and equally annoying to the huntsman and the blunderer; and, in the next place, if you halloo too soon, ten to one the fox heads back into cover. When he is well away through the hedge of a good-sized field, halloo, at the same time raising your cap, "Tally-o aw-ay-o-o!" giving each syllable very slowly, and with your mouth well open; for this is'the way to be heard a long distance. Do this once or twice, and then be quiet for a short spell, and be ready to tell the huntsman, when he comes up, in a few sentences, exactly which way the fox is gone. If the fox makes a short bolt, and returns, it is " Tally-o *back*!" with the " back " loud and clear. If the fox crosses the side of a wood when the hounds are at check, the cry should be " Tally-o over!"

.Foxes.—Study the change in the appearance of the fox between the beginning and the end of a run; a fresh fox slips away with his brush straight, whisking it with an air of defiance now and then; a beaten fox looks dark, hangs his brush, and arche3 his back as he labours along.

With the hounds well away, it is a great point to get a good start ; so while they are running in cover, cast your eyes over the boundary-fence, and make up your mind where you will take it: a big jump at starting is better than thrusting with a crowd in a gap or gateway —always presuming that you can depend on your horse.

Dismiss the moment you start two ideas which are the bane of sport, jealousy of what others are doing, and conceit of what you are doing yourself; keep your eyes on the pack, on your horse's ears, and the next fence, instead of burning to beat Thompson, or hoping that Brown saw how cleverly you got over that rasper!

Acquire an eye to hounds, that is, learn to detect the moment when the leading hound turns right or left, or, losing the scent, checks, or, catching it breast high, races away mute, " dropping his stern as straight as a tobacco-pipe."

By thus studying the leading hound's instead of racing against your neighbours' horses, you see how they turn, save many an angle, and are ready to pull up the moment the hounds throw up their heads.

Never let your anxiety to he forward induce you to press upon the hounds when they are hunting; nothing makes a huntsman more angry, or spoils sport more.

Set the example of getting out of the way when the huntsman, all anxious, comes trotting back through a narrow road to make his cast after a check.

Attention to these hints, which are familiar to every old sportsman, will tend to make a young one successful and popular.

When you are well up, and hounds come to a check, instead of beginning to relate how wonderfully the bay horse or the gray mare carried you, notice every point that may help the huntsman to make his cast—sheep, cattle, magpies, and the exact point where the scent began to fail. It is observation that makes a true sportsman.

As soon as the run has ended, begin to pay attention to the condition of your horse, whose spirit may have carried him further than his strength warranted; it is to he presumed, that you have eased him at every check by turning his nose to the wind, and if a heavy man, by dismounting on every safe opportunity.

The first thing is to let him have just enough water to wash his mouth out without chilling him, The next to feed him—the horse has a small stomach, and requires food often.

At the- first roadside inn or cottage get a quart of oatmeal or wheat-flour *boiled* in half a pail of water— mere soaking the raw oatmeal is not sufficient. I have found the water of boiled linseed used for cattle answer well with a tired horse. In cases of serious distress a pint of wine or glass of spirits mixed with water may be administered advantageously; to decide on the propriety of bleeding requires some veterinary experience; quite as many horses as men have been killed by bleeding when stimulants would have answered better.

With respect to the treatment of hunters on their return, I can do nothing better than quote the directions of that capital sportsman and horseman, Scrutator, in " Horses and Hounds."

"When a horse returns to the stable, either after hunting or a journey, the first thing to be done to him is to take off the bridle, but to let the saddle remain on for some time at least, merely loosening the girths. The head and ears are first to be rubbed dry, either with a wisp of hay or a cloth, and then by the hand, until the ears are warm and comfortable; this will ocoupy only a few minutes, and the horse can then have Ms bit of hay or feed of corn, having previously, if returned from hunting, or from a long journey, despatched his bucket of thick gruel: the process of washing his legs may now be going on, whilst he is discussing his feed of corn in peace; as each leg is washed, it should be wrapped round with a flannel or serge bandage, and by the time the four legs are done with, the horse will have finished his feed of corn. A little hay may then be given, which will occupy his attention while the rubbing his body is proceeded with. I am a great advocate for plenty of dry clean wheat straw for this purpose; and a good groom, with a large wisp in each hand, will in a very short space of time, make a clean sweep of all outward dirt and wet. It cannot, however, be properly done without a great deal of elbow grease as well, of which the present generation are inclined to be very chary. When the body of the horse is dry, a large loose rug should be thrown over him, and the legs then attended to, and rubbed thoroughly dry by the hand; I know the usual practice with idle and knowing grooms is to let the bandages remain on until the legs become dry of themselves, but I also know that there cannot be a worse practice; for horses' legs, after hunting, the large knee-bucket should be used, with plenty of warm water, which will sooth the sinews after such violent exertion, and allay any irritation proceeding from cuts and thorns. The system of bandaging horses' legs, and letting them remain in this state for hours, must tend to relax the sinews; such practices have never gained favour with me, but I have heard salt and water and vinegar highly extolled by some, with which the bandages are to be kept constantly wet, as tending to strengthen the sinews and keep them cool; if, however, used too long or allowed to become dry, I conceive more injury likely to result from their use than benefit. It is generally known that those who have recourse to belts for support in riding, cannot do well without them afterwards, and although often advised to try these extra aids, I never availed myself of them; cold water is the best strength-ener either to man or horse, and a thorough good dry rubbing afterwards. After severe walking exercise, the benefit of immersing the feet in warm water for a short time must be fully appreciated by all who have tried it; but I very much question if any man would feel himself stronger upon his legs the next morning, by having them bandaged with hot flannels during the night Very much may be done by the judicious use of hot and cold water—in fact, more than by half the prescriptions in general use; but the proper time must be attended to as well, for its application. When a horse has had a long and severe day's work, he should not be harassed more than is absolutely necessary, by grooming and dressing; the chief business should be to get him dry and comfortable as quickly as possible, and when that has been effected, a slight wisping over with a dry cloth will be sufficient for that night."

The expenses of horse-keep vary according to the knowledge of the master and the honesty of his groom; but what the expense ought to be may be calculated from the fact that horses in first-rate condition cannot consume more than thirteen quarters of oats and two and a half tons of hay in a year; that is, as to oats, from three to six quarterns a day, according to the work they are doing. But in some stables, horses are supposed to eat a bushel a day every day in the year: there is no doubt that the surplus is converted into beer or gin.

" Upon our return from hunting, every horse had his bucket of thick gruel directly he came into the stable, and a little hay to eat whilst he was being cleaned. We never gave any corn until just before littering down, the last thing at night. The horse's legs were plunged into a high bucket of warm water, and if dirty, soft soap was used. The first leg being washed, was sponged as dry as possible, and then bandaged with thick woollen bandages until the others were washed; the bandages were then removed entirely, and the legs rubbed by hand until quite dry. We used the best old white potatoe oats, weighing usually 45lbs. per bushel, but so few beans that a quarter lasted us a season. The oats were bruised, and a little sweet hay chaff mixed with them. We also gave our horses a few carrots the day after hunting, to cool their bodies, or a bran mash or two. They were never coddled up in hoods or half a dozen rugs at nightv but a single blanket sufficed, which was never so tight but that you might thrust your hand easily under it. This was a thing I always looked to myself, when paying a visit to the stable the last thing at night A tried horse should have everything comfortable about him, but carefully avoid any tight bandage round the body. In over-reaches or wounds, warm water was our first application, and plenty of it, to clean all dirt or grit from the wound; then Fryer's balsam and brandy with a clean-linen bandage. Our usual allowance of corn to each horse per diem was four quarterns, but more if they required it, and from 14 lbs. to 16 lbs. of hay, eight of which were given at night, at racking-up time, about eight o'clock. Our hours of feeding were about five in the morning, a feed of corn, bruised, with a little hay chaff; the horse then went to exercise. At eight o'clock, 4 lbs. of hay; twelve o'clock, feed of com; two o'clock, 2 lbs. of hay; four o'clock, corn; at six o'clock, another feed of corn, with chaff; and at eight o'clock, 8 lbs. of hay; water they could always drink when they wanted it"

I cannot conclude these hints on hunting more appropriately than by quoting another of the songs of the Squire of Arley Hall, Honorary Laureate of the Tarporley Hunt Club:—

" A WORD ERE WE START.

" The order of march and due regulation
That guide us in "warfare we need in the chase ;
Huntsman and whips; each his own proper station—
Horse, hound, and fox, each, his own proper place,

" The fox takes precedence of all from the cover;
 The horse is the animal purposely bred,
After the pack to be ridden, not over—
Good hounds are not reared to be knocked on the head.

" Buckskin's the only wear fit for the saddle ;
Hats for Hyde Park, but a cap for the chase;
In tops of black leather let fishermen paddle,
The calves of a fox-hunter white ones encase.

" If your horse be well bred and in blooming condition,
Both up to the country and up to your weight,
Oh! then give the reins to your youthful ambition,
Sit down in the saddle and keep his head straight.

" Eager and emulous only, not spiteful
Grudging no friend, though ourselves he may beat;
Just enough danger to make sport delightful,

Toil just sufficient to make slumbers sweet !"

# CHAPTER XL

# SKETCHES OF HUNTING WITH FOX-HOUNDS AND HARRIERS.

The Fitzwilliam.—Brocklesby.—A day on the Wolds. — Brighton harriers.—Prince Albert's harriers.

THE following descriptions of my own sport with foxhounds and harriers will give the uninitiated some idea of the average adventures of a hunting-day:—

A DAY WITH THE LATE EARL FITZWILLIAM'S HOUNDS.[15]

" Loo IN, LITTLE DEARIES. LOO IN."

How eagerly forward they rush;
In a moment how widely they spread;
Have at him there, Hotspur. Hush, hush!
'T is a find, or I '11 forfeit my head.
Now fast flies the fox, and still faster
The hounds from the cover are freed,
The horn to the mouth of the master,
The spur to the flank of his steed.
With Chorister, Concord, and Chorus,
Now Chantress commences her song;
Now Bellman goes jingling before us,
And Sinbad is sailing along.

---

15   This sketch was written in 1857.

THE Fitzwilliam pack was established by the grandfather of the present Earl between seventy and eighty years ago; they hunt four days a week over a north-east strip of Northamptonshire and Huntingdonshire—a wide, wild, thinly-populated district, with some fine woodlands; country that was almost all grass, until deep draining turned some cold clay pastures into arable. It holds a rare scent, and the woodland country can be hunted, when a hot sun does not bake the ground too hard, up to the first week in May, when, in most other countries, horns are silenced. The country is wide enough, with foxes enough, to bear hunting six days a week. " Bless your heart, sir," said an old farmer, " there be foxes as tall. as donkeys, as fat as pigs, in these woods, that go and die of old age."

The Fitzwilliam are supposed to he the biggest-boned hounds now bred, and exquisitely handsome. If they have a fault, they are, for want of work, or excess of numbers, rather too fall of flesh; so that at the end of the year, when the days grow warm, they seem to tire and tail in a long run.

Many of the pasture fences are big enough to keep out a bullock; the ditches wide and full of water; bul-finches are to be met with, stiff rails, gates not always unlocked; so, although a Pytchley flyer is not indispensable, on a going day, nothing less than a hunter can get along.

Tom Sebright, as a huntsman and breeder of hounds, has been a celebrity ever since he hunted the Quorn, under Squire Osbaldeston, six-and-thirty years ago. Sebright looks the huntsman, and the huntsman of an hereditary pack, to perfection; rather under than over the middle height; stout without being unwieldy; with a fine, full, intelligent, and fresh-complexioned oval countenance; keen gray eyes; and the decided nose of a Cromwellian Ironside. A fringe of white hair below his cap, and a broad bald forehead, when he lifts his cap to cheer his hounds, tell the tale of Time on this accomplished veteran of the chase.

" The field," with the Fitzwilliam, is more aristocratic than fashionable; it includes a few peers and their friends from neighbouring noble mansions, a good many squires, now and then undergraduates from Cambridge, a very few strangers by rail, and a great many first-class yeoman farmers and graziers. Thus it is equally unlike the fashionable "cut-me-down " multi tude to be met at coverside in the " Shires" par *excellence*, and the scarlet mob who rush, and race, and lark from and back to Leamington and Cheltenham. For seeing a good deal of sport in a short time, the Fitzwilliam is certainly the best, within a hundred miles of London. Yon have a first-rate pack, first-rate hunts-man, a good scenting country, plenty of foxes, fair fences to ride over, and though last not least, very courteous reception, if you know how to ride and when to hold your tongue and your horse.

My fortunate day with the Fitzwilliam was in their open pasture, Huntingdon country.' My head-quarters were at the celebrated " Haycock," which is known, or ought to he known, to every wandering fox-hunter, standing as it does in the middle of the Fitzwiliiam Hunt, within reach of some of the best meets of the Pytchley and the Warwickshire, and not out of reach of the Cottesmore and Belvoir. It is much more like a Lincolnshire Wolds farmhouse than an inn. The guests are regular *habi*tues ; you find yourself in a sort of fox hunting clubhouse, in a large, snug dining-room; not the least like Albert Smith's favourite aversion, a coffee-room; you have a first-rate English dinner, undeniable wine, real cream with your tea, in a word, all the comforts and most of the luxuries of town and country life combined. If needful, Tom Percival will provide you with a flyer for every day in the week, and you will be sure to meet with one or two guests, able and willing, ready to canter with you to cover, explain the chart of the country, and, if you are in the first year of boots and breeches, show you as Squire Warburton sings, how " To sit down in your saddle and put his head straight."

The meet, within four miles of the inn, was in a park by the side of a small firwood plantation. Punctual to a minute, up trotted Sebright on a compact, well-bred

chestnut in blooming condition, the whips equally well mounted on thorough-breds, all dressed in ample scarlet coats and dark cord breeches—a style of dress in much better taste than the tight, short dandified costume of the fashionable hunt, where the huntsman can scarcely be distinguished from the " swell"

Of the Earl's family there were present a son and daughter, and three grand-sons, beautiful boys, in Lincoln green loose jackets, brown cord breeches, black boots, and caps; of these, the youngest, a fair, rosy child of about eight or nine years old, on a thorough-bred chestnut pony, was all day the admiration of the field; he dashed along full of genuine enthusiasm, stopping at nothing practicable.

Amongst others present was a tall, lithe, white-haired, white-moustached, dignified old gentleman, in scarlet and velvet cap, riding forward on a magnificent gray horse, who realised completely the poetical idea of anobleman. This was the Marquess of H known Well forty years ago in fashionable circles, when George IV. was Prince, now popular and much esteemed as a country gentleman and improving landlord. There was also Mr. H , an M.P., celebrated, before he settled into place and " ceased his hum," as a hunter of bishops—a handsome, dark man, in leathers and patent Napoleons; with his wife on a fine bay horse, who rode boldly throughout the day.

In strange countries I usually pick out a leader in some well-knowing farmer; but this day I made a grand mistake, by selecting for my guide a slim, quiet-looking, young fellow, in a black hat and coat, white cords, and boots, on a young chestnut—never dreaming that my quiet man was Alec , a farmer truly, but also a provincial celebrity as a steeplechaser.

The day was mild, cloudy, with a gentle wind. We drew several covers blank, and found a fox, about one o'clock, in a small spinney, from which he bolted at the first summons. A beautiful picture it was to see gallant old Sebright get his hounds away, the ladies racing down a convenient green lane, and the little Fitzwilliam, in Lincoln green, charging a double flight of hurdles. In half-an-hour's strong running I had good reason to rejoice that Percival had, with due respect for the fourth estate, put me on an unmistakable hunter. Our line took us over big undulating fields (almost hills), with, on the flats or valleys, a large share of willow-bordered ditches (they would call them brooks in some counties), with thick undeniable hedges between the pollards. At the beginning of the run, my black-coated friend led me —much as a dog in a string leads a blind man—at a great pace, into a farm-yard, thus artfully cutting off a great angle, over a most respectable stone wall into a home paddock, over a stile into a deep lane, and then up a bank as steep as a gothic roof, and almost as long; into a fifty-acre pasture, where, racing at best pace, we got close to the hounds just before they checked, be tween a broad unjumpable drain and a willow bed—two fine resources for a cunning fox. There I thought it well, having so far escaped grief, to look out for a leader who was less of a bruiser, while I took breath. In the meantime Sebright, well up, hit our friend off with a short cast forward, and after five minutes' slow hunting, we began to race again over a flat country of grass, with a few big ploughed fields, fences easier, ladies and ponies well up again. After brushing through two small coverts without hanging, we came out on a series of very large level grass fields, where I could see the gray horse of the marquis, and the black hat of my first leader sailing in front; a couple of stiff hedges and ditches were got over comfortably; the third was a regular bulfinch, six or seven feet high, with a gate so far away to the right that to make for it was to lose too much time, as the hounds were running breast high. Ten yards ahead of me was Mr. Frank G on a Stormer colt, evidently with no notion of turning; so I hardened my heart, felt my bay nag full of going, and kept my eye on Mr. Frank, who made for the only practicable place beside an oak-tree with low branches, and, stooping his head, popped through a place where the hedge showed daylight, with his hand over his eyes, in the neatest possible style. Without hesitating a moment I followed,rather too fast and too much afraid of the tree, and pulled too much into the hedge. In an instant I found myself torn out of the saddle, balanced on a black-thorn bough (fortunately I wore leathers), and deposited on the right side of the hedge on my back; whence I rose justin time to see Bay Middleton disappear over the next fence. So there I was alone in a big grass field, with strong notions that I should have to walk an unknown number of miles home. Judge of my delight as I paced slowly along—running was of no use—at seeing Frank G returning with my truant in hand. Such an action in the middle of a run deserves a Humane Society's medal. To struggle breathless into my seat; to go off at score, to find a lucky string of open gates, to come upon the hounds at a check, was my good fortune. But our fox was doomed—in another quarter of an hour at a hand gallop we hunted him into a shrubbery, across a home field into an ornamental clump of laurels, back again to the plantation, where a couple and a half of leading hounds pulled him down, and he was brought out by the first whip dead and almost stiff, without a mark— regularly run down by an hour and twenty minutes with two very short cheeks. Had the latter part of the run been as fast as the first, there would have been very few of us there to see the finish.

OK THE LINCOLNSHIRE WOLDS.

I started to meet Lord Yarborough's hounds, from the house of a friend, on a capital Woldpony for cover hack. It used to be said, before non-riding masters of hounds had broadcasted bridle-gates over the Quorn country, that a Leicestershire hack was a pretty good hunter for other counties. We may say the same of a Lincolnshire Wolds pony—his master, farming not less than three hundred and more likely fifteen hundred acres, has no time to lose in crawling about on a punchy half-bred cart-horse, like a smock-frocked tenandt—the farm must be visited before hunting, and the market-towns lie too for off for five miles an hour jog-trot to suit. It is the Wold fashion to ride farming at a pretty good pace, and take the fences in a fly where the gate stands at the wrong corner of the field. Broad strips of turf fringe the road, offering every excuse for a gallop, and our guide continually turned through a gate or over a hurdle, and through half a dozen fields, to save two sides of an angle. These fields contrast strangely with the ancient counties—large, and square, and clean, with little ground lost in hedgerows. The great cop banks of Essex, Devon, and Cheshire are almost unknown— villages you scarcely see, farmhouses rarely from the roadside, for they mostly stand well back in the midst of their acres. Gradually creeping up the Wold—passing through, here vast turnip-fields, fed over by armies of long-woolled Iincoln sheep; there, stubble yielding before from a dozen to a score of pair-horse ploughs, silent witnesses of the scale of Lincolnshire farming— at length we see descending and winding along a bridle-road before us, the pied pack and the gleam of the huntsman's scarlet Around, from every point of the compass the " field " come ambling, trotting, cantering, galloping, on hacks, on hunters, through gates or over fences, practising their Yorkshire four-year-olds. There are squires of every degree, Lincolnshire M.P.'s, parsons in black, in number beyond average; tenant-formers, in quantity and quality such as no other county we have ever seen can boast, velvet-capped and scarlet-coated, many with the Brocklesby hunt button, mounted on first-class hunters, whom it was a pleasure to see them handle; and these were not young bloods, outrunning the constable, astonishing their landlords and alarming their fathers; but amongst the ruck were respectable grandfathers who had begun hunting on ponies when Stubbs was painting great-grandfather Smith, and who had as a matter of course brought up their sons to follow the line in which they had been cheered on by Arthur Young's Lord Yarborough. There they were, of all ages, from the white-haired veteran who could tell you when every field had been inclosed, to the little petticoated orphan boy on a pony, " whose father's farm had been put in trust for him by the good Earl."

Of the ordinary mob that crowd fox-hound meets from great cities and fashionable watering-places, there were none. The swell who comes out to show his clothes and his horse; the nondescript, who may be a fast Life-Guardsman or a fishmonger; the lot of horse-dealers; and, above all, those blase gentlemen who, bored with everything, openly express their preference for a carted deer or red-herring drag, if a straight running fox is not found in a quarter of an hour after the hounds are thrown into cover. The men who ride on the Lincolnshire Wolds are all sportsmen, who know the whole country as well as their own gardens, and are not unfrequently personally acquainted with the peculiar appearance and habits of each fox on foot. Altogether they are as formidable critics as any professional huntsman would care to encounter.

There is another pleasant thing. In consequence, perhaps, of the rarity, strangers are not snubbed as in some counties; and you have no difficulty in getting information to any extent on subjects agricultural and fox-hunting (even without that excellent passport which I enjoyed of a hunter from the stables of the noble Master of the Hounds), and may be pretty sure of more than one hospitable and really-meant invitation in the course of the return ride when the sport is ended.

But time is up, and away we trot—leaving the woods of Limber for the present—to one of the regular Wolds, artificial coverts, a square of gorse of several acres, surrounded by a turf bank and ditch, and outside again by fields of the ancient turf of the moorlands. In go the hounds at a word, without a straggler; and while they make the gorse alive with their lashing stems, there is no fear of our being left behind for want of seeing which way they go, for there is neither plantation nor hedge, nor hill of any account to screen us. And there is no fear either of the fox being stupidly headed, for the field all know their business, and are fully agreed, as old friends should be, on the probable line.

A very faint Tally-away, and cap held up, by a fresh complexioned, iron-gray, bullet-headed old gentleman, of sixteen stone, mounted on a four-year-old, brought the pack out in a minute from the far end of the covert, and we were soon going, holding hard, over a newly-ploughed field, looking out sharp for the next open gate; but it is at the wrong corner, and by the time we have reached the middle of fifty acres, a young farmer in scarlet, sitting upright as a dart, showed the way over a new rail in the middle of a six-foot quickset. Our nag, "Leicestershire," needs no spurring, but takes it pleasantly, with a hop, skip, and jump; and by the time we had settled into the pace on the other side, the senior on the four-year-old was alongside, crying, " Push along, sir; push along, or they'll run clean away from you. The fences are all fair on the line we're going." And so they were—hedges thick, but jumpable enough, yet needing a hunter nevertheless, especially as the big fields warmed up the pace amazingly; and, as the majority of the farmers out were riding young ones destined for finished hunters in the pasture counties, there was above an average of resolution in the style of going at the fences. The ground almost all plough, naturally drained by chalk sub-subsoil, fortunately rode light; but presently we passed the edge of the Wolds, held on through some thin plantations over the demesne grass of a squire's house, then on a bit of unreclaimed heath, where a flock of sheep brought us to a few minutes' check. With the help of a veteran of the hunt, who had been riding well up, a cast forward set us agoing again, and brought us, still running hard, away from the Wolds to low ground of new inclosures, all grass, fenced in by ditch and new double undeniable rails. As we had a good view of the style of country from a distance, we though it wisest, as a stranger, on a strange horse, with personally a special distaste to double fences, to pull gently, and let half-a-dozez young fellows on half-made, heavy-weight four or fire years old, go first. The results of this prudent and unplucky step were most satisfactory; while two or three, with a skill we admired, without venturing to imitate, went the " in and out" clever, the rest, some down and some blundering well over, smashed at least one rail out of every two, and let the " stranger " through comfortably at a fair flying jump. After three or four of these tremendous fields, each about the size of Mr. Mechi's farm, a shepherd riding after his flock on a pony opened a gate just as the hounds, after throwing up their heads for a minute,, turned to the right, and began to run back to the Wolds at a slower rate than we started, for the fox was no doubt blown by the pace; and so up what are called hills there (they would scarcely be felt in Devonshire or Surrey), we followed at a hand gallop right up to the plantations of Brocklesby Park, and for a good hour the hounds worked him round and round the woods, while we kept as near them as we could, racing along green rides as magnificent in their broad spread verdures and overhanging, evergreen walls of holly and laurel as any Watteau ever painted. The Lincolnshire gentry and yeomanry, scarlet coated and velvet capped, on their great blood horses sweeping down one of the grand evergreen avenues of Brocklesby Park, say toward the Pelham Pillar, is a capital untried subject, in colour, contrast, and living interest, for an artist who can paint men as well as horses.

At length when every dodge had been tried, Master Reynard made a bolt in despair. We raced him down a line of fields of very pretty fencing to a small lake, where wild ducks squatted up, and there ran into him, after a fair although not a very fast day's sport: a more honest hunting, yet courageous dashing pack we never rode to. The scarcity of villages, the general sparseness of the population, the few roads, and those almost all turf-bordered, and on a level with the fields, the great size of the enclosures, the prevalence of light arable land, the nuisance of flocks of sheep, and yet a good scenting country, are the special features of the Wolds. When you leave them and descend, there is a country of water, drains, and deep ditches, that require a real water-jumper. Two points specially strike a stranger—the complete hereditary air of the pack, and the attend-ants, so different from the piebald, new-varnished appearance of fashionable subscription packs. Smith, the huntsman, is fourth in descent of a line of Brocklesby huntsmen; Robinson, the head groom, had just completed his half century of service at Brocklesby; and Barnetby, who rode Lord Yarborough's second horse, was many years in the same capacity with the first Earl. But, after all, the Brocklesby tenanted—the Nainbys, the Brookes, the Skipwiths, and other Woldsmen, names " whom to mention would take up too much room," as the "Eton Grammar" says—tenants who, from generation to generation, have lived, and flourished, and hunted under the Pelham family—a spirited, intelligent, hospitable race of men—-these alone ore worth travelling from Land's End to see, to hear, to dine with; to learn from their sayings and doings what a wise, liberal, resident landlord—a lover of field sports, a promoter of improved agriculture—can do in flie course of generations toward " breeding" a first-class tenantry, and feeding thousands of townsfolk from acres that a hundred years ago only fed rabbits. We should recommend those M.P.'s who think fox-hunting folly, to leave their books and debates for a day's hunting on the Wolds. We think it will be hard to obtain such happy results from the mere pen-and-ink regulations of chamber legislators and haters of field sports. Three generations of the Pelhams turned thousands of acres of waste in heaths and Wolds into rich farm-land; the fourth did his part by giving the same district railways and seaport communication. When we find learned mole-eyed pedants sneering at fox-hunters, we may call the Brocklesby kennels and the Pelham Pillar as witnesses on the side of the common sense of English field sports. It was hunting that settled the Pelhams in a remote country and led them to colonise a waste.

There is one excellent custom at the hunting. dinners at Brocklesby Park which we may mention, without being guilty of intrusion on private hospitality. At a certain hour the stud-groom enters and says, " My Lord, the horses are bedded up;" then the whole party rise, make a procession through the stables, and return to coffee in the drawing-room. This custom was introduced by the first Lord Yarborough some half-century ago, in order to break through the habit of late sitting over wine that then was too prevalent.

HARRIERS—ON THE BRIGHTON DOWNS.

Long before hunting sounds are to be heard, except the early morning cub-hunters routing woodlands, and the autumn stag-hunters of Exmoor, harrier packs are hard at work racing down and up the steep hillside and along the chalky valleys of Brighton Downs, preparing old sportsmen for the more earnest work of November—training young ones into the meaning of pace, the habit of riding fast down, and the art of climbing quickly, yet not too quickly, up hill—giving constitutional gallops to wheezy aldermen, or enterprizing adults fresh from the riding-school—affording fun for fast young ladies and pleasant sights for a crowd of foot-folks and fly-loads, halting on- the brows of the steep combs, content with the living panorama.

The Downs and the sea are the redeeming features of Brighton, considered as a place of change and recreation for the over-worked of London. Without these advantages one might quite as well migrate from the City to Regent Street, varying the exercise by a stroll along the Serpentine. To a man who needs rest there is something at first sight truly frightful in the townish gregariousness of Brighton proper, with its pretentious common-place architecture, and its ceaseless bustle and rolling of wheels. But then comes into view first the sea, stretching away into infinite silence and solitude, dotted over on sunny days with pleasure-boats; and next, perpetually dashing along the league of sea-borded highway, group after group of gay riding-parties of all ages and both sexes—Spanish hats, feathers, and riding-habits—*amazones*, according to the French classic title, in the majority. First comes Papa Briggs, with all his progeny, down to the little bare-legged imitation Highlander on a shaggy Shetland pony; then a riding-master in mustachios, boots, and breeches, with a dozen pupils in divers stages of timidity and full-blown to-merity; and then again loving pairs in the process of courtship or the ecstasies of the honeymoon, pacing or racing along, indifferent to the interest and admiration that such pairs always excite. Besides the groups there are single figures, military and civil, on prancing thorough-bred hacks and solid weight-carrying cobs, contrasted with a great army of hard-worked animals, at half-a-crown an hour which compose the bulk of the Brighton cavalry, for horse-hiring at Brighton is the rule, private possession the exception; nowhere else, except, perhaps, at Oxford, is the custom so universal, and nowhere do such odd, strange people venture to exhibit themselves " a-horseback." As Dublin is said to be the car-drivingest, so is Brighton the horse-ridingest city in creation; and it is this most healthy, mental and physical exercise, with the summer-sea yacht excursion*, which constitute the difference and establishes the supe-riority of this marine offshoot of London over any foreign bathing-place. Under French auspices we should have had something infinitely more magnificent, gay, gilded, and luxurious in architecture, in shops, in restaurants, cafes, theatres, and ball-rooms; but pleasure-boat sails would have been utterly unknown, and the horse-exercise confined to a few daring cavaliers and theatrical ladies.

It is doubtless the open Downs that originally gave the visitors of Brighton (when it was Brighthelmstone, the little village patronised by the Prince, by "the Burney," and Mrs. Thrale) the habit of constitutional canters to a degree unknown in other pleasure towns; and the traditional custom has been preserved in the face of miles of brick and stucco. With horses in legions, and Downs at hand, a pack of hounds follows naturally; hares of a rare stout breed are plentiful; and the tradesmen have been acute enough to discover that a plentiful and varied supply of hunting facilities is one of the most safe, certain, and profitable attractions they can provide. Cheltenham and Bath has each its stag-hounds; Brighton does better, less expensively, and pleases more people, with two packs of harriers, hunting four days (and, by recent arrangements, a pack of foxhounds filling up the other two days) of the week; so that now it may be considered about the best place in the country for making sure of a daily constitutional gallop from October to March at short notice, and with no particular attention to costume and a very moderate stud, or no stud at all.

With these and a few other floating notions of air, exercise, and change of scene in my head—having decided that, however tempting to the caricaturist, the amusement of hundreds was not to be despised—I took my place at eight o'clock, at London-bridge station, in a railway carriage—the best of hacks for a long distance—on a bright October morning, with no other change from ordinary road-riding costume than one of Callow's long-lashed, instead of a straight-cutting, whips, so saving all the impediments of baggage. By ten o'clock I was wondering what the " sad sea waves " were saying to the strange costumes in which it pleases the fair denizens of Brighton to deck themselves. My horse, a little, wiry, well-bred chestnut, had been secured beforehand at a dealer's, well known in the Surrey country.

The meet was the race-course, a good three miles from the Parade. The Brighton meets are stereotyped. The Race-course, Telscombe Tye, the Devil's Dyke, and Thunders Barrow are repeated weekly. But of the way along the green-topped chalk cliffs, beside The far-spreading sea, or up and down the moorland hills and valleys, who can ever weary ? Who can weary of hill and dale and the eternal sea ?

To those accustomed to an inclosed country there is something extremely curious in mile after mile of open undulating downs lost in the distant horizon. My day was bright. About eleven o'clock the horsemen and *amazones* arrived in rapidly-succeeding parties, and gathered on the high ground. Pleasure visitors, out for the first time—distinguished by their correct costume and unmistakably hired animals—caps and white breeches, spotless tops and shining Napoleons—were mounted on hacks battered about the legs, and rather rough in the coat, though hard and full of go; but trousers were the prevailing order of the day. Medical men were evident, in correct white ties, on neat ponies and superior cobs ; military in mufti, on pulling steeplechasers; some farmers in leggings on good young nags for sale, and good old ones for use. London lawyers in heather mixture shooting-suits and Park hacks;lots of little boys and girls on ponies—white or cream-coloured being the favourites ; at least one master of far distant fox-hounds pack, on a blood-colt, master and horse alike new to the country and to the sport. Riding-masters, with their lady pupils tittupping about on the live rocking-horses that form the essential stock of every riding-master's establishment, with one or two papas of the pupils— " worthy" aldermen, or authorities of the Stock Exchange, expensively mounted, gravely looking on, with an expression of doubt as to whether they ought to have been there or not; and then a crowd of the nondescripts, bankers and brewers trying to look like squires, neat and grim, among the well and ill dressed, well and ill mounted, who form the staple of every watering-place,— with this satisfactory feature pervading the whole gathering, that with the exception of a few whose first appearance it was in saddle on any turf, and the before-mentioned grim brewers, all seemed decidedly jolly and determined to enjoy themselves.

The hounds drew up; to criticise them elaborately would be as unfair, under the circumstances, as to criticise a pot-luck dinner of beans and bacon put before a hungry man. They are not particularly handsome—white patches being the prevailing colour; and they certainly do not keep very close; but they are fast enough, persevering, and, killing a fair share of hares, show very good sport to both lookers-on and hard riders. The huntsman Willard, who has no " whip " to help him, and often more assistance than he requires, is a heavy man, but contrives, in spite of his weight, to get his hounds in the fastest runs.

The country, it may be as well to say for the benefit of the thousands who have never been on these famous mutton-producing " South Downs," is composed of a series of table-lands divided by barin-like valleys, for the most part covered with short turf, with large patches of gorse and heather, in which the hares, when beaten, take refuge. Of late years, high prices and Brighton demand, with the new system of artificial agriculture, have pushed root crops and corn crops into sheltered valleys and far over the hills, much to the disgust of the ancient race of shepherds.

It is scarcely necessary to observe, that on Brighton Downs there are no blank days, but the drawing is a real operation performed seriously until such a time as the company having all assembled, say at half-past seven o'clock, when, if the unaided faculties of the pack have not brought them up to a form, a shepherd appears as the *Deus ex machine*. In spite of all manner of precautions, the hounds will generally rush up to the point without hunting; loud rises the joyful cry; and, if it is level ground, the whole meet—hacks, hobbie-horses, and hunters—look as if their riders meant to go off in a whirlwind of trampling feet. There is usually a circle or two with the stoutest hare before making a long stretch; but, on lucky days like that of our first and last visit, the pace mends the hounds settle, the ridingmasters check their more dashing pupils, the crowd gets dispersed, and rides round, or halts on the edges, or crawls slowly down the steep-sided valleys; while the hard riders catch their nags by the head, in with the spurs, and go down straight and furious, as if they were away for ever and a day; hut the pedestrians and con-stitutional cob-owners are comforted by assurances that the hare is sure to run a ring back. But, on our day, Pussy, having lain perdu during a few minutescheck, started up suddenly amid a full cry, and rather too much hallooing. A gentleman in large mustachioas and a velvet cap rode at her as if he meant to catch her himself. Away we all dashed, losing sight of the dignity of fox-hunters—all mad as hatters (though why hatters should be madder than cappers it would be difficult to say). The pace becomes tremendous; the pack tails by twos and threes; the valleys grow steeper; the field lingers and halts more and more at each steeper comb ; the lads who have hurried straight up the hillsides, instead of creeping up by degrees blow their horses and come to a full stop; while old hands at Devonshire combs and Surrey steeps take their nags by the head, rush down like thunder, and slily zigzag up the opposite face at a trot; and so, for ten minutes, so straight, that a stranger, one of three in front, cried, "By Jove, it must be a fox !" But at that moment the leading hounds turned sharp to the right and then to the left—a shrill squeak, a cry of hounds, and all was over. The sun shone out bright and clear; looking up from the valley on the hills, nine-tenths of the field were to be seen a mile in the distance, galloping, trotting, walking, or standing still, scattered like a pulk of pursuing Cossacks. The sight reminded me that, putting aside the delicious excitement of a mad rush down hill at full-speed, the lookers-on, the young ladies on ponies, and old gentlemen on cobs, see the most of the sport in such a country as the Brighton Downs; while in a flat inclosed, or wooded country, those who do not ride are left alone quite deserted, five minutes after the hounds get well away.

We killed two more hares before retiring for the day, but as they ran rings in the approved style, continually coming back to the slow, prudent, and constitutional rider3, there was nothing to distinguish them from all other hare-hunts. After killing the last hare there was ample time to get back to Brighton, take a warm bath, dress, and stroll on the Esplanade for an hour in the midst of as gay and brilliant crowd, vehicular, equestrian, and pedestrian, as can be found in Europe, before sitting down to a quiet dinner, in which the delicious Southdown haunch was not forgotten. So ended a day of glorious weather and pleasant sport, jolly—if not in the highest degree genteel.

Tempted to stay another day, I went the next morning six miles through Rottingdean to Telscombe Tye, to meet the Brookside; and, after seeing them, have no hesitation in saying that every one who cares to look at a first-rate pack of harriers would find it worth his while to travel a hundred miles to meet the Brookside, for the whole turnout is perfection. Royalty cannot excel it.

A delicious ride over turf all the way, after passing Rottingdean, under a blue sky and a June-like sun, in sight of the sea, calm as a lake, brought us to the top of a hill of rich close turf, enveloped in a cloud of mist, which rendered horses and horsemen alike invisible at the distance of a few yards; and when we came upon three tall shepherds, leaning on their iron-hooked crooks, in the midst of a gorse covert, it was almost impossible to believo that we were not in some remote Highland district instead of within half an hour of a town of 70,000 inhabitants.

The costumes of the field, more exact than the previous day, showed that the master was considered worthy of the compliment; and when, the mist clearing, tho beautiful black-and-tan pack, all of a size, and as like as peas, came clustering up with Mr. Saxby, a white-haired, healthy, fresh-coloured, neat-figured, upright squire, riding in the midst on a rare black horse, it was a picture that, taking in the wild heathland scenery, the deep valleys below, bright in sun, the dark hills beyond it, was indeed a bright page in the poetry of field sports.

The Brookside are as good and honest as they are handsome; hunting, all together, almost entirely without assistance. If they have a fault they are a little too fast for hare-hounds. After killing the second hare, we were able to leave Brighton by the 3.30 P.M. train. Thus, under modern advantages, a man troubled with indiges tion has only to order a horse by post the previous day, leave town at eight in the morning, have a day's gallop, with excitement more valuable than gallons of physic, and be back in town by half-past five o'clock. Can eight hours be passed more pleasantly or profitably?

PRINCE ALBERT'S HARRIERS.

The South-Western Rail made a very good hack up to the Castle station.

That Prince Albert should never have taken to the Royal stag-hounds is not at all surprising. It requires to be " to the manner born " to endure the vast jostling, shouting, thrusting mob of gentlemen and horse dealers, " legs " and horse-breakers, that whirl away after the un-carted deer. Without the revival of the old Court etiquette, which forbade any one to ride before royalty, his Royal Highness might have been ridden down by some ambitious butcher or experimental cockney horseman on a runaway. If the etiquette of the time of George III.. had been revived, then only Leech could have done justice to the appearance of the field, following impatiently at a respectful distance—not the stag, as they do now very often, or the hounds, as they ought to do—but the Prince's horse's tail.

. Prince Albert's harriers are in the strictest sense of the term a private pack, kept by his Royal Highness for his own amusement, under the management of Colonel Hood. The meets are not advertised. The fields consist, in addition to the Royal and official party from the Castle, of a few neighbouring gentlemen and farmers, the hunting establishment of a huntsman and one whip, both splendidly mounted, and a boy on foot. The costume of the hunt is a very dark green cloth double-breasted coat, with the Prince's gilt button, brown cords, and velvet cap.

The hounds were about fifteen couple, of medium size, with considerable variety of true colours, inclining to the fox-hound stamp, yet very honest hunters. In each run the lead was taken by a houn4 of peculiar and uncommon marking—black and tan, but the tan so far spreading that the black was reduced to merely a saddle.

The day was rather too bright, perhaps, for the scent to lie well; but there was the better opportunity for seeing the hounds work, which they did most admirably, without any assistance. It is one of the advantages of a pack like this that no one presumes to interfere and do Hie business of either the huntsman or hounds. Tho first hare was found on land apparently recently inclosed near Eton; but, after two hours' perseverance, it was impossible to make anything of the scent over ploughed land.

We then crossed the railway into some fields, partly in grass, divided by broad ditches full of water, with plenty of willow stumps on the banks, and partly arable on higher, sloping ground, divided by fair growing fences into large square inclosures. Here we soon found a stout hare that gave us an opportunity of seeing and admiring the qualities of the pack. After the first short burst there was a quarter of an hour of slow hunting, when the hounds, left entirely to themselves, did their work beautifully. At length, as the sun went behind clouds, the scent improved; the hounds got on good terms with puss, and rattled away at a pace, and over a line of big fields and undeniable fences, that soon found out the slows and the nags that dared not face shining water. Short checks of a few minutes gave puss a short respite; then followed a full cry, and soon a view. Over a score of big fields the pack raced within a dozen yards of pussy's scent, without gaining a yard, the black-tanned leading hound almost coursing his game; but this was too fast to last, and, just as we were squaring our shoulders and settling down to take a very uncompromising hedge with evident signs of a broad ditch of running water on the other side, the hounds threw up their heads; poor puss had shuffled through the fence into the brook, and sunk like a stone.

There is something painful about the helpless finish with a hare. A fox dies snarling and fighting.

# CHAPTER XII.

# HUNTING TERMS.

HUNTING terms are difficult to write, because they are often rather sung than said. I shall take as my authority one of the best sportsmen of his day, Mr. Thomas Smith, author of the " Diary of a Huntsman," a book which has only one fault, it is too short; and give some explanations of my own.

HUNTSMAN'S LANGUAGE.

On throwing off.—*Cover hoick! i. e. Hark into cover*
Also—*Eho in*!
 Over the fence.—*Toi over*!
To make hounds draw.—*Edawick*!

Also—Yoi, *wind him! Yoi, rouse him, my boys*!

And to a particular hound—*Hoick, Rector*! Hoick, Bonny Lass!

The variety of Tally-ho's I have given in another place.

To call the rest when some hounds have gone away.—

*Elope forward, aw-ay-woy* !

*If* they have hit off the scent—*Forrid, hoick*!

When hounds have overrun the scent, or he wants them to come back to him.—*Yo-geote*!

When the hounds are near their fox.— *Eloo, at him*!


*Billet.*—The excrement of a fox.

*Burst.*—The first part of a run.


*Burning scent.*—When hounds go so fast, from the good. ness of the scent, they have no breath to spare, and run almost mute.


*Breast high.*—When hounds do not stoop their heads, but go a racing pace.


*Capping.*—To wave your cap to bring on the hounds. Also to subscribe for the huntsman, by dropping into a cap after a good run with fox-hounds. At watering places, before a run with harriers.


*Carry a good head.*—When hounds run well together, owing to the scent being good, and spreading so wide that the whole pack can feel it But it usually happens that the scent is good only on the line for one hound to get it, so that the rest follow him; hence the necessity of keeping your eyes on the leading hounds, if you wish to-be forward.


*Challenge.*—When drawing a fox, the first hound that gives tongue, " challenges."


*Changed.*—When the pack changed from the hunted fox to a fresh one.

*Check.*—When hounds stop for want of scent in running, or over-run it

*Chopped a fox.*—When a fox is killed in cover without running.

*Crash.*—When in cover, every hound seems giving tongue at the same moment: that is a crash of hounds.

*Cub.*—Until November, a young fox is a cub.

*Drawing.*—The act of hunting to find a fox in a cover. or covert, as some term it.

*Drag.*—The scent left by the footsteps of the fox on his way from his rural rambles to his earth, or kennel.Our forefathers rose early; and instead of drawing,hunted the fox by " dragging" up to him.

*Dwelling.*—When hounds do not come up to the huntsman's halloo till moved by the whipper-in, they aresaid to dwell.

Drafted.—Hounds drawn from the pack to be disposed of, or hung, are drafted.

" *Earths are drawn*"—When a vixen fox has drawn out fresh earth, it is a proof she intends to lay up her cubs there.

*Eye to hounds.*—A man has a good eye to hounds who turns his horse's head with the leading hounds.

*Flighty.*—A hound that is not a steady hunter.

*Feeling a scent.*—You say, if scent is bad, " The hounds could scarcely feel the scent.

" *Foil.*—When a fox runs the ground over which he has been before, he is running his foil.

. *Headed.*—When a fox is going away, and is met and driven back to cover. Jealous riders, anxious for a start, are very apt to head the fox. It is one of the greatest crimes in the hunting-field.

*Heel.*—When hounds get on the scent of a fox, and run it back the way he came, they are said to be runningheel.

*Hold hard.*—A cry that speaks for itself, which every one who wishes for sport will at once attend to when uttered by the huntsman.

*Holding scent.*—When the scent is just good enough for hounds to hunt a fox a fair pace, but not enough to press him.

Kennel.—Where a fox lays all day in cover.

Line holders.—Hounds which will not go a yard beyond the scent

Left-handed.—A hunting pan on hounds that are not always right.

Lifting.—When a huntsman carries the pack forward from an indifferent, or no scent, to a place the fox is hoped to have more recently passed, or to a view halloo. It is an expedient found needful where the field is large, and unruly, and impatient, oftener than good sportsmen approve[16].

---

16   The late Sir Richard Sutton, Master of the Quorn, used to say that he liked "to stick to the band and keep hold of the bridle," that is to say, make his pack hold to the line of the fox as long as they could; but there were times when he could not resist the temptation of a sure "holloa," and off he would start at a tremendous pace, for he was always a bruising rider, with a blast or two upon his "little merry-toned horn " which he had the art of blowing better than other people. To his intimate friends he used to excuse himself for these occasional outbreaks by quoting a saying of his old huntsman Goosey (late the Duke of Rutland's)—for whose opinion on hunting matters he had a great

Laid up.—When a vixen fox has had cubs she is said to have laid up.

*Metal*.—When hounds fly for a short distance on a wrong scent, or without one, it is said to be " all metal."

Moving scent.—When hounds get on a scent that is fresher than a drag, it is called a moving scent; that is, the scent of a fox which has been disturbed by travelling.

Mobbing a fox—Is when foot passengers, or foolish

*mute*.—When the pace is great hounds are mute, they have no breath to spare; but a hound that is always mute is as useless as a rich epicure who has capital dinners and eats them alone. Hounds' that do not help each other are worthless.

*Noisy*.—To throw the tongue without scent is an opposite and equal fault to muteness.

Open.—When a hound throws his tongue, or gives tongue, he is said to open.

Owning a scent.—When hounds throw their tongues on the scent

Pad.—The foot of a fox.

Riot.—When the hounds hunt anything beside fox, the word is " Ware Riot"
Skirter.—A hound which is wide of the pack, or a man riding wide of the hounds, is called a skirter. *Stroke of a fox*.—Is when hounds are drawing. It is evi-

respect—" I take leave to say, sir, a fox is a very quick animal, and you must make haste after him during some part of the day, or you will not catch him."—*Letter from Captain Percy Williams, Master of the Rufford Hounds, to the Editor*. jealous horsemen so surround a cover, that the fox is driven into the teeth of the hounds, instead of being allowed to break away and show sport dent, from their manner, that they feel the scent of a fox, slashing their stern significantly, although they

do not speak to it

*Sinking*—A fox nearly beaten is said to be sinking.

*Sinking the wind.*—Is going down wind, usually done by knowing sportsmen to catch the cry of the hounds.

*Stained.*—When the scent is lost by cattle or sheep having passed over the line.

Stooping.—Hounds stoop to the scent.

Slack.—Indifferent A succession of bad days, or a slack huntsman, will make hounds slack.

Streaming.—An expressive word applied to hounds in full cry, or breast high and mute, " streaming away."

Speaks.—When a hound throws his tongue he is said to speak; and one word from a sure hound makes the presence of a fox certain,

*Throw up.*—When hounds lose the scent they " throw up their heads." A good sportsman always takes note of the exact spot and cause, if he can, to tell the huntsman.

*Tailing.*—The reverse of streaming. The result of bad scent, tired hounds, or an uneven pack.

Throw off.—After reaching the " meet," at the master's word the pack is " thrown into cover," hence " throw off."

There are many other terms in common use too plain to need explanation, and there are a good many slang phrases to be found in newspaper descriptions of runs, which are both vulgar and unnecessary. One of the finest descriptions of a fox-hunt ever written is to be found in the account of Jorrocks' day with the " Old Customer," disfigured, unfortunately, by an overload of impossible cockneyisms,. put in the mouth of the impossible grocer. Another capitally-told story of a foxhunt is to be found in Whyte Melville's " Kate Coventry." But the Rev. Charles Kingsley has, in his opening chapter of " Yeast," and his papers in Fraser on North Devon, shown that if he chose he could throw all writers on hunting into the shade. Would that he would give us some hunting-songs, for he is a true poet, as well as a true sports-man!

Another clergyman, under the pseudonym of " Uncle Scribble," contributed to the pages of the *Sporting Magazine* an admirable series of photographs—to adopt a modern word—of hunting and hunting men, as remarkable for dry wit and common sense, as a thorough knowledge of sport. But " Uncle Scribble," as the head of a most successful Boarding School, writes no more.

I may perhaps be pardoned for concluding my hints on hunting, by re-quoting from Household Words an " Apology for Fox-hunting," which, at the time I wrote it, received the approbation, by quotation, of almost every sporting journal in the country. It will be seen that it contains a sentence very similar to one to be found in Mr. Rarey's " Horse Training "—" A bad-tem pered man cannot be a good horse-man."

" TALLY-HO !

" Fox-hunting, I maintain, is entitled to be considered one of the fine arts, standing somewhere between music . and dancing. For ' Tally-ho!' like the favourite eve-ning gun of colonising orators, has been carried round the world.' The plump mole-fed foxes of the neutral ground of Gibraltar have fled from the jolly cry; it has been echoed back from the rocky hills of our island possessions in the Mediterranean; it has startled the jackal on the mountains of the Cape, and his red brother on the burning plains of Bengal; the wolf of the pine forests of Canada has heard it, cheering on foxhounds to an unequal contest and even the wretched dingoe and the bounding kangaroo of Australia have learned to dread the sound.

"In our native land Tally-ho!' is shouted and welcomed in due season by all conditions of men; by the ploughman, holding hard his startled colt; by the wood-man, leaning on his axe before the half-felled oak; by bird-boys from the tops of leafless trees; even Dolly Dumpling, as she sees the white-tipped brush flash before her market-cart in a deep-banked lane, stops, points her whip, and in shrill treble screams * Tally-ho !'

" And when at full speed the pink, green, brown, and black-coated followers of any of the ninety packs -which our England maintains, sweep through a village, with what intense delight the whole population turn out! Young mothers stand at the doors, holding up their crowing babies; the shopkeeper, with his customers, adjourns to the street; the windows of the school are covered with flattened noses; the parson, if of the right sort, smiles blandly, and waves his hand from the porch of the vicarage to half-a-dozen friends; while the surgeon pushes on his galloway and joins for half-an-hour; all the little boys holla in chorus, and run on to open gates without expecting sixpence. As for the farmers, those who do not join the hunt criticise the horseflesh, speculate on the probable price of oats, and tell ' Mis-sis ' to set out the big round of beef, the bread, the cheese, and get ready to draw some strong ale,—' in case of a check, some of the gentlemen might like a bit as they come back.

" It is true, among the five thousand who follow the hounds daily in the hunt-ing season, there are to be found, as among most medleys of five thousand, a certain number of fools and brutes—mere animals, deaf to the music, blind to the living po-etry of nature. To such men hunting is a piece of fashion or vulgar excitement, but bring hunting in comparison with other amusements, and it will stand a severe test. Are you an admirer of scenery, an amateur or artist? Have you traversed Greece and Italy, Switzerland and Norway, in search of the picturesque ? You do not know the beauties of your own country, until, having hunted from Northumberland to Corn-wall, you have viewed the various counties under the three aspects of a fox-hunter's day—the " morning ride," the run,' and ' the return home.'

" The morning ride, slowly pacing, full of expectation, your horse as pleased as yourself; sharp and clear in the gray atmosphere the leafless trees and white farm-houses stand out, hacked by a curtain of mist hanging on the hills in the horizon. With eager eyes you take all in; nothing escapes you; you have cast off care for the day. How pleasant and cheerful everything and everyone looks ! Even the cocks and hens, scratching by the road-side, have a friendly air. The turnpike-man relaxes, in favour of your ' pink', his usual grimness. A tramping woman, with one child at her hack and two running beside her, asks charity; you suspect she is an impostor, but she looks cold and pitiful; you give her a shilling, and the next day you don't regret your foolish benevolence. To your mind the well-cultivated land looks beautiful. In the monotony of ten acres of turnips, you see a hundred pictures of English farming life, well-fed cattle, good wheat crops, and a little barley for beer. Not less beautiful is the wild gorse-covered moor —never to be reclaimed, I hope—where the wiry, white-headed, bright-eyed huntsman sits motionless on his old white horse, sur-rounded by the pied pack—a study for Landseer.

" But if the morning ride creates unexecuted cabinet pictures and unwritten sonnets, how delightful' the find', ' the run' along brook-intersected vales, up steep hills, through woodlands, parks, and villages, showing you in byways little gothic churches, ivy-covered cottages, and nooks of beauty you never dreamed of, alive with startled cattle and hilarious rustics.

" Talk of epic poems, read in bowers or at firesides, what poet's description of a battle could make the blood boil in delirious excitement, like a seat on a long-striding hunter, clearing every obstacle with firm elastic bounds, holding in sight without gaining a yard on the flying pack, while the tip of Reynard's tail disappears over the wall at the top of the hill!

" And, lastly,—tired, successful, hungry, happy,—the return home, when the shades of evening, closing round, give a fantastic, curious, mysterious aspect to familiar road-side objects! Loosely lounging on your saddle, with half-closed eyes, you almost dream — the gnarled trees grow into giants, cottages into castles, ponds into lakes. The maid of the inn is a lovely princess, and the bread and cheese she brings (while, without dismounting, you let your thirsty horse drink his gruel), tastes more delicious than the finest supper of cham- pagne, with a pâté. of tortured goose's liver, that ever tempted the appetite of a humane, anti-fox hunting, poet-critic, exhausted by a long night of opera, ballet, and Roman punch.

"Are you fond of agriculture?—You may survey all the progress and ignorance of an agricultural district in rides across country; you may sound the depth of the average agricultural mind while trotting from cover to cover. Are you of a social disposition ?—What a fund of information is to be gathered from the acquaintances made, returning home after a famous day, ' thirty-five minutes without a check.' In a word, fox-hunting affords exercise and healthy excitement without headaches, or heartaches, without late hours, without the 'terrible next morning' that follows so many town amusements. Fox-hunting draws men from towns, promotes a love of country life, fosters skill, courage, temper; for a bad-tempered man can never be a good horseman.

" To the right-minded, as many feelings of thankfulness and praise to the Giver of all good will arise, sitting on a fiery horse, subdued to courageous obedience for the use of man, while surveying a pack of hounds ranging an autumnal thicket with fierce intelligence, or looking down on a late moorland, broken up to fertility Joy man's skill and industry, as in a solitary walk by the sea-shore or over a Highland hill."

Oh, give me the man to whom nought comes amiss,
One horse or another—that country or this;
Through falls and bad starts who undauntedly still
 Rides up to this motto, " Be with them I will!"
And give me the man who can ride through a run,
Nor engross to himself all the glory when done;

Who calls not each horse that o'ertakes him a screw;
Who loves a run best when a friend sees it too.

WARBURTON of Arley Hall,

# CHAPTER XIII.

# THE ORIGIN OF FOX-HUNTING.

THE origin of modern fox-hunting is involved in a degree of obscurity which can only be attributed to the illiterate character of the originators, the Squire Westerns, who rode all day, and drank all the evening. We need the assistance of the ingenious correspondent of *Notes and Queries*:—

"

It is quite certain that the fox was not accounted a noble beast of chase before the Revolution of 1688; for Gervase Markham classes the fox with the badger in his Cavalrie, or that part of Arte wherein is contained the Choice Trayning and Dyeting of Hunting Horses whether for Pleasure or for Wager. The Third Booke. Printed by Edw. Allde, for Edward White; and are to be sold at his Shop, neare the Little North Door of St Paule's Church, at the signe of the Gun. 1616' He says:—

" 'The chase of the foxe or badger, although it be a chase of much more swiftness (than the otter), and is ever kept upon firm ground, yet I cannot allow it for training horses, because for the most part it continues in woody rough grounds, where a horse can neither con-veniently make foorth his way nor can heed without danger of stubbing The chase, much better than any of these, is hunting of the bucke or stag* especially if they be not confined within a park or pale, but having liberty to chuse their waies, which some huntsmen call " hunting at force." When he is at liberty he will break forth his chase into the winde, sometimes four, five, and six miles foorth right: nay, I have myself followed a stag better than ten miles foorth right from the place of his rousing to the place of his death, besides all his windings, turnings, and cross passages. The time of the year for these chases is from the middle of May to middle of September.' He goes on to say, 'which being of all chases the worthiest, and belonging only Princes and men of best quality, there is no horse too good to be employed in such a service; yet the horses which are aptest and best to be employed in this chase is the Barbary jennet, or a light-made English gelding, being of a middle stature.' ' But to conclude and come to the chase which is of all chases the best for the purpose whereof we are now entreating; it is the chase of the hare, which is a chase both swift and pleasant, and of long endurance; it is a sport ever readie, equally distributed, as well to the wealthie farmer as the great gentleman. It hath its beginning contrary to the stag and bucke; for it begins at Michaelmas, when they end, and is out of date after April, when they first come into season" This low estimate of the fox, at that period, is borne out by a speech of Oliver St John, to the Long Parliament, against Strafford, quoted by Macaulay, in which he declares—' Strafford was to be regarded not as a stag ox hare, but as a fox, who was to be snared by any means and knocked on the head without pity.' The same historian relates that red deer were as plentiful on the hills of Hampshire and Gloucestershire, in the reign of Queen Anne, as they are now in the preserved deer-forests of the Highlands of Scotland.

"When wild deer became scarce, the attention of sportsmen was probably turned to the sporting qualities of the fox by the accident of harriers getting upon the scent of some wanderer in the clicketing season, and being led a straight long run. We have more than once met with such accidents on the Devonshire moors, and have known well-bred harriers run clear away from the huntsmen, after an on-lying fox, over an unrideable country.

" Fox-hunting rose into favour with the increase of population attendant on improved agriculture. In a wild woodland country, with earths unstopped, no pack of hounds could fairly run down a fox.

" I have found in private records two instances in which packs of hounds, since celebrated, were turned from hare-hounds to fox-hounds. There are, no doubt, many more. The Tarporley, or Cheshire Hunt, was established in 1762 for Hare-hunting, and held its first meeting on the 14th November in that year. ' Those who kept harriers brought them in turn.' It is ordered by the 8th Rule, ' that if no member of the society kept hounds, or that it were inconvenient for masters to bring them, a pack be borrowed at the expense of the society.

" The uniform was ordered to be a blue frock with plain yellow mettled buttons, scarlet velvet cape, and double-breasted flannel waistcoat. The coat sleeve to be cut and turned. A scarlet saddle-cloth, bound singly with blue, and the front of the bridle lapt with scarlet.' The third rule contrasts oddly with our modern meats at half-past ten and half-past eleven o'clock: —' The harriers shall not Wait for any member after eight o'clock in the morning.'"As to drinking, it was ordered 'that three collar bumpers be drunk after dinner, and the same after supper; after that every member might do as he pleased in regard to drinking.'

" By another rule every member was ' to present on his marriage to each member of the hunt, a pair of well-stitched leather breeches,'[19] then costing a guinea a pair.

"In 1769, the club commenced Fox-hunting. The uniform was ordered to be changed to ' a red coat, unbound, with small frock sleeve, a green velvet cape, and green waistcoat, and that the sleeve have no buttons; in every other form to be like the old uniform; and the red saddle-cloth to be bound with green instead of blue, the fronts of the saddles to remain the same.,

" At the same time there was an alteration in regard to drinking orders—' That instead of three collar bumpers, only one shall be drunk, except a fox be killed above ground, and then one other collar glass shall be drunk to "Fox-hunting." Among the names of the original members in 1762, we recognise many whose descendants have maintained in this generation their ancestral reputation as sportsmen. For instance, Crewe, Mainwaring, Wilbraham, Smith, Barry, Cholmondeley, Stanley, Grosvenor, Townley, Watkin Williams Wynne, Stanford. But, although the Tarporley Hunt Club has been maintained and thriven through the reigns of George III., George IV., William IV., and Victoria, the pack of hounds, destroyed or removed by various accidents, have been more than once renewed. But the

[19] I think this is a mistake. In a copy of the rules forwarded to me by a Cheshire squire, one of the hereditary members of the club, it is a pair of gloves. But in the notes, the songs and ballads by E. Eger-ton Warburton, Esq., of Arley Hall, it is printed "breeches."

Brocklesby pack has been maintained in the family of the present Earl of Yarborough more than 130 years without break or change of blood; and a written pedigree of the pack has been kept for upwards of 100 years; and it is now the oldest pack in the kingdom. The Cottesmore, which was established before the Brocklesby, has been repeatedly dispersed and has long passed out of the hands of the family of the Noels—by whom it was first established 200 years ago."

By the kindness of Lord Yarborough, I was permitted to examine all the papers connected with his hounds. Among them is a memorandum dated April 20, 1713: it is agreed " between Sir John Tyrwhitt, Charles Pelham, Esq., and Robert Vyner, Esq. (another name well known in modern hunting annals), that the foxhounds now kept by the said Sir John Tyrwhitt and Mr. Pelham shall be joyned in one pack, and the three have a joint interest in the said hounds for five years, each for one-third of the year." And it was agreed that the establishment should consist of "sixteen couple of hounds, three horses, and a huntsman and a boy." So apparently they only hunted one day a week. It would seem that, under the terms of the agreement, the united pack soon passed into the hands of Mr. Pelham, and down to the present day the hounds have been branded with a P I also found at Brocklesby a rough memoranda of the kennel from 1710 to 1746; after that date the Stud Book has been distinctly kept up without a break. From 1797 the first Lord Yarborough kept journals of the pedigree of hounds in his own handwriting; and since his time by the father, the grandfather, and great-grandfather of the present huntsman,

In the time of the first Lord Yarborough, his country extended over the whole of the South Wold country, part of the now Burton Hunt, and part of North Nottinghamshire ; and he used to go down into both those districts for a month at a time to hunt the woodlands. These were, as he told his grandson when he began hunting, only three or four fences between Horn-castle and Brigg, a distance of at least thirty miles.

Sir Thomas Tyrwhitt kept harriers at his Manor House of Aylsby, at the foot of the Lincolnshire Wolds, before he turned them into fox-hounds. A barn at Aylsby was formerly known as the "Kennels." The Aylsby estate has passed, in the female line, into the Oxfordshire family of the Tyrwhitt Drakes, who are so well known as masters of hounds, and first-rate sportsmen ; while a descendant of Squire Vyner, of Lincolnshire, has, within the last twenty years, been a master of fox-hounds in Warwickshire and Worcestershire. Mr. Meyneft, the father of modern fox-hunting, and founder of the Quorn Hunt, formed his pack chiefly of drafts from the Brocklesby.

Between the period that fox-hunting superseded hare-hunting in the estimation of country squires, and that when the celebrated Mr. Meynell reduced it to a science, and prepared the way for making hunting in Leicestershire almost an aristocratic institution, a great change took place in the breed of the hounds and horses, and in the style of horsemanship. Under the old system, the hounds were taken out before light to hunt back by his drag the fox who had been foraging all night, and set on him as he lay above his stopped-earth, before he had digested his meal of rats or rabbits. The breed of hounds partook more of the long-eared, dew-lapped, heavy, crock-kneed southern hound, or of the bloodhound. Well-bred horses, too, were less plentiful than they are now.

But the change to fast bounds, fast horses, and fast men, took place at a much more distant date than some of our hard-riding young swells of 1854 seem to imagine. A portrait of a celebrated hound, Ringwood, at Brocklesby Park, painted by Stubbs, the well-known animal painter in 1792, presents in an extraordinary manner the type and character of some of the best hounds remotely descended from him, although the Cheshire song says:—

" When each horse wore a crupper, each squire a pigtail,
Ere Blue Cap and Wanton taught greyhounds to scurry,
With music in plenty—oh, where was the hurry ?"

But it is more than eighty years since Blue Cap and Wanton ran their race over Newmarket Heath, which for speed has never been excelled by any modern hounds.

And it is a curious fact, that although Somerville, the author of The Chase, died in 1742, his poem contains as clear and correct directions for fox-hunting, with few exceptions, as if it were written yesterday. So that the art must have arrived at perfection within sixty or seventy years. In the long reign of George III the distinction bewteen town and country was much broken down, and the isolation in which country squires lived destroyed. Packs of hounds, kept for the amusement of a small district, became, as it were, public property. At length the meets of hounds began to be regularly given in the country newspapers.

With every change sportsmen of the old school have prophesied the total ruin of fox-hunting. Roads and canals excited great alarm to our fathers. In our time every one expected to see sport entirely destroyed by railroads; but we were mistaken, and have lived to consider them almost an essential auxiliary of a good hunting district,

Looking back at the manner in which fox-hunting has -grown up with our habits and customs, and increased in the number of packs, number of hunting days, and number of horsemen, in full proportion with wealth and population, one cannot help being amused at the simplicity with which Mrs. Beecher Stowe, who comes from a country where people seldom amuse themselves out of doors (except in making money), tells in her " Sunny Memories," how, when she dined with Lord John Russell, at Richmond, the conversation turned on hunting; and she expressed her astonishment " that, in the height of English civilisation, this vestige of the savage state should remain." " Thereupon they only laughed, and told stories about fox-hunters." They might have answered with old Gervase Markham, " Of all the field pleasures wherewith Old Time and man's inventions hath blessed the hours of our recreations, there is none so excellent as the delight of hunting, being compounded like an harmonious concert of all the best partes of most refined pleasures, as music, dancing, running and ryding."

Mrs. Stowe's distinguished countryman, Washington Irving, took a sounder view of our rural pleasures; for he says in his charming " Sketch Book:"—

" The fondness for rural life among the higher classes of the English has had a great and salutary effect upon national character. I do not know a finer race of men than the English gentlemen. Instead of the softness and effeminacy which characterizes the men of rank of most countries, they exhibit a union of elegance and strength, of robustness of frame and freshness of complexion, which I am inclined to attribute to their living so much in the open air, pursuing so eagerly the invigorating recreations of the country."

# CHAPTER XIV.

## THE WILD PONIES OF EXMOOR.

IN England there are so few wild horses, that the following description of a visit I made to Exmoor a few years ago in the month of September, may be doubly interesting, since Mr. Rarey has shown a short and easy method of dealing with the principal produce of that truly wild region.

The road from South Molton to Exmoor is a gradual ascent over a succession of hills, of which each descent, however steep, leads to a still longer ascent, until you reach the high level of Exmoor. The first six miles are through real Devonshire lanes; on each side high banks, all covered with fern and grass, and topped with shrubs and trees; for miles we were hedged in with hazels, bearing nuts with a luxuriance wonderful to the eyes of those accustomed to see them sold at the corners of streets for a penny the dozen. In spring and summer, wild flowers give all the charms of colour to these game-preserving hedgerows; but a rainy autumn had left no colour among the rich green foliage, except here and there a pyramid of the bright red berries of the mountain ash.

So, up hill and down dale, over water-courses—now merrily trotting, anon descending, and not less merrily trudging up, steep ascents—we proceed by a track as sound as if it bad been under the care of a model board of trustees—for the simple reason that it rested on natural rock. We pushed along at an average rate of some six miles an hour, allowing for the slow crawling up hills ; passing many rich fields wherein fat oxen of the Devon breed calmly grazed, with sheep that had eertatnly not been bred on mountains. Once we passed a deserted copper-mine; which, after having been worked for many years, had at length failed, or grown unprofitable, under the competition of the richer mines of Cuba and South Australia. A long chimney, peering above deserted cottages, and a plentiful crop of weeds, was the sole monument of departed glories—in shares and dividends—and mine-captain's promises.

At length the hedges began to grow thinner; beeches succeeded the hazels; the road, more rugged and bare showed the marks where winter's rains had ploughed deep channels ; and, at the turn of a steep hill, we saw, on the one hand, the brown and blue moor stretching before and above us; and on the other hand, below, like a map, the fertile vale lay unrolled, various in colour, according to the crops, divided by enclosures into every angle from most acute to most obtuse. Below was the cultivation of centuries; above, the turnip—the greatest improvement of modern agriculture—flourished, a deep green, under the protection of fences of very recent date.

One turnpike, and cottages at rare intervals, had so far kept up the idea of population; but now, far as the horizon extended, not a place of habitation was to be seen; until, just in a hollow bend out of the ascending road, we came upon a low white farm-house, of humble pretensions, flanked by a great turf-stack (but no signs of corn; no fold-yard full of cattle), which bore, on a board of great size, in long letters, this imposing announcement, " The Poltimore Arms." Our driver not being of the usual thirsty disposition of his tribe, we did not test the capabilities of the one hostelry and habitation on Lord Poltimore's Moorland Estate, but, pushing on, took the reins while our conductor descended to open a gate in a large turf and stone wall. We passed through—left Devon—entered Somerset; and the famous Exmoor estate of 30,000 acres, bounded by a wall forty miles in length, the object of our journey, lay before us.

Very dreary was this part of our journey, although, contrary to the custom of the country, the day was bright and clear, and the September sun defeated the fogs, and kept at a distance the drizzling rains which in winter sweep over Exmoor. We had now left the smooth, rocky-floored road, and were travelling along what most resembled the dry bed of a torrent: turf banks on each side seemed rather intended to define than to divide the property. As far as the eye could reach, the rushy tufted moorland extended, bounded in the distance by lofty, round-backed hills. Thinly scattered about were horned sheep and Devon red oxen. For about two miles we jolted gently on, until, beginning to descend a hill, our driver pointed in the valley below to a spot where stacks of hay and turf guarded a series of stone buildings, saying, " There's the Grange." The first glance was not encouraging—no sheep-station in Australia could seem more utterly desolate; but it improved on closer examination. The effects of cultivation were to be seen in the different colours of the fields round the house, where the number of stock grazing showed that more than ordinary means must have been taken to improve the pasture.

We started on Exmoor ponies to ride to Simon's Bath.

Exmoor, previous to 1818, was the property of the Crown, and leased to Sir Thomas Dyke Acland, who ' has an estate of a similar character close adjoining. He used its wild pasture (at that time it was without roads) for breeding ponies and feeding Exmoor sheep. There are no traces of any population having ever existed on this forest since Roman times. The Romans are believed to have worked iron-mines on the moor, which have recently been re-opened.

Exmoor consists of 20,000 acres, on an elevation varying from 1000 to 1200 feet above the sea, of undulating table-land, divided by valleys, or "combes," through which the River Exe—which rises in one of its valleys—with its tributary, the Barle, forces a devious way, in the form of pleasant trout-streams, rattling over and among huge stones, and creeping through deep pools—a very angler's paradise. Like many similar districts in the Scotch Highlands, the resort of the red deer, it is called a forest, although trees—with the exception of some very insignificant plantations—are as rare as men. After riding all day with a party of explorers, one of them suddenly exclaimed, " Look, there is a man!" A similar expression escaped me when we came in sight of the first tree—a gnarled thorn, standing alone on the side of a valley.

The sides of the steep valleys, of which some include an acre, and others extend for miles, are usually covered with coarse herbage, heather, and bilberry plants, springing from a deep black or red soil: at certain spots a greener hue marks the site of the bogs which impede and at times almost engulph, the incautious horseman. These bogs are formed by springs, which, having been intercepted by a pan of sediment, and prevented from percolating through the soil, stagnate, and cause, at the same time, decay and vicious vegetation. They are seldom deep, and can usually be reclaimed by subsoiling or otherwise breaking the pan, and so drying the upper layers of bog. Bog-turf is largely employed on Exmoor as fuel. On other precipitous descents, winter torrents have washed away all the earth, and left avalanches of bare loose stones, called, in the western dialect, " crees." To descend these crees at a slapping pace in the course of a stag-hunt, requires no slight degree of nerve; but it is done, and is not so dangerous as it looks.

Exmoor may be nothing strange to those accustomed to the wild, barren scenery. To one who has known country scenes only in the best-cultivated regions of England, and who has but recently quitted the perpetual roar of London, there is something strangely solemn and impressive in the deep silence of a ride across the forest Horses bred on the moors, if left to themselves, rapidly pick their way through pools and bogs, and canter smoothly over dry flats of natural meadow; creep safely down the precipitous descents, and climb with scarcely a puff of distress these steep ascents; splash through fords in the trout-streams, swelled by rain, without a moment's hesitation, and trot along sheep-paths, bestrewed with rolling stones, without a stumble: so that you are perfectly at liberty to enjoy the luxury of excitement, and follow out the winding valleys, and study the rich brown and purple herbage.

It was while advancing over a great brown plain in the centre of the moor, with a deep valley on our left, that our young quick-eyed guide suddenly held up his hand, whispering, " Bide on without seeming to take notice; there are the deer." A great red stag, lying on the brown grass, had sprung up, and was gazing on our party—too numerous and too brightly attired to be herdsmen, whom he would have allowed to pass without notice. Behind him were clustered four hinds and a calf. They stood still for some minutes watching our every movement, as we tried to approach them in a narrowing circle. Then the stag moved off slowly, with stately, easy, gliding steps, constantly looking back. The hinds preceded him: they reached the edge of the valley, and disappeared. We galloped up, and found that they had exchanged the slow retreat for a rapid flight, clearing every slight or suspicious obstacle with a grace, ease, and swiftness it was delightful to witness. In an incredibly short time they had disappeared, hidden by undulations in the apparently flat moor.

These were one of the few herds still remaining on the forest In a short time the wild deer of Exmoor will be a matter of tradition; and the hunt, which may be traced back to the time of Queen Elizabeth, will, if continued, descend to the " cart and calf" business.

A sight scarcely less interesting than the deer was afforded by a white pony mare, with her young stock— consisting of a foal still sucking, a yearling, and a two-year-old—which we met in a valley of the Barle. The two-year-old had strayed away feeding, until alarmed by the cracking of our whips and the neighing of its dam, when it came galloping down a steep combe, neighing loudly, at headlong speed. It is thus these ponies learn their action and sure-footedness.

It was a district such as we had traversed—entirely wild, without inclosures, or roads, or fences—that came into the hands of the father of the present proprietor. He built a fence of forty miles around it, made roads, reclaimed a farm for his own use at Simon's Bath, introduced Highland cattle on the hills, and set up a considerable stud for improving the indigenous race of ponies, and for rearing full-sized horses. These improvements, on which some three hundred thousand pounds were sunk, were not profitable; and it is very doubtful whether any considerable improvements could have been prosecuted successfully, if railways had not brought better markets within reach of the district.

Coming from a part of the country where ponies are the perquisites of old ladies and little children, and where the nearer a well-shaped horse can be got to sixteen hands the better, the -first feeling on mounting a rough little unkemped brute, fresh from the moor, barely twelve hands (four feet) in height, was intensely ridiculous. It seemed as if the slightest mistake would send the rider clean over the animal's head. But we learned 60on that the indigenous pony, in certain useful qualities, is not to be surpassed by animals of greater size and pretensions.

From the Grange to Simon's Bath (about three miles), the road, which runs through the heart of Ex-moor proper, was constructed, with all the other roads in this vast extra-parochial estate, by the father of the present proprietor, F. Knight, Esq., of Wolverly House, Worcestershire, M.P. for East Worcestershire (Parliamentary Secretary of the Poor Law Board, under Lord Derby's Government). In the course of a considerable part of the route, the contrast of wild moorland and high cultivation may be found only divided by the carriage-way.

At length, descending a steep hill, we came in sight of a view—-of which Ex-moor and its kindred district in North Devon affords many — a deep gorge, at whose precipitous base a trout-stream rolled along, gurgling and plashing, and winding round huge masses of white spar. The far bank sometimes extended out into natural meadows, where red cattle and wild ponies grazed, and sometimes rose precipitously. At one point, where both banks were equally steep and lofty, the far side was covered by a plantation with a cover of underwood ; but no trees of sufficient magnitude to deserve the name of a wood. This is a spot famous in the annals of a grand sport that soon will be among things of the past—Wild Stag Hunting. In this wood more than once the red monarch of Exmoor has been roused, and bounded over the rolling plains beyond, amid the shouts of excited hunters and the deep cry of the hounds, as with a burring scent they dashed up the steep breast of the hill.

But there was no defiant stag there that day; so on we trotted on our shaggy sure-footed nags, beneath a burning sun—a sun that sparkled on the flowing waters as they gleamed between far distant hills, and threw a golden glow upon the fading tints of foliage and herbage, and cast deep shadows from the white overhanging rocks.

Next we came to the deep pool that gives the name to Simon's Bath, where some unhappy man of that name, in times when deer were more plentiful than sheep, drowned himself for love, or in madness, or both—long before roads, farms, turnip crops, a school, and a church were dreamed of on Exmoor. Here fences give signs of habitation and cultivation. A rude, ancient bridge, with two arches of different curves, covered with turf, without side battlements or rails, stretches across the stream, and leads to a small house built for his own occupation by the father of Mr.D Knight, pending the completion of a mansion of which the unfinished walls of one wing rise like a dismantled castle from the midst of a grove of trees and ornamented shrubs.

. A series of gentle declivities, plantations, a winding, full-flowing stream, seem only to require a suitable edifice and the hand of an artist gardener to make, at comparatively trifling expense, an abode unequalled in luxuriant and romantic beauty. We crossed the stream —not by the narrow bridge, but by the ford ; and, passing through the straggling stone village of Simon's Bath, arrived in sight of the field where the Tattersall of the West was to sell the wild and tame horse stock bred on the moors. It was a field of some ten acres and a half, forming a very steep slope, with the upper path comparatively flat, the sloping side broken by a stone quarry, and dotted over with huge blocks of granite. At its base flowed an arm of the stream we had found margining our route. A substantial, but, as the event proved, not sufficiently high stone fence bounded the whole field. On the upper part, a sort of double pound, united by a narrow neck, with a gate at each end, had been constructed of rails, upwards of five feet in height. Into the first of these pounds, by ingenious management, all the ponies, wild and tame, had been driven. When the sale commenced, it was the duty of the herdsmen to separate two at a time, and drive them through the narrow neck into the pound before the auctioneer. Around a crowd of spectators of every degree were clustered—'squires and clergymen, horse-dealers and farmers, from Northamptonshire and Lincolnshire, as well as South Devon, and the immediate neighbourhood.

These ponies are the result of crosses made years ago with Arab, Dongola, and thorough-bred stallions, on the indigenous race of Exmoors, since carefully culled from year to year for the purpose of securing the utmost amount of perfection among the stallions and mares reserved for breeding purposes. The real Exmoor seldom exceeds twelve hands; has a well-shaped head, with very small ears; but the thick round shoulder peculiar to all breeds of wild horses, which seem specially adapted for inclemencies of the weather; indeed, the whole body is round, com-pact, and well ribbed. The Exmoor has very good quarters and powerful hocks; legs straight, flat, and clean ; the muscles well developed by early racing up and down steep mountain sides while following their dams. In about forty lots the prevailing colours were bay, brown, and gray; chestnuts and blacks were less frequent, and not in favour with the country people, many of whom seemed to consider that the indigenous race had been deteriorated by the sedulous efforts made and making to improve it—an opinion which we could not share after examining some of the best specimens, in which a clean blood-like head and increased size seemed to have been given, without any diminution of the enduring qualities of the Exmoor.

The sale was great fun. Perched on convenient rails, we had the whole scene before us. The auctioneer rather hoarse and quite matter-of-fact; the ponies wildly rushing about the first enclosure, were with difficulty separated into pairs to be driven in the sale section; when fairly hemmed in through the open gate, they dashed and made a sort of circus circuit, with mane and tail erect, in a style that would draw great applause at Astley's. Then there was the difficulty of deciding whether the figures marked in white on the animal's hind-quarters were 8 or 3 or 5. Instead of the regulartrot up and down of Tattersall's, a whisk of a cap was sufficient to produce a tremendous caper. A very pretty exhibition was made by a little mare, with a late foal about the size of a setter dog.[20]

The sale over, a most amusing scene ensued : every man who had bought a pony wanted to catch it. In order to clear the way, each lot, as sold, as wild and nearly as active as deer, had been turned into the field. A joint-stock company of pony-catchers, headed by the champion wrestler of the district—a hawk-nosed, fresh-complexioned, rustic Don Juan—stood ready to be hired, at the moderate rate of sixpence per pony caught and delivered. One carried a bundle of new halters; the others, warmed by a liberal distribution of beer, seemed as much inspired by the fun as the sixpence. When the word was given, the first step was to drive a herd into the lowest corner of the field in as compact a mass as possible. The bay, gray, or chestnut, from that hour doomed to perpetual slavery and exile from his native hills, was pointed out by the nervous anxious purchaser. Three wiry fellows crept cat-like among the mob, sheltering behind some tame cart-horses; on a mutual signal they rushed on the devoted animal; two—one bearing a halter—strove to fling each one arm round its neck, and with one hand to grasp its nostrils while the insidious third, clinging to the flowing tail; tried to throw the poor quadruped off its balance. Often they were baffled in the first effort, for with one wild spring the pony would clear the whole lot, and flying with streaming mane and tail across the brook up the field, leave the whole work to be recommenced. Sometimes when

[20] According to tradition, the Exmoor ponies are descended from horses brought from the East by the Phoenicians, who traded there with Cornwall for metals.

the feat was cleverly performed, pony and pony-catchers were to be seen all rolling on the ground together; the pony yelling, snorting, and fighting with his fore feet, the men clinging on like the Lapithæ and the Centaurs, and how escaping crushed ribs or broken legs it is impossible to imagine. On one occasion a fine brown stallion dashed away, with two plucky fellows hanging on to his mane: rearing, plunging, fighting with his fore feet, away he bounded down a declivity among the huge rocks, amid the encouraging cheers of the spectators : for a moment the contest was doubtful, so tough were the sinews, and so determined the grip of Davy, the champion; but the steep bank of the brook, down which the brown stallion recklessly plunged, was too much for human efforts (in a moment they all went together into the brook), but the pony, up first, leaped the opposite bank and galloped away, whinnying in short-lived triumph.

After a series of such contests, well worth the study of artists not content with pale copies from marbles or casts, the difficulty of haltering these snorting steeds — equal in spirit and probably in size to those which drew the car of Boadicea—was diminished by all those un-caught being driven back to the pound ; and there, not without furious battles, one by one enslaved.

Yet even when haltered, the conquest was by no means concluded. Some refused to stir, others started off at such a pace as speedily brought the holder of the nalter on his nose. One respectable old gentleman, in gray stockings and knee-breeches, lost his animal in much less time than it took him to extract the sixpence . from his knotted purse.

Yet in all these fights there was little display of vice; it was pure fright on the part of the ponies that made them struggle so. A few days1 confinement in a shed; a few carrots, with a little salt, and gentle treatment, reduces the wildest of the three-year-olds to docility. When older they are more difficult to manage. It was a pretty sight to view them led away, splashing through the brook—conquered, but not yet subdued.

In the course of the evening a little chestnut stallion, twelve hands, or four feet in height, jumped, at a standing jump, over the bars out of a pound upward of five feet from the ground, only just touching the top rail with his hind feet.

We had hoped to have a day's wild stag hunting, but the hounds were out on the other side of the country. However, we had a few runs with a scratch pack of harriers after stout moorland hares. The dandy school, who revel in descriptions of coats and waistcoats, boots and breeches, and who pretend that there is no sport without an outfit which is only within the reach of a man with ten thousand a year, would no doubt have been extremely disgusted with the whole affair.. We rose at five o'clock in the morning and hunted puss up to her form (instead of paying a shilling to a boy to turn her out) with six couples, giving tongue most melodiously.

Viewing her away we rattled across the crispy brown moor, and splattered through bogs with a loose rein, in lunatic enjoyment, until we checked at the edge of a deep " combe." Then—when the old yellow Southerner challenged, and our young host cheered him with " Hark to Reveller, hark! "—to hear the challenge and the cheer re-echoed again from the opposite cliff; and—as the little pack in full cry again took up the running, and scaled the steep ascent—to see our young huntsman, bred in these hills, go rattling down the valleys, and to follow by instinct, under vague idea, not unmixed with nervous apprehensions of the consequences of a slip, that what one could do two could, was vastly exciting, and amusing, and, in a word, decidedly jolly. So with many facts, some new ideas, and a fine stock of health from a week of open air, I bade farewell to my hospitable hosts and to romantic Exmoor.

# POSTSCRIPT.

## THE HUNTING MAN'S HEALTH.

WITHOUT health there can be no sport. A man at the commencement of the hunting often requires condition more than his horse, especially if engaged in sedentary occupations, and averse to summer riding or walking. Of course the proper plan is to train by walking or riding. I remember, some years ago, when three months of severe mental occupation had kept me entirely out of the saddle, going out in Northamptonshire, fortunately admirably mounted, when the hounds were no sooner in cover than they were out of it, " running breast high," five minutes after I had changed from my seat in a dog-cart to the saddle. We had thirty-five minutes' sharp run, without a check, and for the latter part of the run I was perfectly beaten, almost black in the face, and scarcely able to hold my horse together. I did not recover from this too sudden exertion for many days. Those who are out of condition will do well to ride, instead of driving to cover.

In changing from town to country life, between the different hours of rising and hearty meals—the result of fresh air and exercise—the stomach and bowels are very likely to get out of order. It is as well, therefore, to be provided with some mild digestive pills: violent purges are as injurious to men as to horses and more inconvenient.

The enema is a valuable instrument, which a hunting man should not be without, as its use, when you are in strong exercise, is often more advisable than medicine.

But one of the most valuable aids to the health and spirits of a hard-riding man is the Sitz Bath, which, taken morning and evening, cold or tepid, according to individual taste, has even more advantageous effects on the system than a complete bath. It braces the muscles, strengthens the nerves, and tends to keep the bowels open. Sitz baths are made in zinc, and are tolerably portable; but in a country place you may make shift with a tub half-filled with water. In taking this kind of bath, it is essential that the parts not in the water should be warm and comfortable. For this end, in cold weather, case your feet and legs in warm stockings, and cover your person and tub with a poncho, through the hole of which you can thrust your head. In default of a poncho, a plaid or blanket will do, and in warm weather a sheet If you begin with tepid water, you will soon be able to bear cold, as after the first shock the cold disappears. The water must not reach higher than your hips, rather under than over; The time for a Sitz bath varies from ten to twenty minutes, not longer, during which you may read or smoke; but then you will need sleeves, for it is essential that you should be covered all the time. I often take a cup of coffee in this bath, it saves time in breakfasting. In the illustration, the blanket has been turned back to show the right position.

THE HOT-AIR OB INDIAN BATH.

In case of an attack of cold or influenza, or a necessity for sweating off a few pounds, or especially after a severe fall, there is no bath so effective and so simple as the hot-air or Indian bath. This is made with a wooden-bottomed kitchen chair, a few blankets, a tin cup, and a claret-glass of spirits of wine. For want of spirits of wine you might use a dozen of Price's night lights.

Take a wooden-bottomed chair, and place it in a convenient part of the bed-room, where a fire should be previously lighted. Put under the chair a narrow metal cup or gallipot, if it will stand fire filled with spirits of wine. Let the bather strip to his drawers, and sit down on the chair with a fold of flannel under him, for the seat will get extremely hot—put on his knees a slop-basin, with a sponge and a little cold water, Then take four blankets or rugs, and lay them, one over his back,one over his front, and one on each side, so as to cover him closely in a woollen tent, and wrap his head up in flannel or silk—if he is cold or shivering put his feet in warm water, or on a hot brick wrapped in flannel. Then light the spirits of wine, which will very soon make a famous hot-air bath. By giving the patient a little cold water to drink, perspiration will be encouraged; if be finds the air inconveniently hot before he begins to perspire, he can use the sponge and slop-basin to bathe his chest, &c.

When the perspiration rolls like rain from his face, and you think he has had enough, have a blanket warmed at the fire, strip him, roll him in it, and tumble him into bed. In five or ten minutes, you can take away the blanket and put on his night shirt—give him a drink of white wine whey, and he will be ready to go to sleep comfortably.

This bath can be administered when a patient is too ill to be put in a warm bath, and is more effective. I have seen admirable results from it on a gentleman after a horse had rolled over him.

It can also be prepared in. a few minutes, in places where to get a warm bath would be out of the question.

In the illustration, the blanket is turned back, to show the proper position, and by error the head is not covered.

### The Codes Of Hammurabi And Moses
### W. W. Davies

QTY

The discovery of the Hammurabi Code is one of the greatest achievements of archaeology, and is of paramount interest, not only to the student of the Bible, but also to all those interested in ancient history...

**Religion**     ISBN: *1-59462-338-4*     **Pages:132**
*MSRP $12.95*

### The Theory of Moral Sentiments
### Adam Smith

QTY

This work from 1749. contains original theories of conscience amd moral judgment and it is the foundation for systemof morals.

**Philosophy**  ISBN: *1-59462-777-0*     **Pages:536**
*MSRP $19.95*

### Jessica's First Prayer
### Hesba Stretton

QTY

In a screened and secluded corner of one of the many railway-bridges which span the streets of London there could be seen a few years ago, from five o'clock every morning until half past eight, a tidily set-out coffee-stall, consisting of a trestle and board, upon which stood two large tin cans, with a small fire of charcoal burning under each so as to keep the coffee boiling during the early hours of the morning when the work-people were thronging into the city on their way to their daily toil...

**Pages:84**

**Childrens**   ISBN: *1-59462-373-2*     *MSRP $9.95*

### My Life and Work
### Henry Ford

QTY

Henry Ford revolutionized the world with his implementation of mass production for the Model T automobile.  Gain valuable business insight into his life and work with his own auto-biography... "We have only started on our development of our country we have not as yet, with all our talk of wonderful progress, done more than scratch the surface. The progress has been wonderful enough but..."

**Pages:300**

**Biographies/**    ISBN: *1-59462-198-5*     *MSRP $21.95*

## The Art of Cross-Examination
## Francis Wellman

QTY

I presume it is the experience of every author, after his first book is published upon an important subject, to be almost overwhelmed with a wealth of ideas and illustrations which could readily have been included in his book, and which to his own mind, at least, seem to make a second edition inevitable. Such certainly was the case with me; and when the first edition had reached its sixth impression in five months, I rejoiced to learn that it seemed to my publishers that the book had met with a sufficiently favorable reception to justify a second and considerably enlarged edition. ..

**Reference**    **ISBN: *1-59462-647-2***

**Pages:412**
*MSRP $19.95*

## On the Duty of Civil Disobedience
## Henry David Thoreau

QTY

Thoreau wrote his famous essay, On the Duty of Civil Disobedience, as a  protest against an unjust but popular war and the immoral  but  popular institution  of slave-owning. He did more than write—he declined to  pay his  taxes,   and  was hauled off to gaol in consequence. Who can say how much  this  refusal  of  his hastened the end of the war and of slavery ?

**Law**    **ISBN: *1-59462-747-9***

**Pages:48**
*MSRP $7.45*

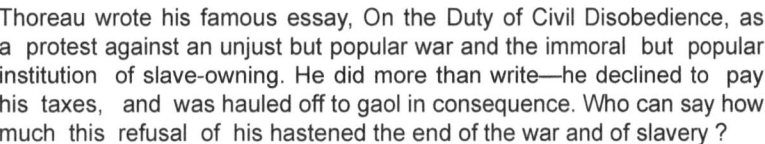

## Dream Psychology Psychoanalysis for Beginners
## Sigmund Freud

QTY

Sigmund Freud, born Sigismund Schlomo Freud (May 6, 1856 - September 23, 1939), was a Jewish-Austrian neurologist and psychiatrist who co-founded the psychoanalytic school of psychology. Freud is best known for his theories of the unconscious mind, especially involving the mechanism of repression; his redefinition of sexual desire as mobile and directed towards a wide variety of objects; and his therapeutic techniques, especially his understanding of transference in the therapeutic relationship and the presumed value of dreams as sources of insight into unconscious desires.

**Psychology**    **ISBN: *1-59462-905-6***

**Pages:196**
*MSRP $15.45*

## The Miracle of Right Thought
## Orison Swett Marden

QTY

Believe with all of your heart that you will do what you were made to do. When the mind has once formed the habit of holding cheerful, happy, prosperous pictures, it will not be easy to form the opposite habit.  It does not matter how improbable or how far away this realization may see, or how dark the prospects may be, if we visualize them as best we can, as vividly as possible, hold tenaciously to them and vigorously struggle to attain them, they will gradually become actualized, realized in the life. But a desire, a longing without endeavor, a yearning abandoned or held indifferently will vanish without realization.

**Self Help**    **ISBN: *1-59462-644-8***

**Pages:360**
*MSRP $25.45*

QTY

**The Rosicrucian Cosmo-Conception Mystic Christianity** *by Max Heindel*  ISBN: *1-59462-188-8*  **$38.95**
*The Rosicrucian Cosmo-conception is not dogmatic, neither does it appeal to any other authority than the reason of the student. It is: not controversial, but is: sent forth in the, hope that it may help to clear...*  New Age/Religion Pages 646

**Abandonment To Divine Providence** *by Jean-Pierre de Caussade*  ISBN: *1-59462-228-0*  **$25.95**
*"The Rev. Jean Pierre de Caussade was one of the most remarkable spiritual writers of the Society of Jesus in France in the 18th Century. His death took place at Toulouse in 1751. His works have gone through many editions and have been republished...*  Inspirational/Religion Pages 400

**Mental Chemistry** *by Charles Haanel*  ISBN: *1-59462-192-6*  **$23.95**
*Mental Chemistry allows the change of material conditions by combining and appropriately utilizing the power of the mind. Much like applied chemistry creates something new and unique out of careful combinations of chemicals the mastery of mental chemistry...*  New Age Pages 354

**The Letters of Robert Browning and Elizabeth Barret Barrett 1845-1846 vol II**  ISBN: *1-59462-193-4*  **$35.95**
*by Robert Browning and Elizabeth Barrett*  Biographies Pages 596

**Gleanings In Genesis (volume I)** *by Arthur W. Pink*  ISBN: *1-59462-130-6*  **$27.45**
*Appropriately has Genesis been termed "the seed plot of the Bible" for in it we have, in germ form, almost all of the great doctrines which are afterwards fully developed in the books of Scripture which follow...*  Religion/Inspirational Pages 420

**The Master Key** *by L. W. de Laurence*  ISBN: *1-59462-001-6*  **$30.95**
*In no branch of human knowledge has there been a more lively increase of the spirit of research during the past few years than in the study of Psychology, Concentration and Mental Discipline. The requests for authentic lessons in Thought Control, Mental Discipline and...*  New Age/Business Pages 422

**The Lesser Key Of Solomon Goetia** *by L. W. de Laurence*  ISBN: *1-59462-092-X*  **$9.95**
*This translation of the first book of the "Lemegton" which is now for the first time made accessible to students of Talismanic Magic was done, after careful collation and edition, from numerous Ancient Manuscripts in Hebrew, Latin, and French...*  New Age/Occult Pages 92

**Rubaiyat Of Omar Khayyam** *by Edward Fitzgerald*  ISBN:*1-59462-332-5*  **$13.95**
*Edward Fitzgerald, whom the world has already learned, in spite of his own efforts to remain within the shadow of anonymity, to look upon as one of the rarest poets of the century, was born at Bredfield, in Suffolk, on the 31st of March, 1809. He was the third son of John Purcell...*  Music Pages 172

**Ancient Law** *by Henry Maine*  ISBN: *1-59462-128-4*  **$29.95**
*The chief object of the following pages is to indicate some of the earliest ideas of mankind, as they are reflected in Ancient Law, and to point out the relation of those ideas to modern thought.*  Religion/History Pages 452

**Far-Away Stories** *by William J. Locke*  ISBN: *1-59462-129-2*  **$19.45**
*"Good wine needs no bush, but a collection of mixed vintages does. And this book is just such a collection. Some of the stories I do not want to remain buried for ever in the museum files of dead magazine-numbers an author's not unpardonable vanity..."*  Fiction Pages 272

**Life of David Crockett** *by David Crockett*  ISBN: *1-59462-250-7*  **$27.45**
*"Colonel David Crockett was one of the most remarkable men of the times in which he lived. Born in humble life, but gifted with a strong will, an indomitable courage, and unremitting perseverance...*  Biographies/New Age Pages 424

**Lip-Reading** *by Edward Nitchie*  ISBN: *1-59462-206-X*  **$25.95**
*Edward B. Nitchie, founder of the New York School for the Hard of Hearing, now the Nitchie School of Lip-Reading, Inc, wrote "LIP-READING Principles and Practice". The development and perfecting of this meritorious work on lip-reading was an undertaking...*  How-to Pages 400

**A Handbook of Suggestive Therapeutics, Applied Hypnotism, Psychic Science**  ISBN: *1-59462-214-0*  **$24.95**
*by Henry Munro*  Health/New Age/Health/Self-help Pages 376

**A Doll's House: and Two Other Plays** *by Henrik Ibsen*  ISBN: *1-59462-112-8*  **$19.95**
*Henrik Ibsen created this classic when in revolutionary 1848 Rome. Introducing some striking concepts in playwriting for the realist genre, this play has been studied the world over.*  Fiction/Classics/Plays 308

**The Light of Asia** *by sir Edwin Arnold*  ISBN: *1-59462-204-3*  **$13.95**
*In this poetic masterpiece, Edwin Arnold describes the life and teachings of Buddha. The man who was to become known as Buddha to the world was born as Prince Gautama of India but he rejected the worldly riches and abandoned the reigns of power when...*  Religion/History/Biographies Pages 170

**The Complete Works of Guy de Maupassant** *by Guy de Maupassant*  ISBN: *1-59462-157-8*  **$16.95**
*"For days and days, nights and nights, I had dreamed of that first kiss which was to consecrate our engagement, and I knew not on what spot I should put my lips..."*  Fiction/Classics Pages 240

**The Art of Cross-Examination** *by Francis L. Wellman*  ISBN: *1-59462-309-0*  **$26.95**
*Written by a renowned trial lawyer, Wellman imparts his experience and uses case studies to explain how to use psychology to extract desired information through questioning.*  How-to/Science/Reference Pages 408

**Answered or Unanswered?** *by Louisa Vaughan*  ISBN: *1-59462-248-5*  **$10.95**
*Miracles of Faith in China*  Religion Pages 112

**The Edinburgh Lectures on Mental Science (1909)** *by Thomas*  ISBN: *1-59462-008-3*  **$11.95**
*This book contains the substance of a course of lectures recently given by the writer in the Queen Street Hall, Edinburgh. Its purpose is to indicate the Natural Principles governing the relation between Mental Action and Material Conditions...*  New Age/Psychology Pages 148

**Ayesha** *by H. Rider Haggard*  ISBN: *1-59462-301-5*  **$24.95**
*Verily and indeed it is the unexpected that happens! Probably if there was one person upon the earth from whom the Editor of this, and of a certain previous history, did not expect to hear again...*  Classics Pages 380

**Ayala's Angel** *by Anthony Trollope*  ISBN: *1-59462-352-X*  **$29.95**
*The two girls were both pretty, but Lucy who was twenty-one who supposed to be simple and comparatively unattractive, whereas Ayala was credited, as her Bombwhat romantic name might show, with poetic charm and a taste for romance. Ayala when her father died was nineteen...*  Fiction Pages 484

**The American Commonwealth** *by James Bryce*  ISBN: *1-59462-286-8*  **$34.45**
*An interpretation of American democratic political theory. It examines political mechanics and society from the perspective of Scotsman James Bryce*  Politics Pages 572

**Stories of the Pilgrims** *by Margaret P. Pumphrey*  ISBN: *1-59462-116-0*  **$17.95**
*This book explores pilgrims religious oppression in England as well as their escape to Holland and eventual crossing to America on the Mayflower, and their early days in New England...*  History Pages 268

QTY

**The Fasting Cure** *by Sinclair Upton*                                                          ISBN: *1-59462-222-1*   **$13.95**

*In the Cosmopolitan Magazine for May, 1910, and in the Contemporary Review (London) for April, 1910, I published an article dealing with my experiences in fasting. I have written a great many magazine articles, but never one which attracted so much attention...  New Age/Self Help/Health Pages 164*

**Hebrew Astrology** *by Sepharial*                                                          ISBN: *1-59462-308-2*   **$13.45**

*In these days of advanced thinking it is a matter of common observation that we have left many of the old landmarks behind and that we are now pressing forward to greater heights and to a wider horizon than that which represented the mind-content of our progenitors...                Astrology Pages 144*

**Thought Vibration or The Law of Attraction in the Thought World**            ISBN: *1-59462-127-6*   **$12.95**

*by William Walker Atkinson*                                                          *Psychology/Religion Pages 144*

**Optimism** *by Helen Keller*                                                          ISBN: *1-59462-108-X*   **$15.95**

*Helen Keller was blind, deaf, and mute since 19 months old, yet famously learned how to overcome these handicaps, communicate with the world, and spread her lectures promoting optimism. An inspiring read for everyone...                Biographies/Inspirational Pages 84*

**Sara Crewe** *by Frances Burnett*                                                          ISBN: *1-59462-360-0*   **$9.45**

*In the first place, Miss Minchin lived in London. Her home was a large, dull, tall one, in a large, dull square, where all the houses were alike, and all the sparrows were alike, and where all the door-knockers made the same heavy sound...                Childrens/Classic Pages 88*

**The Autobiography of Benjamin Franklin** *by Benjamin Franklin*            ISBN: *1-59462-135-7*   **$24.95**

*The Autobiography of Benjamin Franklin has probably been more extensively read than any other American historical work, and no other book of its kind has had such ups and downs of fortune. Franklin lived for many years in England, where he was agent...                Biographies/History Pages 332*

| | |
|---|---|
| **Name** | |
| **Email** | |
| **Telephone** | |
| **Address** | |
| | |
| **City, State ZIP** | |

☐ **Credit Card**                    ☐ **Check / Money Order**

| | |
|---|---|
| **Credit Card Number** | |
| **Expiration Date** | |
| **Signature** | |

*Please Mail to:   Book Jungle*
*PO Box 2226*
*Champaign, IL 61825*
*or Fax to:         630-214-0564*

## ORDERING INFORMATION

**web***: www.bookjungle.com*
**email***: sales@bookjungle.com*
**fax***: 630-214-0564*
**mail***: Book Jungle  PO Box 2226  Champaign, IL 61825*
**or PayPal** *to sales@bookjungle.com*

*Please contact us for bulk discounts*

## DIRECT-ORDER TERMS

**20% Discount if You Order
Two or More Books**
Free Domestic Shipping!
Accepted: Master Card, Visa,
Discover, American Express